The Dublin Driver Mysteries by Catie Murphy

DEAD IN DUBLIN

DEATH ON THE GREEN

DEATH OF AN IRISH MUMMY

DEATH IN IRISH ACCENTS

DEATH BY IRISH WHISKEY

Death by
Irish Whiskey

Catie Murphy

Kensington Publishing Corp.
www.kensingtonbooks.com

Pronunciation Guide

Irish names will often trip up English-speaking readers because we try to map English letter sounds and combinations onto a language never intended to use them. The trickier names and phrases in *Death by Irish Whiskey* are pronounced and translated as followed:

Niamh = Neev

Go raibh maith agat = thank you (gur-uv MAH ah-guth)

Uisce beatha = water of life; whiskey (ISH-keh BA-ha)

An Garda Síochána = police (ahn garda sheeow-kana)

Diarmuid = Dearmad

Taoiseach = teashuck; the political leader of Ireland

CHAPTER 1

Angus McConal died in the punch bowl, which Megan couldn't help think was a fitting end for a boxer.

She made the mistake of saying so out loud, and her girlfriend's gaze, blazing with fury, nearly ended Megan, too. She hissed, "I didn't mean to!" by which she meant she didn't mean to be present for another presumable murder, rather than she didn't mean to say something horrifically inappropriate in the moment.

Jelena hissed, "You never mean to!" back, and stalked away in a show of gorgeous, long-legged rage. She didn't go very far, because Detective Garda Paul Bourke was ordering convention center security to block off the exits as he crouched beside Angus McConal's body.

As if the boxer's dramatic collapse, his gasping for air, and the horrid final sound he had made wasn't enough to be certain he was dead, Bourke checked his pulse, waiting a long, weary moment before dropping his chin to his chest and exhaling deeply. Then he rose and asked for something to cover the body with. A pale-faced member of staff got a tablecloth from under the bar.

They spread it over McConal's unmoving form, and as it settled with a soft billow, Detective Bourke took a heartbeat to meet Megan's eyes with a warning look.

Megan muffled a completely irrational desire to defend herself. She hadn't *done* anything! She nodded anyway. Bourke couldn't have said "Stay out of it, Megan," any more clearly if he'd spoken aloud.

"He's never dead," her uncle said at Megan's elbow, genuine shock staining his usually jovial voice. "Sure and he can't be dead, Megan."

"I'm sorry, Uncle Rabbie. Come on, we should probably move away from the body, at least. The guards will be here any minute." Megan cast a grim look of her own toward Paul and corrected herself: "More guards."

Paul—tall, slim, sandy-red of hair—wasn't on duty. No one was on duty tonight, except maybe Niamh O'Sullivan. Her megawatt movie star charm was at the Dublin Whiskey Festival's opening party as part of the promotion for Harbourmaster Whiskey, a new brand she and Megan's uncle Rabbie had gone in on together. Rabbie was the harbormaster in question, newly retired after decades of being the man behind everything in and out of Sligo's harbor on the western side of the country.

Rabbie had always struck Megan as the quintessential Irishman, sharply blue of eye and equally sharp of wit, with a well-tended mane of white hair and a fierceness to his smile. He was fit, even in his seventies, and full of vigor, exactly the kind of older image that Ireland wanted to project to the world. His years in the shipping industry seemed to have offered him the chance to meet every single person in Ireland. He was certainly on a first-name basis with an awful lot of them. Technically speaking, he was Megan's second cousin once removed, but "uncle" covered the generation gap more comfortably, and Megan always thought of him that way.

He was also pale with disbelief as she walked him away from Angus McConal's body. "I knew him when he was a lad," the older man said in real dismay. "His granda would bring him around and talk him up when he did well in the fights. What happened, Megan?"

"I don't know." Megan bit her tongue on saying she would find out. She had been involved in four murder cases now—more if she allowed herself to think about the fact that more than one person had died in at least two of those cases—and she was absolutely not supposed to be in the proximity of any *more* murders. No civilian was, of course, but in descending order, Jelena, Detective Bourke, and the entire Irish police force were going to line up to kill *her* if she got entangled in another one. "I'm sure Paul will figure it out quickly."

"He was a competitor!" Rabbie said desperately. "His whiskey was up against ours! Are they going to think Niamh and I killed him?"

Megan's eyebrows rose and she turned to look at her uncle. "I don't know, Uncle Rabbie. Should they? Do you have some kind of beef I don't know about?"

For a moment his expression wobbled, reminding Megan that although she'd been in Ireland for most of five years now, she still tended toward some very American expressions. It wasn't that the Irish didn't know what the phrase "some kind of beef" meant. It just wasn't common parlance in this part of the world. Then Rabbie said, "I wouldn't, no," almost sullenly, like a child caught on the cusp of misbehaving.

"Rabbie?" Megan heard the warning in her question, and her uncle's jaw set.

"There's no story with myself and himself, and I'll thank you not to poke and prod at me like I was one of your mysteries," the older man snapped. "I'm only after getting a shock with this happening."

Megan drew a breath, then exhaled it again, knowing a losing fight when she saw one. If it turned out to be important, she—or the guards—would ferret it out of Rabbie later.

Chaos had erupted around them while she spoke with Rabbie, and it was probably a measure of Megan's exposure to unexpected dead bodies that she hadn't really noticed. Now, though, with Rabbie clamming up, she had a moment to take in the panicked situation surrounding her.

The Dublin Whiskey Festival had grown large enough over the past several years to hold its opening evening at the convention center, a Celtic Tiger venue overlooking the River Liffey and the harp-shaped Samuel Beckett Bridge. The organizers regarded opening night as a gala event, rolling out a red carpet and everything. Well, a gold one, technically, in keeping with the whiskey theme. It snaked outside, in front of the CCD's tall, angled glass windows, and across the broad convention center ground floor, just in case the weather turned desperate. Its path led people to the escalators, sending them upstairs to a genuinely spectacular crystal-and-mirror-lined bar. Everyone, even Megan, who was mostly there because she had a limo license and had driven all her friends over that evening, was dressed to the nines.

The crush of people in tuxedoes and evening gowns trying to reach the escalators looked peculiarly familiar, as did the huddled groups of people who had already given up on escaping and were either crying or staring with ghoulish fascination at Angus McConal's body lying next to the upended punch bowl. The sound was astonishing, a combination of hysterical sobs, angry shouts, and the buzz of urgent gossip. Megan frowned briefly at the gathering, trying to think of what was familiar about it, then choked on a laugh.

It looked like a movie. This many well-dressed people panicking and running for the doors was straight out of a film scene. Megan, unable to help herself, moved to the glass-walled railings and looked down at the ground floor, searching for the actual, real-life movie star among them.

Niamh had worn red so she would stand out against the gold carpet, and it had worked perfectly. Everyone else in the building might have been in black-and-white, compared to her vibrant brilliance. She had been called to stay on the gold carpet for photographers, and was still there, now fending off reporters who smelled blood in the water.

From above, she appeared poised, grieving, confused, comfortable, compliant, and confident all at once, even as people shouted questions at her and stuck their microphones or cameras in her face. Megan couldn't imagine how she coped with it on a normal day, never mind now, thrust into the middle of an unexpected crisis.

Paul Bourke's voice rose. Megan turned away from watching Niamh to listen to the police detective as he asked people to put their phones away and to please not post on social media right now. He might as well have asked the tide not to rise, but Megan admired the fact that he even made the effort.

A few people did put their phones away, their expressions either sheepish or mortified, depending on their level of guilt. Most didn't, and one young woman pushed her way to the front of the crowd circling Angus's body, and began talking into her phone. She looked about eleven years old from Megan's early-forties vantage point, but an actual tween would have adults supervising her, and Paul wasn't that lucky in this situation.

Podcaster Hannah Flanagan came from a genuinely well-respected whiskey family in Ireland, her family's distillery going back nearly two hundred years. She was twenty-two, not eleven, but she was baby-faced by nature and had wispy blond hair and large blue eyes that played into her looking younger than she really was. Megan was surprised she'd gone into podcasting instead of acting, because she absolutely did *not* have a face meant for radio.

She did have a voice meant for it, though: low and smoky with a bit of a purr to it, like two centuries of family whiskey had distilled itself into her vocal cords. She knew *everything* about whiskey. Not just her family's, but about all of it, everywhere, as far as Megan could tell. That was what she talked about on her podcast, and either her voice or her topic were so fascinating that she'd racked up a host of awards and global sponsorships. She'd been born with a silver spoon in her mouth, to be sure, but she'd turned it into a whole cutlery set.

Megan winced and smirked simultaneously at her own terrible metaphor, then made her way toward Hannah, hoping to interrupt her recording. Then a trickle of warning chilled her spine and she stopped before she got to the young woman. Podcasters recorded everything, and the last thing Megan wanted was to end up as a "murder driver" segment on an internationally renowned broadcast.

More to the point, the last thing *Jelena* wanted was for Megan to end up on a globally-popular podcast. Other people were crowding up to Hannah anyway, trying to get a word in edgewise in hopes that *they* would end up famous. Megan turned away, looking through the crowd for her girlfriend.

Jelena was a point of stillness in the agitation. She'd found a chair and sat with her face in her hands and her curly hair falling from its updo to cascade around her fingers. Megan's heart twisted so hard she felt dizzy. This was not what she'd promised as their night out. It was supposed to be rubbing elbows with the beautiful, the wealthy, and the famous, not finding themselves stuck in the convention center in the world's biggest locked-room mystery.

She sighed, then braced herself to go offer her girlfriend support or accept the brunt of a scolding she didn't necessarily deserve, but wouldn't blame Jelena for. People *did* have a horrible tendency to drop dead around Megan, and that just wasn't normal.

"Meghaaaan?" A shrill voice, albeit used at less volume than usual, cut through the noise and a petite woman rushed through the crowd to embrace Megan unexpectedly. "Meghaaaan, I did not know you would be here! How could you not drive me tonight when you are wearing my suit! I cannot forgive you! Oh, but I must, you are too beautiful to be angry at. Meghaaan, what is going on? I am here for a party and to promote my whiskey, yes? And now someone is dead? You must fix this, Meghaaan! You must fix it now!"

Megan said, "I—" faintly, then paused to recalibrate before she even tried to say anything else. After a few seconds, she managed, "Hello, Ms. de la Fuente," which she thought was safe enough, and which bought her a little more time to organize her thoughts.

Carmen de la Fuente was probably the richest person Megan had ever personally met. As far as Megan could tell, she lived her entire life going from one exclusive party to another, hosting several of them along the way, and surrounding herself with staggeringly beautiful women whom she spent outrageous amounts of money on dressing in fanciful, gorgeous ways. Megan had driven her once early in her career at Leprechaun Limos, and had apparently charmed the little Spanish woman. Carmen—who rarely, to the best of Megan's recollection, said *Megan* with fewer than three "a" sounds—had announced that Megan would drive her everywhere from then on, and paid accordingly for the privilege of having her favorite driver whenever she was in Dublin.

And Megan was, in fact, wearing her suit. Carmen had had the gold suit *made* for Megan to wear when she drove Carmen, and while her boss normally wouldn't let anybody drive while out of uniform, even Orla made exceptions for Carmen de la Fuente. It was by far the fanciest thing Megan owned, and she actually felt a stab of guilt at wearing it while *not* driving Carmen. "I didn't know you were in town."

Carmen sniffed. "I called dreadful Ms. Keegan and she told me you weren't answering your phone. I was forced to take a helicopter from the Weston Airport to the convention center."

Megan had to bite the inside of her cheek very hard to keep from laughing out loud. It was true Orla had rung her, but she'd already been driving Rabbie, Jelena, Niamh, and Paul to the whiskey gala, and hadn't picked up. "I didn't even know there was a helicopter landing site at the convention center."

Carmen fluttered a hand, implying that such middling details were unimportant for someone as rich as she was. Megan lifted her gaze again—she wasn't tall, but she could look over Carmen's head easily—and glanced around for the usual bevy of beauties following Carmen. "You don't seem to have an entourage tonight."

The tiny, wealthy woman's entire expression melted into what, despite her theatrical persona, seemed to be genuine grief. "Isabella left me. I am not a serious enough person for her. What is the point in frivolous beauty if you have no one to share it with?"

Megan had no idea who Isabella was, and spent a moment wondering if she would know if she kept up with the tabloid gossip columns. It didn't really matter, though. "I'm sorry to hear that. And— I'm sorry, did you say you were here to promote *your* whiskey?" There were several new whiskeys competing for the best new whiskey award, but she was sure she would have noticed if Carmen de la Fuente's name was attached to one of them.

"Shh." Carmen pursed her lips and put her finger to them, managing a smile at the same time. "The Midnight Sunrise is mine, no? For ten years we have sat it in casks to see what would come of it, and now it is ready. But I am only the money, not the face." Another flicker of distress went through her brown eyes, although she kept the smile in place. "Again, I am not serious enough. Whiskey is serious business, and ours is, mmm, dark? A dilettante is not the right face to sell it."

"Midnight Sunrise," Megan echoed in surprise. There was a Northern Irish actor attached to that, an older man with a great voice and a steely gaze. She could see how he would sell whiskey in a way

Carmen couldn't, although unlike Carmen, he wasn't here for the opening gala. "I didn't know that was you."

"Shh," Carmen said again, lightly, before her face fell and she looked toward Angus McConal's body. Megan glanced toward him, too, and wasn't surprised to discover he'd been covered, and that convention center security surrounded the body so no one could take any more pictures. "What happened, Meghan?" For once she mostly dropped the drawn-out vowels, which made Megan smile a little sadly.

"I don't know. I'm not going to find out, either. That's the gardaí's job."

"He wasn't a nice man," Carmen said, still in that light voice. "But he did not deserve to die in a whiskey punch bowl."

"You knew him?" Megan asked before she could stop herself, then actually physically bit her tongue to keep from asking more questions.

Carmen only needed the one, though. "Oh yes. Only a little, but yes. A friend with very bad taste in men dated him for a little while, and brought him to some of my parties. I told her she could not bring him again after he hit a man and the head of my security threw him off the yacht."

Megan said, "Good grief. Was everyone okay?"

"The man who got hit was very angry, but unharmed. My security man, tonight when Angus died, he smiled."

Megan's stomach sank. "He's here?"

Carmen's eyes widened. "Of course. I am very rich, Meghan. I go almost nowhere without a security team."

"Right. No, of course you don't. Come with me, please, Carmen. I need you to talk to someone." Megan offered her elbow, because Carmen would like that, and it would help if she was happy when Megan told Paul Bourke she'd found his first potential suspect in Angus McConal's death.

CHAPTER 2

Detective Paul Bourke had been made for skinny suits, and a slim-cut tuxedo looked even sharper on him than his usual pinstripes did. Megan had seen him in the tux before—at one of Carmen's parties, in fact—but she was still impressed with how well he looked in it. Which was the point of formal wear, she supposed: it should always stun, even if the person in it had tight shoulders and a tense jaw as she approached. There were a lot of people who wanted to escape the convention center, and the only thing standing between them and their departure was Detective Bourke's authority as a police officer. He was at the head of the escalators, politely and firmly refusing to let an older white man with an impatient air go past.

He still managed a brief, if thin, smile for Carmen. "Ms. de la Fuente."

"Detective Bourke." Carmen's own smile nearly

rivaled Niamh's for a moment. "It's very nice to see you again."

Megan kept her eyebrows from rising with effort. She hadn't expected Carmen to remember Paul, although she'd approved of him at the yacht party they'd met at.

"You, too." Bourke's gaze flickered to Megan, then back to Carmen. "I don't mean to be rude, but I assume Megan brought you over here for a reason."

"Her head of security has a history with McConal, and is here tonight," Megan said almost apologetically.

Bourke's blue eyes went eagle-sharp as Carmen let out a dramatic gasp. "Meghaaan! No! You cannot think—!"

"I don't think *anything*," Megan said as strenuously as she dared. "That's why I'm bringing you to Detective Bourke. He's the one who's supposed to be thinking in this situation."

"Megan . . ." Paul managed not to groan, but it was a near thing. "Go get somebody from the center's security team, please. I should talk to Ms. de la Fuente's bodyguard, but I can't leave you here to block the escalator. You have no authority."

"No, but I have a mean right hook," Megan said brightly. Paul's expression went completely flat and she mumbled, "Right, going to find security." She scurried off to the people surrounding McConal's body, leaving Carmen with Paul. A moment later one of the convention center security team, a guy about twice as wide across the shoulders as Paul, went to take Paul's place at the head of the escalators. The older man decided he had better things to do than argue with a security guy who could be mistaken for a wall, and sulked off to his well-dressed date. Megan, feeling like she'd put quite enough in motion, turned to go find Jelena.

Jelena was already there, her full lips pressed tight as she looked down at Megan, whose heart lurched again. Despite having slid her hands into them, Jelena's tight-wound black curls were still mostly piled on top of her head, dripping around her cheeks and nape more than before, maybe, but still flawless. Earrings the same color as her angry aquamarine eyes dangled from her lobes, and she was tall and entirely too gorgeous in a flowing jade dress borrowed from Niamh. "Why were you talking to Paul?"

"So that *he* could do the investigating on something that Carmen mentioned," Megan said firmly. "Because I'm staying *out* of it, Yella."

A trace of softness crept into Jelena's anger, and after a moment she sighed, then pulled Megan into her arms. "I'm sorry. I don't mean to be suspicious. I just don't like this, Megan."

"I know." Megan almost said *I don't either*, but her gaze darted to the sheet-covered body, and she wondered if that was true.

What she definitely did like, though, was Jelena Kowal, and getting involved in murders and *staying* involved with Jelena were long-term incompatible. "Pretty soon we'll be able to get out of here and go home to the dogs and forget this even happened, okay, babe?"

Jelena hesitated before nodding, and Megan

knew the incident certainly wouldn't be forgotten. Not by either of them, truthfully, but she could pretend.

A commotion downstairs drew everyone's attention, people moving from a wide semicircle around the body to pressing up the glass-lined railing so they could look down and see what was going on. More guards had arrived, and gossip rag photographers were snapping shots of Niamh in her glamorous red dress and glittering jewelry, surrounded by police. The gardaí had their hands in front of camera lenses and offered glares that bordered on threats, but there were far more cameras than there were police, and flashes lit up the glass wall behind them.

A handful of gardaí came up the escalators two at a time. The older man who thought his whims took priority over everything else immediately approached one of the guards, who began interrogating him on his connection to the dead man. Absolute outrage filled the older man's voice as it lifted enough for half the convention hall to hear him: "I am *Sean Byrne*, you utter gombeen. I *sponsor* the whiskey festival."

"Sure and you're eager to get out of here for a man who just had one of the talent die at his feet," the guard said with unflappable calm into a silence that started as a rush of murmured sound and cut off like someone had pushed a button, because no one wanted to miss a word of what was going down. "I'd think a man of your stature would be crying for the guards, not scarpering off to try to put distance between himself and the crime. Now why is it you'd be doing that, I wonder?"

A choked-off sound of laughter rippled through the convention center. Sean Byrne flushed with anger. "I've nothing to hide! I've nothing to do with this tragedy! I've—" A little too late he realized dozens of people had their phones out, filming. His entire demeanor changed instantly, real outrage suddenly drowned beneath a wash of elder statesman charm. "I've only got to get to Angus's wife, don't you see. Someone's got to give her the news, and I wouldn't want it to be the media or the likes of your own self."

A snarl came through the last words, and the guard, a robust man in his late twenties, smiled into it. "Wouldn't it be madness, then, if I were to say to you that I'm often along to tell the bereaved about their loss? A calming presence, has Garda Barry Dunne, that's what they say. So I'm sure you'll understand it when I tell you to step off, Mr. Byrne, and we'll get to yis in our own good time. Also," he added, blithely, "Angus hasn't got a wife, you ignorant muppet."

Whatever hope the onlookers had of keeping quiet was lost in a center-wide cackle. Sean Byrne flushed deep enough red that he appeared to be on the edge of combustion. With visible effort, he arranged his expression into one that suggested he'd stepped in something unpleasant, and spun away with a sniff of dismissal that would do an outraged toddler proud.

Megan whispered, "Honestly, would you have known that was the guy who sponsored the whiskey festival?"

"I thought it was the Guinness family," Jelena admitted, then wrinkled her nose. "Although now that I say it aloud, why would the Guinness family sponsor a whiskey festival?"

"Because they sponsor a lot of stuff. I mean, now that you've said it aloud I hear it too, but still, I totally would have believed Guinness sponsored the whiskey festival." Megan paused thoughtfully. "Is there a Guinness whiskey?"

"I don't know, but you have the internet in your pocket, so you could find out if you wanted to," Jelena said.

Megan reached for her phone, which was actually in a tiny glittery gold purse that matched her outfit, then let it go. "Probably doesn't matter. Not unless Ireland's richest family has decided to start murdering people over a new whiskey brand."

"There's no way Guinness is Ireland's richest family. The Ryanair guy is definitely richer." Jelena actually did get out her phone and looked it up, then made a face. "I never even heard of any of the richest people here except for him. Guinness doesn't even make the top ten. Did you know there are like twenty Irish billionaires?"

"Well, that's an embarrassing policy failure." Megan wasn't sure how they'd gotten to discussing billionaires, but it meant she wasn't trying to investigate McConal's death, so she would be happy to keep talking about them until they were allowed to leave. Some of the newly arrived guards were taking pictures of, and examining, McConal's body, while others gave the impatient, rubbernecking crowd some of what they wanted, and began escorting them downstairs, or into the huge auditorium. Megan didn't think it was coincidence that somehow, Sean Byrne and his companion kept getting shuffled farther back in the line.

Not that it mattered, because people were clearly not being allowed to leave. They were just being removed from the crime scene itself and separated for ease of interviewing. At a conservative guess, there were a thousand people at the gala. Megan said, "We're going to be here all night," as she realized it.

"I am not wearing the right shoes to stand around all night," Jelena said grimly.

Megan looked at Jelena's feet, then at her own. They were both in heels—Megan couldn't actually wear her gold pantsuit without them, because the hems were so long—and Jelena had made the most of her height by wearing four-inch stilettos. "If we go over there," she said with a nod toward the far side of the bar, "maybe we'll get streamlined into a group that gets to go sit down in the auditorium while we wait to be interviewed."

"I have nothing to say in an interview!"

"Me either, so hopefully it won't take long. I wish we could get Niamh out of there, though." Their film star friend was still downstairs at the center of a maelstrom, graciously answering questions, but Megan could see the tension in the lines of her smile and the way her gaze kept going to one side or the other like she was looking for a way out. "The paparazzi must have something better to do than harass her."

"I should be down there with her." Rabbie Lynch came back to Megan's side. He'd aged in the past half hour, and moved like he needed to sit down. "This shouldn't be on her at all. The one woman in all of Ireland you introduced me to, and this is her thanks for it."

"Oh, now that's not fair," Jelena protested. "Megan introduced me to you, too."

"She did, and I'll be thanking her for the rest of me days," Rabbie said, rallying briefly. "An old man surrounded by beautiful young women. I couldn't ask for more. But with no ill intent meant, me darling, Niamh's a wee little bit more famous than you are."

"Thank goodness," Jelena said fiercely. "I don't want to be famous. Niamh can bring glamour to the brand. I just want to have a nice little house and a normal life."

Megan felt the weight of Jelena *not* looking at her, and tried to hide a wince. She didn't particularly want notoriety or fame herself, but she'd gained a certain degree of both over the past few years, to the point that she had an actual hashtag-slash-nickname of her own: "murder driver." The only person who liked it less than Jelena was Megan's boss, Orla. Then again, being the company that employed the murder driver had done wonders for Leprechaun Limo's bottom line, so Orla's complaints seemed increasingly like posturing.

Rabbie, oblivious to Megan's line of thought, carried on with increasing expansiveness. "Without her we'd never have gotten Harbourmaster to the competition."

"I wouldn't say that," Megan said, more amused than objecting. "Harbourmaster would have done just fine without Niamh. It's a good whiskey."

"It would have done fine," Rabbie agreed, "but

yer wan elevates the promotion, and you know it, love."

"Well, that *was* the point of introducing you," Megan said under her breath. "Look, I don't know, Uncle Rabbie, do you know any of the paparazzi down there? Maybe you could shame them into leaving her alone by saying you'll give out to their mums, or something."

Interest creased Rabbie's face and he leaned over the rail, examining the gathered reporters. "There's Aidan Collins with the *Daily Star*, but I wouldn't know most of the others. They're not Irish," he said apologetically. "I only know everyone in Ireland."

"Some of them do nothing but follow Niamh around," Jelena said. "I don't know how Paul lives with it."

All three of them turned their attention back to Paul Bourke, who was in quiet, grim-looking discussion with another guard. They both stood a few feet away from McConal's body, where a woman in a forensics jacket was finishing taking pictures and doing what looked to Megan like rifling through the dead man's pockets. She said, "See, I don't think I could do that," out loud, and spread her hands at Jelena's glance. "Despite it all, I don't think I'm cut out to be a cop, is what I'm saying. I'm just a bad luck magnet."

"You and Jessica Fletcher," Rabbie muttered.

"*Murder, She Drove,*" Megan agreed. Jelena made a disapproving sound and Megan offered an apologetic smile that her girlfriend clearly didn't buy. A lot of people had been cleared off the balcony by then, and a determined-looking guard was simultaneously guiding a couple near Megan toward the auditorium, and eyeing Megan warningly. They would clearly be given their marching orders next.

The forensics woman took a folded sheet of paper from Angus's breast pocket, opened it, and looked up sharply, her eyebrows elevated. "Detective Bourke." She stood, handing him the paper, which Paul took, glanced at, nodded, then double-took at before whipping toward Megan, Jelena, and Rabbie. "Bloody *hell*, Megan!"

"What?" Megan took a couple of startled steps forward, genuinely unsure of what she could have done this time. A woman who had been near McConal since he'd fallen reached for the paper Paul held, but he flicked it out of her way without seeming to realize he'd done so. A few long steps took him to Megan's side, where he thrust the paper at her, although he didn't let her touch it. Almost before she got a glimpse of its contents, he flicked it toward Rabbie, snapping, "And what have you got to say about this, Mr. Lynch?"

Rabbie Lynch snapped, "Not a word, laddie, and ye'd best keep a civil tongue in your head or I'll be ringing your mam to speak to her about your attitude!" before Megan put her hand on his arm and whispered, "Take it down a notch, Uncle Rabbie. Paul, did I really see . . ."

The police detective turned the paper toward her again, and Megan's stomach churned into a ball of nauseous confusion as she read it again, confirming what she thought she'd seen.

Angus McConal had died with the Harbourmaster Whiskey recipe in his pocket.

CHAPTER 3

U ncle Rabbie, what . . ." Megan stopped there, because she couldn't imagine what to say next.

"Well, I didn't put it there, did I!" Rabbie's face flushed red with indignation, and unexpected guilt flashed through Megan.

"I didn't mean to say you had. I just—why does Angus McConal have your recipe?"

"I don't know, but don't go showing it to the world!" Rabbie made a motion like he'd snatch the paper from Paul's hands, although the police detective moved it away and folded it over, hiding the words.

"The guards will be needing to talk to you, Mr. Lynch."

"Well, I'll be needing to talk to the guards! We've kept that recipe secret for years! This could ruin us! This—" A little too late, Rabbie clearly re-alized what he was saying and what it could mean.

His jaw dropped and he took a step backward, physically distancing himself from the implication he'd drawn. "Oh, no, I'd never. I wouldn't kill him. The man could lay me out with a single punch!"

Megan grimaced, and although Paul kept his expression more or less steady, she rather thought he was hiding a grimace of his own. "He could beat me up" wasn't exactly the defense Rabbie meant it to be, especially since whatever had happened to Angus, he clearly hadn't been killed through outright physical violence.

The woman who had tried to get the paper before was suddenly there, between Paul and Rabbie, with fury blazing in her eyes. "You've done this!" she shrieked. "You've killed Angus McConal, you filthy bastard, you always hated his father and this is the way you've had your revenge!" She hauled off and slapped Rabbie, the sharp crack of sound silencing everything else in the convention center.

Rabbie staggered, as much from shock, Megan thought, as the power of the blow. He put his hand to his cheek, stunned to silence for the first time that Megan could remember, and for a few seconds simply stared at the woman who'd hit him. She was dark-haired in a shade that Megan recognized from the drugstore shelves, and her makeup tended toward the gothy, which rather suited her.

Then Rabbie, his tone more astonished than aggrieved, said, "Erin Ryan, what would your father think of you assaulting one of his oldest friends? He'd roll in his grave, he would. What's the story, lass?"

Megan bit back an *oh!* of recognition. Erin Ryan was Angus McConal's manager, and had been for twenty years. She was also at least in her mid-forties, hardly young enough to be called "lass," even by Rabbie, who had a solid twenty years on her. Megan would have been tempted to slap him again just for that, but apparently Erin had vented her spleen, because rather than respond verbally to Rabbie, she broke down and began crying.

Someone stepped up, put their arms around her shoulders, and steered her away. For long seconds, silence continued to reign, although voices began to pick up and murmur to one another as gossip and suppositions were shared. Paul, after a measured beat, said, "And did you hate Mr. Mc-Conal's father, Mr. Lynch?"

"I did," Rabbie said without hesitation. "He was a mean man, was Owen McConal. That's nothing to do with the boy, though."

"The boy," Paul said, "was thirty-seven. Why would you want revenge against his father, through him or otherwise?"

"I swear to you that I have never had an ill thought against Angus McConal," Rabbie said. "His father was bad to a woman I cared about, but he's dead these twenty-five years and more, too, and all my anger is long gone. Even if it wasn't, I would never have taken it out on Angus."

"Right." Paul stared at him a long moment, then dragged in a deep breath. "We'll need to bring you in to have a talk. You and the rest of your t—"

He broke off, blanching, and Megan saw his gaze dart to the balcony. From where they stood, neither of them could see beyond it, but Niamh was still down there.

Niamh, his girlfriend, and also part of the Harbourmaster Whiskey team.

A bubble of cold dismay rose and burst in Megan's stomach as Paul said, "*Feck,*" more vigorously than she'd ever heard him swear before.

"She's only the face, Paul," Megan said, as if it might help, but he gave her a dark look in return.

"She'll still be caught up in it, as she has to be. I have to recuse myself. I have to step away right now." He turned abruptly and handed the recipe to another guard, his voice low and frustrated as he explained the situation in a few brief words.

The other guard's eyes widened, a combination of horror, sympathy, and excitement chasing each other across his face. Someone, Megan thought, would get the lead on this case who wouldn't have otherwise. Given the high profile nature of the victim's death, it might make someone's career. She wondered if it would be Dervla Reese, who had taken over the last case when Paul had been compromised, or if a new guard would get involved.

Her stomach dropped again. This was the second time in a row that Detective Bourke *had* been compromised in a case, or at least, compromised in a case that Megan was also involved in. That couldn't be good for *his* career.

Paul muttered, "I'm going downstairs to be with Niamh," and brushed past, leaving Megan with Jelena, Carmen, Rabbie, and the guard she didn't know. A squeak of protest broke in her throat, and Paul gave her a significant glance as he reached the head of the escalator.

He couldn't possibly have just flickered his gaze between her and the guard, Megan thought as he disappeared downstairs. He couldn't have been telling her to keep on top of things, could he? Inspector Detective Paul Bourke of the Garda Síochána wasn't giving her the go-ahead to investigate a murder because he wasn't going to be able to do it himself.

No. No, obviously, he wasn't. She was reading things in. He probably just wanted her to stay out of it. That had probably been a warning, not a suggestion.

Jelena, at her elbow, breathed, "He did *not* just tell you to keep an eye on things," and a terrible combination of delight and dismay churned through Megan's belly until she pulled a maniacal grin.

"I'm sure he didn't."

"*Megan.*"

"I'm trying, Yella!"

Her girlfriend sighed from the bottom of her soul and said something in Polish. For the space of a heartbeat, Megan considered asking for a translation, but really, the tone was enough. Jelena's faith in Megan's ability to stay out of a murder investigation was . . .well, Megan didn't think it was nonexistent, but it was certainly limited. Given that this time her cousin and one of her best friends was involved, and that the detective she trusted was off the case . . .

Megan herself sighed and repeated, "I'm trying," more quietly, and finally looked back toward the cop Paul had left in charge.

He was comparatively young, probably in his late twenties, and didn't have any of the insignia of a police detective. Megan imagined there would

be another detective on-site soon—one who was
actually on duty, instead of there for pleasure and
caught up in the tragedy—but for the time being,
she could see a slight wideness in the garda's eyes
that suggested he was in over his head. His nostrils
were a little too flared, and a muscle bunched in
his jaw. Altogether, he struck Megan as the kind of
person inclined to take uncertainty out in belliger-
ence.

Megan had the fleeting, unkind thought that
maybe it was just as well that the boxer known to
have a temper was the victim. A minute ago, even
her own Uncle Rabbie, faced with a completely
nonaggressive, and even technically off-duty cop,
had been ready to put up a fight. She could all too
easily imagine Angus McConal fraying out of control when faced with an even mildly aggressive cop
asking if he'd been involved in a murder.

All the fight had drained out of her uncle now,
though. Lines she'd never particularly noticed
were carved deeper in his face, and his shoulders
rounded in a way they never had before. For the
first time that she'd known him, he looked old.
She didn't believe he'd had anything to do with
McConal's death, but that would require proof.

She winced and mumbled, "But I guess everything to do with whiskey requires proof," aloud,
even though she was fairly confident it wouldn't
make sense to anyone else.

Jelena gave her a pained look, and Megan bit
the inside of her cheek, trying not to laugh at herself. "I'm sorry. I was thinking—"

"That you'd need proof to show Rabbie was innocent," Jelena said with more humor than Megan

expected, given the circumstances. A wave of fondness rose in Megan's chest, followed closely by an equally strong wash of concern. Jelena knew her well enough to follow her thoughts from silence through a terrible pun. Megan didn't want to lose that.

Which meant that even if Paul *had* been giving her signals to keep an eye on things, she really couldn't, because Jelena had made it clear she'd had more than enough of Megan's mystery-solving. "The police will do their job," she said, again mostly to herself.

Jelena's eyebrows rose. "Yes, they will. Uncle Rabbie will be fine."

The note of relief and approval in her voice warmed Megan, but she still couldn't help glancing around, trying to take in what was going on around them.

Despite the best efforts of the handful of gardaí who were on the scene, a lot of people still clumped together, some mute with horror, but far more whispering to each other about the situation. The whiskey heiress, Hannah Flanagan, was talking into her phone, presumably recording her thoughts and reactions for a podcast later. Megan bet her ratings would be through the roof for that episode.

Carmen de la Fuente's security guy had rejoined her and was doing an excellent job playing the part of a wall that separated Carmen from the riffraff. He was bald, strong-jawed, and had an almost perfectly square shoulder-to-hip ratio. Megan didn't think he was much more than an inch taller than she was, and bet there were a lot of people who decided short and squat meant he wasn't particularly dangerous. She also bet those people were painfully wrong.

No one had yet taken Sean Byrne, the event organizer, away. His well-dressed date, a gray-blond white woman in her mid-fifties, had joined him again and stood with one hand tucked over his folded arms. Her expression was extremely tight, and Megan wondered if that light touch was keeping him under control, or at least, reminding him to remain in control.

There were two other competitors in the best new whiskey category. One of them, a florid man in his forties, sat on the floor next to the escalators, weeping. Megan racked her brain for the man's name and couldn't come up with it. "Yella, do you remember who he is?"

Jelena squinted toward the sobbing competitor, her lips pursing as she thought. "Danny something. Keane?"

"Right, he's the Keane Edge whiskey." Megan looked for the last of the competitors, then glanced back at Keane. "I wonder why he's so upset. Do you think they were close?"

"I think no matter who wins the competition now, it'll be overshadowed by McConal's death, or McConal will get the sympathy vote and win posthumously. I'd say that's what's got him in bits."

Megan bobbed a nod, but also muttered, "Not if McConal was stealing recipes. I mean, he won't win, in that case," as she looked around for the final competitor. She knew they were a married couple, and that one of the husbands was into whiskey, and the other was into graphic design.

Their surname was Murphy and, in following with the Irish meaning of the name, their brand was Sea Warrior Whiskey. Megan, somewhat guiltily because she felt she should be all-in on the Harbourmaster brand, thought their label had by far the most visual appeal of any of the competitors. But the husbands appeared to have already been shuffled into one of the conference rooms that the police were still trying to sort everyone into.

Which was *fine*, because that was the gardaí's job, not Megan's. It didn't matter what she thought of how anybody reacted to McConal's death. Paul *definitely* hadn't been giving her a signal about it before, because that would be, as the Irish would say, mental. "I wonder if it was a good idea for him to go down there with her. Her picture's going to be all over everything in another five minutes, and so will his. I bet the last thing anybody needs is to be reminded that Niamh O'Sullivan's boyfriend is a cop."

Jelena glanced toward the downstairs, but shrugged. "Too late now. If you haven't solved it already, we should go into the auditorium."

"So I stop trying?" Megan asked with a faint smile.

She did not get a smile in return. Jelena only nodded, and started making her way toward the line where officers were guiding people into the seats to wait. Megan touched Rabbie's arm and tilted her head. "You want to come sit down with us? I'm sure you'll be on the short list of people they want to talk to first, so maybe when that's over we can all get out of here."

Rabbie, red with worry, nodded and followed them to the auditorium. They were on the second level, high enough to appreciate the size of the place. People were seated in small bunches, far enough away from one another that talking about the events of the evening with anyone other than their immediate group would be both awkward and very obvious. The sense of decorum that the huge auditorium carried lent a greater difficulty to shouting across its spaces, so mostly it was filled with quiet murmurs and anxious or curious looks.

A young woman with her curly light brown hair in an upsweep waved at them, and Megan, recognizing the Harbourmaster team's marketing guru, murmured, "There, with Willow," and Jelena led them down toward the girl. Willow Hartley wasn't yet thirty, and when Megan had met her earlier, had come across as confident, savvy, and quick with a line. Now, however, her brown eyes were enormous with worry. "This is one of the scariest things that's ever happened to me."

"Let's hope it stays that way. It'll be fine." Megan smiled at her briefly, glancing back to see the guard who'd directed them to seats making a note of who and where they were before he left again.

Jelena folded her arms across her chest as she sat next to Willow. "I hate this, Megan."

"I know." Megan, sitting beside her, with Rabbie settling on her other side, offered Jelena her hand and was relieved when Yella wound her fingers through hers. "But you and I didn't have anything to do with this, and they'll clear Uncle Rabbie soon enough and we can all go home." She nudged Rabbie's shoulder with her own, hoping to make him smile. "Well, unless you've got a deep, dark secret you're keeping about Angus McConal, in which case, we're screwed."

Rabbie turned a stricken look on her and Megan's stomach sank through the floor.

CHAPTER 4

"Rabbie! Not twenty minutes ago you told me there was no beef!" Megan remembered his expression had wobbled at the time. She'd thought it had to do with the American-ness of the phrase, but she was suddenly much less sure. "What's the story? What are you not telling me?"

"There's nothing between Angus McConal and myself!" There was a kind of precision in how Rabbie Lynch spoke, as if he was being careful to choose his words so he wasn't actually lying.

Megan pulled her hands down her face until she felt like the *Scream* painting. "So who *is* there something between?"

"It was a long time ago, and there was neither anything wrong with what we did, nor anyone hurt, nor anything come of it!"

"Rabbie!" Megan wailed. "What are you talking about?"

A deep pink blush began to crawl up from below Rabbie's collar. "Bridey McConal and I had a relationship not long after her husband died. Angus couldn't keep mad at his ma, but he never forgave me for it."

On Jelena's far side, Willow's eyes popped as if the idea of Rabbie ever having had a lover was beyond comprehension. At her age, it might be: he was decades older than she, and the idea that he'd ever been meaningfully younger was probably too much for her to contemplate. While she goggled, Jelena sucked her cheeks in and slid a glance toward Megan, who found herself trying not to grin. "A relationship." She could practically *hear* her uncle refusing to call it an affair, because of the sordid implications the word often carried. "How long did this relationship last? How old was Angus?"

Rabbie's skin gradually became florid, until his blue eyes bulged in the heat of his face. "It lasted a few months. The lad was eleven or so, and raging at the idea that his ma could move on, but I said it to your detective and I'll said it to you. Owen McConal was not a nice man, Megan. Him dying young likely saved Bridey the same fate."

"Ah." Megan sat back and scrubbed her hands over her face. "Why did it end?"

"Because she chose her son over me," Rabbie said simply. "The only choice she could make, and I've never blamed her for it, though there's many times I've regretted it."

"But his grandfather still brought him around?" Jelena asked quietly. "You said that, earlier. That he brought him around and talked him up after his matches."

"Joe Boyle was Bridey's da," Rabbie said. "I think he hoped Angus would come around to me after a while."

Megan nodded, still mostly into her hands. "Did Angus know what kind of man his father was?"

She glanced up in time to see Rabbie bare his teeth. "You know how that kind of man can be. He wanted Angus to think the world of him, so he never threatened or hit her when the lad was around, and he was careful about where he left bruises. He'd have been pleased the boy grew up to make a living through his fists."

"Was Angus that kind of man himself? I know there were allegations." Megan reached for her phone, thinking she would look up some of the headlines she'd seen splashed across the tabloids, but Rabbie's face said a lot.

Then to Megan's surprise, Willow said more.

"He was. The accusations were made to go away, but I—I know people who were involved with him. There have been choices made and so I wouldn't want to say more to protect people's privacy, but . . ." Willow offered a stiff shrug of her thin shoulders. "He wasn't a good person."

Megan let out a long breath and sank into her seat, working her way through that careful confirmation. "That probably expands our circle of suspects. That's probably good for you."

"Except he had our recipe on him when he died," Rabbie said grimly.

"But why?" Jelena sounded both baffled and reluctantly engaged. "What good does having the Harbourmaster whiskey recipe do anybody? Whiskey takes a long time to make, doesn't it? The aging process? So unless he had it for years, he couldn't have been planning to try claiming Rabbie'd taken *his* recipe, and what else would he be doing with it?"

"Using it in a blend? Or . . ." Megan's knowledge of whiskey ended with the idea that it was aged and sometimes blended, so she couldn't suggest anything more. "Or maybe they were going to pretend it was theirs, and that Harbourmaster had stolen it years ago? But who gave it to them?" She sat up straighter, which was more comfortable in the glittering golden pantsuit she wore anyway, and looked around the auditorium like the answer lay in the little gatherings of people there. "Rabbie, how big is your team? I don't know if three people can develop a new whiskey or if it takes forty. I don't even know how you actually tell one whiskey from another most of the time. It all burns the lining off my throat."

"Anybody with a grain mash and a barrel can make whiskey," Rabbie said with a sniff. "Making *good* whiskey is an art. Making a new, unique, palatable flavor that will appeal to the masses is a blend of art and science and," he said, tone falling as if he'd lost the high ground, "takes a load of people who know what they're competing against and what they're reaching for. There's eight of us who have been working on Harbourmaster for years, and Niamh."

"Does Niamh even have access to the recipe?"

Rabbie shook his head, and Megan sighed with relief. "So that's one person who couldn't have shared it. It's a start."

"What if someone analyzed it?" Jelena asked. "Can you tell how a whiskey has been made by doing a chemical analysis?"

"No," Rabbie said, then bobbled his hand. "Yes. To a point, love, but not enough to replicate a recipe. It'd tell you the difference between an American bourbon and a Scotch, but not one Irish malt from another."

Megan and Jelena's gazes met for a moment before Jelena, clearly unwilling but unable to stop herself, giggled. Willow, empathetic, put a hand on Jelena's arm. "*Right?*"

Rabbie frowned between them, verging on offended. "What?"

Jelena smiled at Megan's uncle. "I'm sorry, Rabbie. I barely understood any of that. I thought bourbon was something else. Why is it called bourbon if it's a whiskey? And I know there are things called malt whiskeys, but I don't know what it means. I did know Scotch was whiskey," she added almost defensively, but Megan grinned at her in complete understanding, and Rabbie brightened for the first time in several minutes, obviously happy to impart his wisdom to someone.

"Bourbon is a particular kind of American whiskey. All whiskey starts with a grain mash, you know that?"

Jelena, still with a smile lingering, said, "We drink vodka made from rye, so yes, I know that."

Megan blinked. "I thought vodka was made from potatoes."

"That too," Jelena said, "but Poland had rye before it had potatoes."

"Fair."

"Bourbon is made from a corn mash and aged in new barrels," Rabbie said in the tone of a man afraid he would lose his audience if he chose the wrong details to share with them. "Scotch is from malted barley and has to be aged in oak barrels. To be an Irish whiskey, it's got to be of malted *and* unmalted barley. And other ingredients, of course, for any whiskey, and then—" He hesitated, eyeing the fading interest in Jelena's expression, and concluded, "Then it's distilled, usually three times for Irish whiskey, before it's aged to alter its flavor, depending on the barrel used."

Megan, brightly, said, "I knew that part!" and Rabbie smiled crookedly at her.

"It's what most people know, I'd say. So to develop a new whiskey, especially one that isn't blended—most of them are—you have to have people who know their whiskeys, and have a sense of how the end product will taste when you take it out of the barrel three or more years after it's gone in. Otherwise you've wasted a lot of time, and maybe a lot of money."

"How long have you been working on Harbourmaster?" Megan asked in astonishment.

"Seventeen years." Rabbie's smile fled. "Since Angus was twenty, if you want to look at it that way, and I've heard rumor his own brand has been in the making a decade. By ten years ago, we were certain enough of our recipe that it could have been sold or stolen, Megan."

"He wouldn't be carrying around a recipe that

said it was Harbourmaster's, though, if he'd had it that long," Megan objected. "Would he?"

"Maybe someone planted it on him." Jelena pressed her lips together as if they'd betrayed her with the suggestion. Megan fought back the impulse to say "See? This is how it starts!" to her, but this *was* how it started. Wondering, or being concerned, or just spitballing ideas about what could have happened, was how she'd ended up involved in four murder cases already. Even Jelena had fallen a little way down that rabbit hole in the last case—in fact, Megan wouldn't have solved it without her—but she so clearly didn't want to be engaged with it that Megan felt guilty that she'd had an idea.

Rabbie, oblivious to Megan's conflicted feelings, shook his head as if in disbelief. "Sure and who would do that, though? Why?"

"Someone who wanted to point the police in the wrong direction," Megan said. "And it would still be someone who had access to the Harbourmaster recipe. Assuming it's the real recipe."

Utter relief swept Rabbie's face. "It mightn't be, mightn't it? I didn't get a good look at it, only that it had our name on it. Ah, Jaysus, Megan, you're a lifesaver. I'd hate to think any of the team would betray us, and it would make more sense that they wouldn't. It's not only my time and money that's gone into Harbourmaster, ye know."

"We wouldn't." Willow's eyes were huge. "We could never, Rabbie. I know I'm only new to the team, but everybody loves you, Mr. Lynch. We'd never betray you."

Megan started with, "Well, I don't know that it

isn't—" but Rabbie was already dedicated to the idea it wasn't even their recipe, and wouldn't hear a word she had to say. She glanced at Jelena, whose gaze was a mix of warning and wry. Megan read it clearly enough: she thought Megan should leave it alone, and understood why she might not be able to. Megan sighed and spread her hands, letting it go. If it wasn't the actual Harbourmaster recipe, they'd find out soon enough, and if it was, the few hours' peace of mind the suggestion had provided would probably be good for Rabbie.

"Sorry." A woman's warm voice spoke behind Megan and a flash of dismay shot through Jelena's expression. Megan, grimacing, mouthed a name at her, and Jelena responded with a nod so tiny Megan wouldn't have seen it if she hadn't been looking for it.

Then she schooled her expression and turned to look up at Hannah Flanagan, the podcasting whiskey heiress with the smoky voice that Lauren Bacall would have envied. Flanagan was dressed in sparkling sky blue, which made her look even younger than her baby-faced features did on their own, and she had a cutely apologetic pout that made Megan realize that she was playing into her childish appearance. She had a strappy purse over her shoulder, but held her phone in one hand, a recording app disappearing as the screen went dark. "You're Megan Malone, right? The murder driver. And Rabbie Lynch of Harbourmaster Whiskey is your uncle? I'm Hannah Flanagan of *Flanagan's Flights* podcast. I'll only take a minute of your time."

"No," Megan said in her most Texas accent.

"You won't take any of our time." She turned her back on Hannah again and watched Rabbie's eyes bug at her abruptness. Jelena, her own eyes wide, bit the inside of her cheek, and Megan could almost hear Flanagan recalibrating behind her.

After a few seconds, the podcaster tried again, this time saying, "Mr. Lynch, I don't know if you're familiar with *Flanagan's Flights*, but I'm—"

Megan said, "*No,*" again, and this time stood up. She wasn't particularly tall, even in heels, and Flanagan had a couple inches on her, but getting between clients and anybody else was occasionally a literal part of Megan's job. Shoulders squared and voice firm, she said, "Ms. Flanagan, I understand you're doing your job, but I also understand that at the moment, we're in the very early stages of what appears to be a murder investigation, and the absolute last person *anyone* potentially involved—and that includes every competitor in this year's roster—should be doing is talking to someone whose ratings increase every time somebody says something stupid or sensational. I'm sure that after this is resolved, everyone would love to be on your podcast to rehash it all, but this is not the time."

She spoke loudly and clearly on purpose, making sure her voice carried across the auditorium. People turned to look, which was what she wanted, particularly since a couple of those people were, in fact, competitors, and they should listen to her advice.

Color flushed along Flanagan's cheeks and cords stood out in her neck, as if she'd never encountered someone unwilling to be interviewed. Megan had the fleeting thought that, given the young woman came from money and was independently successful and famous, it could literally be true. The wealthy, in her experience, were frequently baffled by people not doing what they expected of them. "Thank you for your time, Ms. Flanagan."

Flanagan, unaccustomed to having the script reversed on her, automatically said, "Yes, of course, my pleasure," before frowning. Megan sat and turned her back on the young woman again, deliberately dismissing her, and from the corner of her eye, saw Hannah slowly walk away.

Both Willow and Rabbie had the horrified expression common to Irish faces when Megan had done something unspeakably and unforgivably *American*. Willow hadn't yet recovered when a guard came to get her for her interview, and all of them were silent, watching the young woman climb the steps behind the guard.

"Sure now, that wasn't necessary," Rabbie said uncertainly. "She's only a young wan."

"If you mean Willow, we all have to go through the interview process. If you mean Hannah Flanagan, she's old enough to profit off this incident," Megan replied acerbically. "I'm your driver tonight, Uncle Rabbie. Part of my job is defusing situations that might bite you on the ass later."

"And she's very good at it," Jelena said with admiration. "No wonder I think you're hot, *bejb*."

Megan grinned. "It's the pantsuit, isn't it? You like a woman in gold."

Jelena took a breath to respond, then murmured, "So does the woman who bought it for you," as Carmen swept down the auditorium stairs from where she and her bodyguard had been sitting.

"You see, Ramon," Carmen was saying as they approached, "Meghaaaan would be an excellent bodyguard, you do not need to be so tall and *male* to protect me!"

Only someone as tiny as Carmen could think Ramon was tall. Megan grinned at him, but nothing even vaguely resembling a smile cracked his visage. It looked like nothing resembling a smile had *ever* crossed his face, although she remembered Carmen saying her bodyguard had smiled at the news of Angus McConal's death. She tried to imagine it, failed, and had her attention drawn to his employer as Carmen drawled, "Meghaaan! You were magnificent with that pretty vulture, and so Ramon will tell you everything he knows about Angus McConal."

It turned out Ramon's expression *could* change, because pained resignation flickered over it. Megan shook her head and lifted a hand. "Really, that's not necessary. I'm not an investigator, after all. If you've talked to the police, that's enough."

Carmen sniffed. "Please. Everyone knows there are things you do not tell the police."

Jelena swore in Polish, raised her hands to the sky, then turned away and folded her arms, clearly indicating she would have nothing to do with any of this.

Megan shook her head, honestly trying to keep her promise to Jelena, and trying not to think about whether Paul really had given her a "keep an ear open" look, earlier. "Carmen, no, really, I can't."

The tiny rich woman said, "Ramon," imperiously, and with a sigh, her bodyguard began to talk.

CHAPTER 5

"Angus McConal should never have been made into a boxer," the bodyguard said. Like Carmen, he had a Spanish accent, although his, while thicker, was also somehow less noticeable, because he didn't lean into the trills and vowels the way Carmen did. "It taught him the answer to everything was at the end of his fist. Violence is the only language he understood. Men like that should be put down."

Megan blinked, and not just because that was an unwise thing to say about a man who had just presumably been murdered. Something less than amusement glinted in Ramon's gaze. "You think that's a strange thing for someone on a security detail to say."

"Well . . . yes."

"In this line of work, if it comes to violence,

you've already lost control of the situation. It should never go that far. And," he said with a flicker of his gaze across the auditorium, like he was keeping an eye out for danger, "I should have said people, not men. But men are more often a physical threat."

"What was your relationship with McConal?"

His nose wrinkled slightly. "We had no relationship. I worked security for the fights, a long time ago, and watched him coming up. He was a very good fighter, but he could not leave it in the ring."

"He was an Olympic champion," Megan objected. "If he had trouble keeping his temper under control, that would have been news, wouldn't it?"

Ramon's expression turned almost pitying, just for a moment. "Do you know how much money goes into those fighters, Señora Malone? Do you know who puts the money up?"

Megan winced. "Allegedly, yeah. At least the second part." There were consistent rumors of notoriously deep criminal links to Irish boxing. More than one local champion had distanced themselves from their roots, and sometimes even the country, to try to break the associations. "So you're saying they'd have covered up any . . ." She took a very deep breath, trying to choose noninflammatory words, as if there was someone to protect in the here and now. "Any missteps. But wouldn't that be hard in the Olympic village, or anywhere there's a lot of media coverage? People have mobile phones and record everything now."

"When the world is watching, you keep a volatile athlete under very tight control," Ramon said. "Even then it isn't always enough. And in public . . ." He shrugged his massive shoulders. "You must see the headlines, señora. Angus McConal has been in them for fights in the pubs more than fights in the ring, lately."

"Carmen said you threw him out of one of her parties."

His nostrils flared. "I wouldn't have let him in, if I'd been on the door. I threw him into the harbor." He paused, considering her momentarily. "You were at that party, I think."

Megan's eyebrows shot up. "I've only been to one of Carmen's parties! The costume party?" She had only realized after arriving in the gold pant-suit she now wore that she had been dressed—by Carmen, who had been surrounded by other women in similar garb—as a very modern take on a Disney princess. Paul Bourke had been her date for the evening and by coincidence, had worn the dark blue that matched her princess's gold. Like Belle and the Beast. Carmen, to Megan's amuse-ment, had approved.

An almost-invisible smile flickered across Ramon's face. "He came as a gobshite."

A laugh burst from Megan's throat and echoed across the auditorium as she clapped her hand over her mouth. "You're a funny man, señor—I'm sorry, I don't know if Ramon is your first or last name."

"Sanchez. Ramon Sanchez."

"Señor Sanchez, then. What did she want you to tell me, though, that she wouldn't tell the police?"

The head of Carmen's security glanced at her,

then sighed as she leaned in to murmur—or as close to murmuring as Carmen could come— "Meghan is the murder driver, Ramon. She is a safe person to tell things to. She is not police, but she cares for justice."

Ramon sucked his teeth, then nodded. "It was a long time ago and not important enough anymore to matter, Señora Malone. But it would look bad to the police."

Megan, trying not to notice Jelena's stiff shoulders, nodded with understanding. "What happened?"

"Fights are sometimes fixed," Ramon said cautiously. "You hear things, working security."

The pieces fell into place easily enough. "You lost a lot of money on McConal when he won a fight he was supposed to throw? Or the other way around? I guess it doesn't matter."

"Sí, yes. A long time ago. Too long to remember how much money, even. And if I had been going to kill him for it, I would have made sure he stayed down, in the harbor. But authorities don't like fixed fights, or betting on them with insider information. I would rather . . ." He shrugged his broad shoulders again. "Not mention it."

"Hopefully it won't become relevant, but if it does, you should tell somebody who's actually in authority. You know that, right?"

Ramon grimaced. Apparently his stoic expression was reserved for when he was actually guarding Carmen, and not when talking about personal things. "It might be enough for you to know— from an anonymous source—that many of his early losses were fixed. That his big win in Barcelona was calculated. The underdog, coming up for the title."

"I'm sorry. I don't know about Barcelona. I don't really follow boxing."

"It was the making of a champion," Rabbie said quietly, startling her. She'd mostly forgotten he was there, focused on Ramon's story. "He'd been coming up in the ranks for a few years, fighting on the smaller circuits. Mostly winning, but he'd had a streak of losses, only broken by enough wins to get him into the ring with an older star on the downside of his career. They went ten rounds, and it was the stuff of legend. McConal knocked the other man out a heartbeat before the bell. Sixteen months later he won the Olympic gold."

"Wow. And it was set up?"

"I wouldn't say the gold was," Rabbie replied cagily, but Ramon nodded.

"The losing streak, the underdog win, sí, yes. He was a good fighter," he emphasized. "It's all he *was* good at. But I did bet on him and would prefer the police not know."

Megan nodded and finally risked a glance toward Jelena, whose shoulders were stiff with frustration. She turned her attention back to Ramon for a moment, promising, "If it somehow comes up, I'll mention it as something I'd heard. I'll try to keep your name out of it."

"Gracias, Señora Malone. I see why Carmen likes you, too."

"Because she looks *muy linda* in her gold suit," Carmen trilled happily. "Good, now we can go."

"The police are still going to want to interview you!"

Carmen waved a hand dismissively as she rose. "I am rich." She swanned off, Ramon at her hip, and Megan was left wanting to protest, but also fairly certain that Carmen's airy confidence that her wealth would protect her from much inconvenience was largely accurate.

"See," she said hopefully to Jelena, "it wasn't really anything. Nothing that's probably ever going to come up."

Jelena said, "Megan," then bared her teeth and shook her head, looking away. "Never mind. Not here. Not now."

"Ah, sure and it's not Megan's fault," Rabbie tried. "It's only that she's gone and gotten herself a reputation, isn't it. And people like to talk to Americans. They're so . . . *friendly*."

He said it as if it was more of a curse than a blessing. Megan ducked her head, grinning. Ireland held two predominant American stereotypes: the ugly, rude one, and the garishly noisy, talk-to-everybody friendly one. She'd gotten mileage out of both in the years she'd lived in Ireland, although her version of "ugly" American was pretty low-key, mostly doing things like having the audacity to shut Hannah Flanagan down.

"Friendly is fine," Jelena said tightly. "Involved in another murder investigation isn't."

"I'm not, though. As soon as we can get out of here, Jelena, I swear I won't have anything else to do with it. I can't even report in to Paul on this one, so I don't know what good it would do for me to try investigating anyway."

"You'd never leave me hanging," Rabbie said with an audible gasp of worry in his voice.

Guilt surged through Megan. It must have shown on her face, because Jelena groaned, slumping in her seat, which was terrible for her gown. "Fine, go on. I won't be able to stop you anyway. Rabbie is your family. Maybe I shouldn't even try."

"Jelena . . ." An entirely different guilt rolled through Megan and she reached for Jelena's hand. The other woman let her take it, although she sighed. A couple of men started moving down their row of the auditorium as Megan ducked her head to kiss Jelena's knuckles. "I'm sorry. I don't know why this keeps happening around me."

"Because you're good at it," Jelena said morosely, before a frown drew a line between her eyebrows and she straightened to stare at Megan like she'd become someone new. "You're not just good at it. It's—what's the English word? In Polish it would be *osobliwy*. Peculiar. Unusual." She snapped her fingers, searching for the word. "Unnatural. Un . . ."

"Uncanny?" Megan asked and Jelena snapped her fingers again, then pointed at her.

"That's it. Yes. *Rodzanice* has chosen you to help the dead."

"Rodzanice?" Megan actually looked around, as if someone she didn't know might be standing nearby, waiting for an introduction.

"Fate. The Fates, you would say, I think. I thought they had let you go after the third one, but then the fourth, and now this. You've been marked, Megan.

There's nothing I can do." Jelena slumped again, now frowning toward the stage like it might have answers to an unexpected question.

"Well, okay, but I don't believe in fate, and—" The men who had entered their row walked all the way up to them, and Megan looked up with a scowl of her own, ready to run them off.

"I'm sorry," one of them said. "I'm Jacob Murphy. This is my husband, John. We're the—"

"Sea Warrior Whiskey," Megan said with a barely contained groan. "Right. You're competitors."

Jacob Murphy smiled apologetically. He was tall-ish and slim, losing his hair but not trying to hide it, and his husband was short and well-built with a marquee jawline that the rest of his features didn't quite live up to. He picked up where Jacob had left off, although he both sounded and looked less apologetic than his husband. "We couldn't help overhearing you saying no one should talk to Ms. Flanagan. That's clear enough in retrospect, but in all the excitement, we already had. Do you think it's going to cause a problem?"

Megan bit back the impulse to demand why they were asking *her*. It wasn't as if she had any genuine insight into what was happening.

No, she just had a loud American voice, and she'd deliberately used it to bray an opinion across the whole auditorium, thus establishing herself as an authority of some sort. And if anyone knew she was the murder driver, that would add to the perception she knew what she was talking about. She sighed, dug deep for her manners, and tried to produce a reassuring smile. "I'm sure it'll be all right, Misters Murphy."

The taller of the pair, Jacob, grinned, then actually chuckled. "I don't think I've heard anybody say that before. Not with confidence, anyway. There's usually some fumbling around with 'Mr. Murphys' or Mr. and Mr., but I think I like *misters*, plural."

Megan crooked a smile back at him. "It felt efficient. C'mere to me, I was just suggesting no one talk to her because in this kind of situation you shouldn't talk to the press in general, and podcasters can arguably be considered a kind of journalist."

John Murphy smiled, more reluctantly than his husband had. "It's strange hearing 'come here to me' in an American accent like your own."

"I'm trying so hard to teach myself to use Irish phrases," Megan said wryly. "I've mostly got 'lads' down in favor of 'guys,' but it's harder to switch out 'come here to me' for 'listen.' I'm getting there, though."

"How long have you been in Ireland?"

"Almost five years now. Long enough that you'd think I'd be losing my accent, but I work with a lot of Americans."

Both men nodded and Jacob said, "A lot of us like to listen to American accents anyway, so hold on to it if you can." He glanced at his husband, then back at Megan. "I don't think we said anything incriminating to Ms. Flanagan. Only how sorry we were about McConal's death, and how shocked, and that we hoped it would be explained soon."

"Jacob even had the grace to wish her luck in the competition," John said with a note between fondness and exasperation. "I'll never know how I landed myself a man so polite."

"Your flawless jawline," Jacob replied easily, and John smiled and rolled his eyes with the comfortable response to a familiar line.

"I'm sure it'll be fine," Megan assured them both. "The police will sort it out and I assume you don't have any kind of grudge against Angus Mc-Conal."

"Nothing beyond hoping he loses the competition and we win," John said. "Which is as much horse I have in the race with regards to Mr. Lynch here, too."

Jacob immediately said, "And we wish you the best of luck with Harbourmaster, too, Mr. Lynch," which got another faintly exasperated smile, and a look at Megan as if to say 'see what I have to deal with?' from his husband.

"Well, may the best whiskey win," Rabbie said in as broad an accent as Megan had ever heard from him, and he was rarely above laying it on thick. He stood to shake his competitors' hands, then swallowed with visible worry as he looked up the auditorium aisle.

A pair of guards jogged down to stop at their row, expressions neutral with a side of grim. "If you'll come with us, Mr. Lynch, we'd like to talk to you now."

"Sure and my niece can come with me," Rabbie asked, sounding much older than he had a few seconds earlier. Megan stood, hoping decisive action would lead to inevitable acceptance, but the guards exchanged glances and one shook his head.

"I'm sorry, Mr. Lynch, but the detective in charge made it expressly clear that Ms. Malone wasn't to join us. If you'll come with us?"

Rabbie's shoulders hunched as he stepped into the aisle, and the look he gave Megan was that of a helpless, frightened old man as he was taken away.

CHAPTER 6

It was nearly three in the morning before they were all released, although Jelena left as soon as the guards let her, murmuring, "The dogs are going to think we're dead," as she called a taxi to bring her home.

Megan waited until first Paul, who, like she and Jelena, was not a person of interest in the investigation, then Niamh, and finally Rabbie were allowed to leave the convention center. Sean Byrne, the man running the festival, was one of the few people still there when they all staggered their way to the parking garage so Megan could drive them home.

"We can walk," Paul protested. "Niamh's apartment is just across the river."

"Are you prepared to carry me, then?" Niamh demanded tartly. Like all of them, she had to be exhausted. Unlike the rest of them, though, she still looked flawless. Megan wondered if there was a way to *act* like you didn't look tired. If there was, the film star had mastered it. "There's a reason I had Megan pick us up from just across the river. I'm not walking a kilometer in these." She lifted a foot, displaying gorgeous four-inch red heels.

Paul gazed at the shoe, at Niamh's pursed lips, and finally at Megan. "I'm an eejit, obviously. We'll take the lift."

"Good choice." Megan climbed into the back of the limo with the other three, and for a few tired moments they all just gazed at one another as if an answer of some kind would appear among them if they waited long enough. Megan finally said, "Is everyone okay, at least?"

Niamh pressed her fingertips into the corners of her eyes, the gesture of a weary woman who didn't want to spoil her makeup. "Is it wrong of me to be glad I *don't* have a film coming out right now? By the time the next one is out, hopefully this will all have blown over. I'm all right, although 'Did you have anything to do with the murder' isn't usually a question you get in the pressers."

Paul put his arm around her and tucked her close so he could rest his mouth against her hair. "Suspicious death. There's no proof it's a murder, yet."

Everyone in the car, including Niamh, turned ironically disbelieving looks on the police detective, who grimaced apologetically. "All right, I hear what you're not saying, but the man *could* have had a heart attack or an aneurysm."

"With the Harbourmaster whiskey recipe in his pocket?" Rabbie demanded.

"Well, now, an aneurysm wouldn't care," Paul began, but twisted another pained expression and waved his hand, dismissing his own commentary. "But no, probably not. Did you learn anything, Megan?"

"*Were* you telling me to keep my ears open, then?" she asked, caught between surprise and an uprising of delight. "Nothing useful, I don't think. The Murphys ran their mouths off at Hannah Flanagan, so you might want to get her recordings for the evening. Carmen's bodyguard said McConal was at that party on her boat that we went to."

Relieved horror shot across Paul's face. "Thank God we didn't meet up with him. I'd hate to have anything linking me to him, under the circumstances."

Niamh, rather miserably, said, "I'm so sorry," to him and Paul blinked in confusion, then groaned and shook his head, nestling close again.

"You don't link me to him. I just can't work the case until you're cleared. And maybe not then," he admitted. "But you're not really a person of interest, Nee. I'm not sure Rabbie is, either."

Rabbie shot a guilty look at Megan, who groaned. "About that . . ." She did the talking for her uncle, explaining about his decades-ago relationship with Angus's mother, but petered off into silence as Paul's expression went increasingly stony.

"I thought you said *nothing useful*, Megan!"

"I forgot about that bit!"

"You f—" Paul bit back the objection and scrubbed a hand over his face. "You'd better start taking notes instead of relying on memory."

"I'm not supposed to be a note-taker in this kind of situation!"

A brief silence filled the back of the limo before Paul mumbled, "Right. I forgot."

Megan sighed explosively. "Jelena didn't."

A fresh wince crawled across Paul's face. "No, I'm sure she didn't. Did you tell Detective Reese about your relationship with McConal's mother, Mr. Lynch?"

"I've told you more than once you're a grown man now and can call me Rabbie," Megan's uncle said with the faint amusement of a man who knew he would never be heeded in this. The amusement faded fast, though. "I did, yes. I thought it'd be my head Megan would have if I didn't."

"It sure would have been," Megan said without meaning it.

Paul, though, nodded. "That was the right thing to do. They'll find it out anyway, so better not to hide it. All right. I'm out of this, I can't be asking questions. Maybe you'd better drive us home, Megan. I'm sorry."

"You'd better," Niamh said with a wrinkle of her nose. "My publicist has been calling for two hours and it's only ten PM there, so she could keep it up for hours yet. I'd rather get some sleep before I talk to her. We're going to be in all the papers in the morning," she warned Paul.

"I'm sure we're already all over the gossip sites. Fortunately, you're only gorgeous and half of them will forget about the murder to talk about your fashion sense instead."

Megan chuckled and got out so she could get in

the driver's seat, saying, "He's not wrong," over
her shoulder. "Maybe they'll have solved it all by
morning, anyway."

They had not solved it all by morning.

Jelena was up early enough to go to the gym.
Megan normally would have joined her, but after a
four AM bedtime, she didn't even know Jelena was
gone until the dogs barked, welcoming her back.
Megan staggered out of the bedroom toward the
scent of brewing coffee in the kitchen and Jelena
met her with, "Rabbie's still sleeping in the guest
bedroom. They're saying McConal died of anaphylactic shock. Apparently it was fairly commonly
known that he had a kiwi allergy."

Megan, barely awake enough to walk in a straight
line, blinked thickly at her girlfriend, then sat on
the floor with a thump and invited Dip, the slightly
larger of her two Jack Russells, into her lap. He was
almost entirely white, with a brown muzzle that
looked, to Megan, like he'd been dipped in chocolate. His sister, Thong, was *not* entirely white with a
thong-like mark over her bum. Megan had just
thought "Dip Thong" was funny, because they were
the only two from their litter, and diphthongs were
a sound made from only two letters.

No one else thought she was funny, and she
thought that was funny, too.

Dip licked her chin and Megan rubbed the top
of his head, eliciting envy from Thong, who came
to join them. After a minute, Jelena handed a cup
of coffee down to Megan, who had to push Dip's

face out of the way to take a sip, but after that, was able to scrape together enough coherency to say, "I didn't know he had an allergy. Was there . . ."

Working her way through the question required more coffee. She took another sip, and then another, before starting over again. "Was there kiwi in the punch bowl? Was it a fruit punch? It mostly tasted like whiskey and honey to me. Why was he drinking it if it was a fruit punch and he had a fruit allergy?"

"You were driving, so you only had a sip," Jelena pointed out. Megan put Dip on the floor, moved Thong out of her lap, put Dip back on the floor, moved Thong again, and wailed as Dip crawled into her lap another time. Jelena, traitorously, only grinned and watched her try to escape the dogs without risking putting her coffee cup down. "But no, it wasn't a fruit punch, or it wasn't supposed to be. But how many people are going to notice, much less go into anaphylactic shock if somebody pours a can of kiwi juice into a bowl of whiskey punch?"

"I don't know." Megan finally scooted on her butt toward the table, put the coffee on it, removed the dogs from her lap, and crawled into one of the chairs. "I guess we could make a giant bowl and start putting kiwi juice in until we notice the change in flavor."

"That is the strangest way I've ever had someone ask to get drunk with me."

Megan laughed into her coffee and gave Jelena a smile over the cup's rim. "But did it work?"

"No. We couldn't possibly drink enough to justify the cost of making a punch bowl."

"It wouldn't have to be the size of the one at the convention center!" That had been a cut glass bowl, glittery enough to pass for crystal, but Megan wasn't sure anybody had ever made crystal punch bowls that big. It held a couple of gallons of liquid, which sounded like a lot, but there had been hundreds of people at the party. That bowl had always had at least one, and sometimes two, people bringing pitchers of premixed punch to pour into it, just to keep it full. Aloud, as the thought struck her, Megan said, "Just about anybody could have poured kiwi juice into the bowl, or into the pitchers the punch was being carried in."

"But there wouldn't have been any point unless they knew McConal was coming to get a drink," Jelena pointed out, then bared her teeth as she visibly realized she was being drawn into the discussion. The expression faded, though, as if she remembered she was the one who'd brought it up in the first place. "You wouldn't want to keep spiking it on the chance he stopped by for some punch."

"So you'd want to see who he'd been talking to. Whether anybody suggested they get a drink. And whether they stayed with him on the way to the table, or whether they had an accomplice." Megan paused, then put her forehead against the coffee cup. "All of which the police will be looking into."

Jelena came over to the table and sat across from Megan, snaking a hand toward her. Megan put her cup down and tangled her fingers with Jelena's. "At least we know Rabbie wasn't talking to McConal at any point, so he couldn't have led him to his death."

"You don't really think your uncle has anything

to do with it." Jelena, despite being sweaty from
her gym workout, with little curls stuck to the sides
of her neck and forehead, looked beautiful to
Megan. The highlights of her gray workout gear
matched the aquamarine of her eyes, and her
cheeks were still flushed a pretty pink. Megan
squeezed her hand and sighed.

"No, but it doesn't matter what I think. It matters what the police can prove. So I'm looking for
what shows he's innocent."

A little smile crept across Jelena's face. "How
about that affair, though?"

Megan groaned and laughed all at once, and
put her head on the kitchen table. "On one hand,
go Uncle Rabbie. On the other . . . okay, what's the
worst spin you can think of for a decades-old affair
with Angus McConal's mother?"

"Let's see." Jelena pulled her hand back to pick
up her own coffee and contemplate it. "Rabbie,
feeling guilty about the affair, shared the Harbourmaster recipe with Angus to give him a decent
base for his whiskey blend and one of the other
Harbourmaster team found out and killed Angus
over it."

Megan lifted her head to look at her girlfriend
with admiring horror. "That *is* a terrible spin."

"It means Rabbie's probably next, too."

The admiration drained away, leaving only the
horror. "God, I hope not."

"Well, what's your worst take? No, Dip." Jelena
nudged the terrier down from where he'd stood,
front paws on her leg, to see if there was anything
on the table a small dog might want to have. His
ears drooped and he got down again. A moment

later an audible *flop* sounded beneath the kitchen table, followed by a deeply put-upon sigh. Thong gave Megan a reproachful look before going to comfort her brother in his time of need.

"Um. I don't think I can top yours. Mrs. McConal secretly had Rabbie's love child, and that child, now an adult who has grown up in their famous older brother's shadow, is trying to clear a path to inheriting all the fortune that both Rabbie and Angus have separately built?"

"Oooh, that's good. Of course, it also probably means Rabbie's next."

"Great. Wonderful. Terrific. Let's just lock him in the bedroom, okay? He can stay nice and safe in there until we've got it sorted out."

Jelena said, "Mmm. I'm not going to lock that door. But if that's the story, bad timing on the killer's part. They should have waited until either Rabbie or Angus had *won* the competition. There'd be a lot more fortune that way."

"Okay, so they're trying to destroy the legacies of those who ruined their lives and never cared about them?"

"There we go, that's better. Although how do we get to ruined lives from where we are?"

"Oh, you know, widowed mother giving birth two years after her husband dies, the scandal of it all and everything. It wouldn't be nearly as big a deal now, but thirty years ago?"

"Ah, yes, right. Catholic Ireland." Jelena spoke with the wry understanding of a woman who had grown up in a predominantly Catholic country herself. "Things have changed so much sometimes I forget how they were, even though none of it was very long ago. And some of it is still now. But I think neither of our theories is true. I think someone else killed Angus McConal, and that no matter what I hope, you're going to spend the next few days or weeks figuring out who."

Guilt spasmed through Megan, cutting her breath off. "It's just that it's Rabbie, Yella. He's family."

"And if it wasn't Rabbie, it would be that it's Niamh and Paul, and if it wasn't Niamh and Paul, it would be that someone had died at your feet and you wanted to know what had happened, or that someone was willing to tell you a secret that could unlock the case, because you *aren't* a garda. And even if it wasn't for all of those—those *exceptions*—then I think you would still be an instrument of the *rodzanice*. Of fate. I don't think I'm a particularly superstitious woman, Megan—"

Megan, not meaning to interrupt, but also appreciating the strength of superstition in Ireland, breathed, "But you wouldn't disturb a fairy ring if you found one," and Jelena exhaled a laugh.

"No. I wouldn't. And I wouldn't move an elf-stone to make way for a bypass, either, and neither would you."

Neither, as it had turned out, would a lot of people in Ireland; a highway's path actually *had* been altered, years earlier, to avoid cutting down a local legend "fairy tree." It was broadly considered to have been both absurd and the only possible choice to make. Jelena put that aside with a short motion of her hand that made Dip hop up again, hoping somebody would give him lovies. She smiled faintly and scratched the top of his head, sending his tail thumping. "I don't have to be superstitious to see this keeps happening. Maybe it *is* superstitious to think it's the hand of fate, but Megan, do you have a better explanation?"

"I don't." Megan fell silent a moment, finishing her coffee and searching for the right thing to say. "I mean, you're right. This isn't normal. Hardly anybody goes about their lives running into murdered bodies every few weeks or months. Probably even fewer of them stick around to try to figure out what happened. Jelena, if I could stop this—"

"You wouldn't."

"I *would*. I know you don't like it, and it's not exactly the most comfortable way to live my life, you know? I'd rather be normal. Ordinary. Not the murder driver."

"I think you believe that, but I think if you truly rejected it, fate would find another vessel. But I also think fate doesn't make mistakes like that. Fate chooses the ones who can, and will, do the task they're given. So *rodzanice* chose you."

"I—" Megan blinked at Jelena, slightly taken aback. "Well, how *do* I reject it, then? I thought most 'fated one' stories had a whole thing about how the chosen one runs away and is stuck doing it anyway, so they accept their fate?"

A thin smile ran across Jelena's face. "Sometimes they just accept it and do their best with the fate they've been handed. I think you're that kind of chosen one." Her smile broadened a little. "Most of the ones who run away are young and haven't yet learned that life will catch up to you. You're old."

Megan laughed. "I'm forty-three!"

Jelena nodded serenely. "Old, for a chosen one."

"You read way too many fantasy novels," Megan announced. "Did you think all of this through at the gym this morning? I should have gotten up and gone with you so you'd have been too distracted by my hot bod to think."

"Your hot bod didn't come to bed until four," Jelena replied, still serenely. "If you'd gone to the gym at six, I would have been distracted by you dropping a weight and having to go to A and E for a broken foot."

Megan breathed, "I will never learn to call the emergency room the A and E."

"*Accidents* and *emergencies*," Jelena said. "It's not that hard, Megan."

"I know, I know, it's just the hopelessly American part of me. Anyway, see, I should have gone to the gym and dropped a weight and broken my foot, because then I'd be in a cast and couldn't solve a mystery. Fate would be thwarted."

Jelena stood and kissed her on the way to get another cup of coffee. "It's never that simple."

CHAPTER 7

It might not be that simple, but it wasn't that complicated, either. Megan, slurping her way through a third cup of coffee in as many hours, was incredibly grateful she didn't have to work today. She'd be dangerous behind the wheel with this little sleep. She was also obscurely annoyed that Paul was off the case so she couldn't have tidbits she wasn't supposed to know slipped to her. If she was fated to solve mysteries, surely fate would be more helpful than that.

Rabbie lurched out of the guest room before she'd finished the third cup. His bloodshot eyes spoke of exhaustion, but his tone was agitated. "Did you see about McConal's death? Have you ever heard of someone being allergic to kiwi? I didn't even know anyone ate them," he said grimly. "I thought they were endangered."

Megan paused, taking that in, then paused longer,

trying to figure out how to respond. She eventually said, "The fruit, Uncle Rabbie. He was allergic to the kiwi fruit?"

"Megan," her uncle said, exasperated, "are ye telling me there's a small, flightless *fruit* called a kiwi?"

She bit her lower lip hard, trying to hold back a choked laugh. It took long seconds to reply, "I assume it's flightless, yes," more or less normally, although her voice broke a little as she added, "I've never heard of an independently powered flying fruit."

Rabbie stared at her, first in confusion, then murderously before taking a cup of coffee and swept out of the kitchen with the grace of aged, offended dignity. Megan, giggling helplessly, texted Paul and Niamh to ask if they were familiar with the small, flightless kiwi fruit. A moment later Paul sent an exceptionally realistic "photograph" of a kiwi fruit in full flight, its stubby little wings spread over an exposed green fruit belly, and Megan laughed so hard she had to run to the bathroom to pee. Jelena yelled, "What?" from the kitchen and Megan, still laughing, shouted, "It wasn't really that funny!" back at her. "I'm just really tired!"

Jelena said something that sounded suspiciously like "Americans," and Megan, post-toilet, was in the bedroom strongly considering going back to sleep for a couple of hours when her phone rang again, her boss's number coming up.

Megan answered with, "I'm a danger to myself and others right now, I can't drive," and got a dismissive sniff from Orla Keegan in response.

"I wouldn't want ye to. There's a mob at the

garage, a load of 'em, half of them clamoring for an interview with the murder driver and the other half screeching about how you're an opponent of free speech and hate podcasters." Orla's inner city accent came on thicker and thicker with each word, until a deep breath followed the last of them. "What the hell is a podcaster?"

"Um, podcasts are online programs about all kinds of different topics. Podcasters are the people who do them. I must have riled up Hannah Flanagan's fan base by telling the other competitors not to talk to her."

"Isn't Hannah Flanagan that wee girl whose da is a country singer?"

Megan choked on a laugh for the second time in five minutes. "No. That's Hannah Montana, and she's actually named . . . never mind. Are you calling because you want me to come take the heat, or to stay away?"

"I want to know what kind of mess you've gotten me into this time!"

"Oh! Angus McConal, the boxer? Died at the whiskey festival opening gala last night. Right in front of me," Megan added as an afterthought.

"You're cursed." Orla had said that before, but this time it was spoken as a simple matter of fact, a detail that couldn't be overlooked but was also no longer worth raging about. "It's as plain as that. You're cursed."

"Jelena thinks I'm an instrument of fate," Megan offered. That sounded better than being cursed.

She could essentially hear Orla considering it as a possibility, although another sniff dismissed it. "Cursed or fated, it's the same thing so. I'd say stay away, unless you're looking for a segment on *Six One.*"

"I have never once been looking for a feature on the evening news," Megan promised. "Hopefully they'll have all cleared out by tomorrow and I can pick up my shift like I'm supposed to."

"Well, if you'll get off your arse and solve the case, they will." Orla hung up and Megan sat gazing at the phone a while. Next thing she knew Paul Bourke would be calling to tell her to get to work on the murder.

The phone rang with Paul's picture coming up. Megan shrieked, fumbled the phone, wincing as it bounced across the floor, then had to scramble to get it before Thong, barking her fool head off, came rushing into the bedroom to protect Megan from whatever had alarmed her. Megan fended her off with a hand, pressed the answer button, and said, "Paul?" nervously.

"It's Niamh, my battery died. Paul's still sleeping," Niamh O'Sullivan said cheerfully. "He said the best way to avoid getting in trouble with this whole mess was to sleep through it, but I'm after activating movie star time and think I'm grand altogether with four hours of sleep."

"Movie star time. Is that what you call it when you have to do pressers from four in the morning Eastern time to two AM Pacific?"

"And when you have to shoot all night and still be on set fresh as a daisy at six," Niamh agreed. "So who do you like for McConal's murder?" She put on a New York accent for the question, hitting the vowels so flawlessly Megan would have believed she was a Brooklyn native, if she hadn't known better.

"Are you practicing for a part, or are you just amazing? You're just amazing. And I don't like anybody for it—"

"Really?" Niamh went back to sounding Irish, and disappointed. "I was sure you'd have it all sorted by now."

"I don't have enough information! I mean—not that I'm trying to solve it, but—"

"But that's exactly what you mean. Even Paul hopes you'll figure it out. He doesn't want it to be Rabbie, you know. Tell you what." A sly note crept into Niamh's voice. "Why don't we go get some more information?"

Staking out a lunchtime whiskey tasting in the Meeting House Square with three hours of sleep under her belt was not the *wisest* thing Megan had ever agreed to, but swanning in with Niamh made it one of the most *entertaining* things she'd ever done. Niamh didn't often use her celebrity to get preferential treatment, but in this case she swept up to the young man at the gate and declared, "I'm here for the tasting," with a conspiratorial charm.

The poor kid, who was about twenty and as pale an Irishman as Megan had ever seen, recognized her with a visible drop of his jaw, then fumbled the paperwork he was holding. A truly impressive blush shot up from below his collar and rushed for his hairline like it had a schedule to keep, and he stuttered, "I'm sorry, Ms. O'Sullivan, but you're not on the guest list."

Niamh leaned in and Megan thought it was

good she wasn't wearing something low-cut, or the poor lad would have expired on the spot. Still in the same conspiratorial tone, but softer, more intimate, the actress said, "Well, now, sure and of course I'm not, am I? It's hard enough getting to these things without the paparazzi following me everywhere. If I announce I'm going to be in a public space, it's madness. C'mere to me now, Diarmuid, I'm one of the competitors, aren't I? Go on and ask, they'll tell you to let me in."

Diarmuid, who didn't seem to be wearing a name tag, turned an even more profound shade of deep tomato red at hearing his name on Niamh O'Sullivan's lips, and shook his head. His voice was little more than an awestricken rasp. "No, sure, it's grand so. Please come in, Ms. O'Sullivan. And your, uh, guest."

Megan had to give the kid props for managing to extend the invitation to her—for even *noticing* her—when it was clear he'd have been emotionally unable to prevent Niamh from bringing Megan in with her. She smiled her thanks, but Niamh dropped him a quick wink and blew a kiss at him, and Megan was fairly certain that she entirely ceased to exist in Diarmuid's world. The starry-eyed youth let them through the gate, then, in a burst of seize-the-moment hope, blurted, "Ms. O'Sullivan? Could I—a picture? Maybe? Please?"

Megan swore Niamh's eyes sparkled even more than usual as she turned back to the young man. "Promise me you won't post it until after the whiskey tasting is over?"

He didn't so much nod as tremble with agreement. His hands shook so badly as he got his phone that Niamh gently took it from him and handed it to Megan. "Would you?"

"Of course." She took several pictures, in all of which Niamh looked utterly perfect and in most of which Diarmuid looked like an awkward, starstruck teenager. At the last moment, though, Niamh said something that made him laugh, and the final picture was a genuinely terrific one of both of them. He took the phone back, saw that picture, beamed, and reluctantly returned to his job after offering a flurry of thanks.

"He wasn't wearing a name tag," Megan said as they walked down the steps into the square itself. "How on earth did you know what his name was?"

"It was at the top of the guest list. *Diarmuid's Sheet, one to three* PM."

"Oh, you *are* good."

"I *am* on the guest list," Niamh added. "There's usually a VIP version they don't let people see for paparazzi reasons. But that was more fun."

Megan laughed. "You made his day, anyway."

"Sometimes being famous is great," Niamh admitted. "All right, where will we start?"

The Meeting House Square was a lively space in the heart of Temple Bar for markets, film festivals, live performances, and hanging out. There were arts spaces on most of its sides—the Irish Film Institute, the National Photographic Gallery, a children's cultural center, and more—and Megan came down to the Saturday food market as often as she could, getting takeaway meals of shrimp-fried noodles and small bottles of local apple juice that she always drank in one go because they were so good.

Today the mid-November sun was bright and surprisingly warm, pouring down over tables laid out with walkable aisles between them. Backdrops and posters announced who the vendors were, and whiskey bottles were laid out on white table-cloths, sunlight glimmering gold through them. People maneuvered around pillars and sat, singly or in crowds, on the benches scattered around the sides of the square, but far more were engaged with the vendors, tasting whiskeys and chattering beneath the banners that proclaimed the entire event a part of the Dublin Whiskey Festival. Megan said, "Lots of people here," and Niamh wrinkled her nose.

"It used to hold more booths and tables, before they put the umbrellas up. I have a love-hate relationship with them."

Megan glanced upward at the tremendous pillars that supported four upside-down "umbrellas" high above the square's floor. They were furled now, but could open into huge overlapping petals that protected the square from Ireland's inclement weather. They'd been there since before she moved to Ireland, so to her mind, they belonged, but Niamh went on. "We used to all crush in here like mad things when we were young. It's not that you can't now, and it's not even the umbrellas I don't like. It's the bollards. I know the pillars need to be protected from a delivery van accidentally running into them, but it still feels like they take up so much *room*." She gave a dramatic sigh, then shrugged. "On the other hand, the square gets so much more use now that everything doesn't get rained out."

Megan put a hand on her friend's shoulder and solemnly said, "The price of progress, Niamh. The price of progress. Besides," she added in a more chipper tone, "if they hadn't dug it all up to put the umbrellas in, they wouldn't have found the Viking shipyard under our feet."

"I think it was just a couple of houses," Niamh disagreed, but lifted her feet as if trying not to step on the Viking remains below. "What I can't get over is they were built on an island. We're standing on an island, or what was an island before they filled it in and paved things over."

"The Poddle is right below us." Megan couldn't stop herself from doing the same thing, lifting her feet like she was avoiding the river beneath them. "The entire idea of cities built over rivers does my head in."

"Don't look at a map of Cork, then," Niamh warned. "It's all islands held together by filler and pavement."

Megan made a note to look at a map of Cork as soon as possible, but for the moment, they had other things on their minds. Ireland boasted a *lot* of whiskey distilleries, and while Megan was certain they weren't all represented at the tasting event, the sheer number of them made it feel like every maker in the country had shown up.

The best whiskey competitors had booths spread through the market space, as far apart from one another as they could go, but there was also, up on the stage at the side of the square, a tasting table for all of the new whiskeys. The entire event had a fairly steep price tag to attend, and a punch card to allow attendees up to five tasters at the various

booths, but the new whiskey tasting table had a
ticket of its own. Megan recognized a few of the
people up there: the festival manager, Sean Byrne,
was one of them, as was the gray-blond woman
he'd been with the night before. Erin Ryan, Mc-
Conal's manager who had slapped Rabbie the previous evening, was up there, too, and Willow, the
PR manager for Harbourmaster, was giving her a
hug. Overall, though, Megan thought they probably mostly weren't people of interest in Angus Mc-
Conal's death.

Of course, she couldn't be sure of that if she
didn't go talk to them. "Think you can bank on
your, er, bankability to . . . this sentence started out
better in my head."

Niamh laughed, the big, rich sound that Megan
secretly believed would have made her a movie
star even if she'd looked like a drunken ox. "Lean
on my bankability, maybe? Anyway, yes, I do. Let's
go play good-cop-bad-cop."

Megan glanced at her literally movie-star-gorgeous
friend and grinned. "I'm gonna assume you'll be
the good cop. We wouldn't want to mess with your
image."

"You assume correctly. Also, you've actually solved
murders, I've just played detectives on TV." Niamh
paused. "Okay, I played two murder victims early
in my career, which is even less like detecting than
playing a detective. So you be the bad cop."

"Or," a woman's voice behind them said, "you
don't be *any* cop."

A sinking feeling of guilt in her stomach, Megan
turned to face Detective Garda Dervla Reese.

CHAPTER 8

Dervla Reese was a strongly built woman with equally strong red hair, wrangled, as it had been the first time Megan had met her, into a bun of such quantity as to express its natural curls, even if they were currently contained. She was in her early thirties at the most, freckled, and nowhere *near* as inclined to accept Megan's shenanigans as Paul Bourke was.

She had also obviously met Niamh before and was not in the least starstruck. Either that or she was a far better actor than young Diarmuid at the gate had been. Whichever it was, she gave Niamh a short nod of greeting, but kept the bulk of her attention on Megan. "And what is it you think you'll be detecting, Ms. Malone?"

Megan offered a grimace that was meant to be a smile. "Whether my uncle is going down for murder?"

"That," Dervla Reese said with barely a change of expression, "is my job, not yours. Will I be escorting you off the premises?"

After five years in Ireland, Megan just about gotten to the point of organically understanding that the "will I" phrasing usually meant "can I," as in *Will I help you?* was to be understood as *Can I help you?* All too often, though, even in the best of circumstances, the snide teenage American in her still wanted to respond with "I dunno, *will* you? How am I supposed to know what you *will* do?"

These were not the best of circumstances. In this particular case, Dervla's question was less a "can I" than a threat to actually do so, and Megan mouthing off would absolutely get her escorted out of the Meeting House Square. She took a deep, careful breath, making sure her teenage self was firmly locked down, and said, "No, Detective. That won't be necessary. Niamh and I aren't here to cause any trouble."

"Ms. Malone," Dervla said, still in that steady, take-no-nonsense tone, "please don't imagine you're pulling one over on me. I'm sure you're not here with the intention of causing any trouble. What I want is to hear you're not here to do any investigating, and that you won't be."

Unreasonable irritation flashed through Megan. Most people would have accepted the implication that "no trouble" meant "no detecting."

On one hand, that kind of attention to detail meant Dervla Reese was probably good at her job. On the other hand, Megan didn't want to straight-up lie to a police officer. And on the third hand, she wasn't going to stop poking around, either, even if it could potentially lead to being arrested for interfering with an ongoing investigation. Although that probably wouldn't happen, as Megan did usually get around to telling the police what she'd figured out. Not necessarily in a timely fashion, but she *did* tell them.

While she was trying to figure out how to respond, Niamh said, "Detective, you obviously know I'm in a relationship with Detective Bourke. Neither Megan nor I have any intention of doing anything that will reflect badly on him."

Dervla's brown gaze flickered to Niamh. "That's still not a promise to keep out of it, Ms. O'Sullivan."

Niamh smiled, but not the megawatt movie star smile that she could unleash to devastating effect. This was more ordinary: rueful, polite, and accepting, rather than trying to railroad somebody with her presence. "No, it's not. But people are intrigued by Megan, and they have an amazing tendency to admit the most outrageous things to me. Since I'm peripherally involved in this mess, I'd just as soon use my powers for good. If anyone says *anything* interesting to us, I promise we'll report it to you."

By then, a number of people had noticed Niamh O'Sullivan's presence at the event, and were gathering around, taking pictures, elbowing each other, murmuring, giggling; all the things fans did when they suddenly found themselves cheek by jowl with a star. Megan was suddenly certain Niamh had spoken up so people would hear, and recognize, her voice. She'd wanted the attention.

Detective Reese seemed to realize that at the

same time, and her expression grew dour as she further realized she'd been outplayed. It was one thing to escort Megan Malone, known by a handful as the Murder Driver, off the premises. It was a whole different thing to evict Niamh O'Sullivan, Movie Star, especially from an event Niamh actually had a completely legitimate, even expected, reason to be at.

She exhaled heavily, taking half a step back. "Have a pleasant afternoon, Ms. O'Sullivan. Ms. Malone." Then she turned and moved through the crowd, who were happy enough to let her go so they could get closer to Niamh.

Niamh caught Megan's eye and shot a look toward one of the competitor's personal tables in the far corner from where they were. Megan breathed, "You sure?" and Niamh nodded, then turned from Megan to the gathering fans, a smile blossoming across her face.

"All right, ten minutes, all of yis, d'yah hear me so? A quick picture, no autographs, and I'll thank yis all to wait until *after* I'm gone from the tasting to post them!" She sounded so Dub that Megan laughed as she squished away from the group of fans to approach the table Niamh had suggested she start with.

Daniel Keane of Keane Edge Whiskey was the one competitor Megan hadn't spoken to the night before. He still looked ragged, hollows under his eyes and his pale skin pasty, reminding Megan that the man had been in bits in the wake of McConal's death. An interesting conclusion leaped to her mind, although she'd certainly never heard so much as a rumor that the boxing champion was bisexual, and she knew nothing at all about Keane himself.

She tucked her bisexual disaster theories aside, fairly certain they weren't true, and waited until he was done talking to a young couple who had clearly already had too much to drink. Willow Hartley went by, offering a smile but not stopping to talk. Like Hannah, Willow's youth had seen her through the late night looking none the worse for wear. Megan bit back the impulse to call, "Enjoy it while you can!" after the young woman, then grinned at the idea. Willow would think she'd lost her mind.

The slightly inebriated young couple finally left the Keane Edge table, and Megan stepped forward, offering a hand. "Mr. Keane. I'm Megan Malone."

Keane took it with a weak smile. "If it isn't yourself. I heard you giving out to that young wan last night, and admonishing the lot of us not to talk to her. Danny Keane. It's grateful I am, actually. Had you not been railing at us to keep our mouths shut I might have spoken with her. She's a winning way about her."

Megan privately thought that Hannah Flanagan's "winning way" was mostly being a pretty young woman who would, for the sake of her podcast, pay attention to a paunchy middle-aged man and hang on his every word like it was gospel. Saying so, however, wouldn't win her any friends, and Niamh had just gone to the trouble of saying people liked Megan. She wouldn't want to prove her friend wrong. "I really haven't talked to her, but I know her podcast is popular. How are you doing, with all of this . . ." She circled a hand, hoping Keane would decide for himself what "this" meant.

"Poorly," he replied with surprising frankness. "How's your uncle? Everybody knows Rabbie Lynch," he said before Megan could express surprise, although she wouldn't have, because everybody *did* seem to know Rabbie. Keane knowing he was her uncle—or close enough—was a little more unexpected, but given the previous evening's events, not all that astonishing.

"Shocked," she said, because it was true. "This is all more than any of us bargained for. He knew Angus when he was young. Did you know him at all?"

"Only in passing." Danny Keane poured a wee dram of his own whiskey into one of the thimble-sized plastic tasting cups and offered it to Megan. "As much as anyone developing a new whiskey knew each other, I'd say. To the auld lad?" He touched a second thimble to Megan's, and they both swallowed the tiny drinks.

"Not that he was so old," Megan said, trying to put the right amount of regret into her voice. Then her eyebrows rose and she glanced at the thimble she'd drunk from. "That's quite good."

A laugh popped from Keane's chest like he'd forgotten he could do that. "I'll trust you're using 'quite' like an American there and say thank you."

Megan chuckled. "I was, yes." The British, particularly, used "quite" when they meant "fairly," or "a little;" Americans tended to use it to mean "very." She hadn't ever particularly noticed where the Irish landed on that particular separation-by-a-common-language, but Keane was obviously aware of it. "I don't mean to be rude, but you seemed devastated last night."

Keane exhaled until he seemed to have shrunk two sizes. "Look here, I won't lie to you. This has been a long, hard road for me, and I've no backers like some of the bigger brands do. I'd say the Murphys are close to in the same boat as I am, but they've a double income and no children, and John Murphy is a savvy businessman, so they've a little more cash to spare. My wife is raging mad at this whole business, and I can't even say as I blame her. If Keane Edge was to win, our whole world would be different, but with McConal's death, even if I do, it's his own whiskey that will fly off the shelves, not mine."

"I thought about that last night," Megan admitted. "It's going to overshadow everyone, isn't it?"

"And to make it worse, I heard he had your uncle's recipe on him when he died." Keane slid a glance at Megan, clearly trying to see whether the rumor had enough truth to get a reaction out of her.

She breathed a laugh of her own and shrugged. "Wouldn't it be better for everybody if his was a rip-off? I'd think they wouldn't bring it to market, in that case."

Keane's eyebrows lifted. "You might be right. Ah, sure now, I don't know. I only wish it hadn't happened. You're never with the police, now, are you? I saw you talking to that detective woman."

"She was expressly telling me to butt out," Megan said with a grin.

"Here now and it's a fine job you're doing of that. I'll be sure to tell her you didn't ask a thing about any of this, only complimented my whiskey and went on your way, if she comes knocking again."

"She gave you the third degree already?"

"First degree, at worst, I'd say. If there's a connection between myself and himself, it's one I wouldn't even know about my own self." His gaze shifted beyond Megan for a moment and he pulled together a smile. "Now, it's herself coming to the table, and if I'm caught talking to the competition she'll have my head, she will."

Megan, assuming this "herself" was his wife, glanced over her shoulder to see an unexpectedly fit woman about Keane's own age approaching. Her jaw was set and her stiff way of moving suggested she was on the edge of emotionally shattering, but she would, by God, look good doing it. Keane had evidently married up. "Right so. I'll talk to you later, Mr. Keane. Or I won't, I suppose. Good luck with the competition."

He gave her a weak smile reminiscent of the one he'd started the conversation with, and Megan hied herself off down the aisle before Mrs. Keane got to the table. She still overheard the woman's sharp, "What was all of that about? Got your eye on another woman, do you, Danny?"

Megan's eyebrows shot up and she couldn't help glancing back. Fortunately, Mrs. Keane was focused on her husband, who drooped in place and shook his head like a defeated man. Megan breathed, "I wonder what *that's* all about," and slipped deeper into the crowd, not wanting to draw Mrs. Keane's attention.

The temptation to send Niamh over to talk to him was mighty, though. She might be able to figure out if Danny Keane was having an affair, and her fame would probably put Mrs. Keane on the back foot. Just as she glanced around for Niamh, the film star stepped up to her from the other side, tucking her arm through Megan's. She had acquired most of a new wardrobe in the minutes since Megan had last seen her, and now wore a Whiskey Festival baseball cap pulled low over very large sunglasses, and a matching hooded sweatshirt that obscured her from jawline to mid-thigh. "Secret movie star disguise activated," she murmured. "Now if you'll just stand between me and everyone else, I should be able to go unnoticed long enough for most of them to forget I was here."

"I thought we were going to lean on your marketability to get up on the stage without paying seventy quid for tickets. How can we do that if you're in disguise?"

Niamh pursed her lips. "First, it's not the seventy quid that's the problem—"

Megan laughed. "Maybe not for you!"

"—it's the fact that the tickets are sold out, and second, on our approach I'll shed the disguise and rise up like a butterfly from the chrysalis. Did you talk to Danny Keane?"

"I did. I want you to go see if he's having an affair. He didn't seem like the sort, to me, but his wife went after him for talking to another woman, so maybe I'm just not his type."

"How do you know I am?"

"You're like David Bowie, Niamh. You're everybody's type. Just go come on to him or something. He thought Hannah Flanagan had a winning way about her, so if he's susceptible, I'm sure he'll fall for it."

Niamh pulled her sunglasses down half an inch and gave Megan a flat look over the rims. "You want me, a famous woman known to have a boyfriend, to go flirt with some rando at a whiskey festival?"

"It sounds terrible when you put it like that, but . . . yes."

"It is terrible!" Nonetheless, with another semiserious glare that she hid behind her sunglasses, Niamh marched off to do as she'd been asked. Megan followed a few steps behind her, both so she could listen in and just in case Niamh needed someone to actually step in if a fan noticed her.

A minute later, Danny Keane, clearly thunderstruck, said, "Ms. O'Sullivan," in a hoarse voice. "What are you doing here?"

Niamh sounded positively saucy as she said, "Checking out the competition, of course," in a near-purr. "It's *such* a pleasure to meet you, Mr. Keane. Why don't you tell me about your whiskey?"

His wife, still at the booth, snorted audibly. "Get away with you, lassie. You're out of my husband's league and not even the devil himself could make anybody think otherwise."

Megan, trying a thimble of whiskey from the vendor she'd ended up in front of, coughed on the drink as Niamh switched tactics without missing a beat, her purr all for Mrs. Keane, now. "Surely a woman as lovely as yourself couldn't think anyone was out of her husband's league, Mrs. Keane?"

"*I'm* out of his league. Now get out of here your own self before I make sure everybody knows

Niamh O'Sullivan's making an arse of herself with my husband."

Daniel Keane said, "Maggie," weakly, but Niamh flounced off, joining Megan after a roundabout path to her side.

"You're right," she said as soon as she got back to Megan. "He already thinks she's too good for him, so I don't think he's the type to have an affair. I'd say she also thinks she's too good for him, though, so *she* might be."

"Well, unless she was having one with Angus Mc-Conal, I don't see how that does us any good."

Niamh smiled impishly. "Why don't we go ask his manager?"

CHAPTER 9

"I can't imagine she'll talk to us." Megan turned toward the stage as if Erin Ryan might still be up there with Sean Byrne. She was, actually. Talking with the gray-haired woman who appeared to be Byrne's keeper, although the second woman left after patting Ryan's arm. "Sure," Megan decided, ill-advisedly. "Let's do that. And if we land a hit, we tell Detective Reese."

They moved through the crowd, Megan nodding as the Murphy husbands looked up from their booth and recognized her. Hannah Flanagan was up on the stage now, chatting with Byrne, Ryan, and others, all with her phone out and no doubt recording. Megan wondered if the police were encouraging her to interview everyone, presumably with the intention of using her recordings later.

Her pretty baby face tightened with irritation as

Megan climbed the steps, but underwent a complete change as Niamh pulled her baseball cap off and tucked her sunglasses into a pocket. "Ms. O'Sullivan."

The way she spoke the name positively gushed with hero worship. Niamh gave her a wink and a smile very much like she'd offered to Diarmuid-at-the-gate earlier. "Ms. Flanagan. I'm sure you'll understand when I say my publicist would have my head if I let you record our conversations, so if you don't mind . . ." Her eyebrows lifted in flawless expectation. Hannah, blushing almost as brightly as Diarmuid had, actually held up the phone, made a show of closing all the apps, and put it in her handbag like it might bite her.

Niamh beamed at her. "Thanks so much, chicken. You're a star."

Hannah, positively teary with awe, whispered, "You know my name."

"Of course I do. I like to keep an eye on Ireland's up-and-coming talent. Keeps me on my toes." Niamh winked again, then breezed past Hannah to offer a hand to Sean Byrne. "I'm sorry we didn't get to meet properly last night, Mr. Byrne. I heard poor Mr. McConal had been poisoned. What a terrible shock for everyone."

Erin Ryan snapped, "He wasn't poisoned! He had an allergic reaction, and whoever did it is going to pay!"

If she was grieving, Megan thought, she expressed it through rage. She wore metallic blue, dark enough be considered appropriate for mourning, but rather too glittery for the average expectation of such. Like almost everyone else who'd been immedi-

ately swept up in the investigation, her eyes were
hollow with a lack of sleep, and her gothy makeup
now had a macabre vibe.

Niamh, with every evidence of sincerity, laid a
gentle hand on Erin's arm for a moment. "Of course.
I knew that. I suppose I thought of it as a poisoning because whomever did this clearly knew he'd
have a deadly reaction. I'm truly so sorry for your
loss, Ms. Ryan. You two were together a long time,
weren't you?"

Megan couldn't say Erin Ryan's rage melted
away under Niamh's touch, but it certainly faded.
She said, "Twenty years," hoarsely, and abruptly
pulled her arm across her eyes, wiping tears away.
"He was my first client. You never forget your first.
He was like family to me. He was family. I don't
know how I'll go on without him."

"Oh, come now, chicken." Niamh put her arm
around Erin's shoulder. "You've had to be so
brave. Everyone's looking to you, aren't they?
They all want answers, and of course they expect
you to have them, with no one at all thinking of
your loss and your grief. You poor love. I don't
know how you've borne it. Here, sit down with me
and tell me all about it." She guided Erin to a chair
at the back of the stage, as out of the public eye as
was possible, and to Megan's complete astonishment, McConal's manager dissolved into devastated
tears on Niamh's shoulder. Apparently people really
did open up to her.

"That," Sean Byrne said very softly, at Megan's
side, "is a hell of a performance."

Megan, genuinely unsure of what he meant,
said, "Whose?" and the festival manager chuckled.

"Good question. I'd have said Ms. O'Sullivan's, but then I'd have said Erin Ryan was cold as a snake, too, and didn't have a tear to shed anywhere in the whole deep, dark depths of her soul." Like almost everyone else, Byrne was haggard around the edges, the result of too little sleep and too much commotion. He still managed to look at her with a degree of amusement. "You don't belong up here, Ms. Malone. No matter how popular your uncle is, or how famous your friend is, you didn't buy a ticket to the taster menu. But you get into a lot of places you're not meant to be, don't you?"

"It's a gift." Megan smiled briefly. "Are you going to throw me off the stage on my ear?"

"Oh, I think we have more than enough dramatics going on up here right now. I wouldn't want to draw any more attention. Excuse me." He went to the side of the stage where several people were now waiting, and gave them a hearty welcome. "C'mon now, lads, sit down and let us tell you a little about each of our competition whiskeys today. With us right now we have Hannah Flanagan of the new Flanagan Blend, and Megan Malone of the Harbourmaster Whiskey team. Most of our other competitors are available to speak to in the market today—"

"And one of 'em's dead! The one we was all looking to meet!" The lad who spoke couldn't have been more than twenty-five, and had the belligerent air that made Megan instantly define him as a langer. *Langer* covered a lot of territory as a term, but most generously could be regarded as *raging idiot*, or possibly *disgraceful twit*. Several of the langer's companions giggled, partially out of nerves and partially, she thought, out of thinking he was genuinely funny.

Sean Byrne didn't *do* anything, she thought. He didn't exhale, he didn't straighten, he didn't make any particular physical change to his demeanor, but he went from being a friendly, welcoming older gentleman to a deeply disappointed patrician figure whose grim expression went a long way toward quelling their amusement. "It's true that the festival, the boxing world, and Ireland have all suffered a devastating loss with Angus McConal's death," he said with a world of sorrow in his voice. "If your tickets were purchased on the understanding you would unquestionably meet Mr. McConal, the festival is prepared to offer you refunds, although they would not normally be made available, as I'm sure you're aware from the terms and conditions of the purchase. If, however, you wish to proceed with the tasting, please be assured that we are all as devastated as you are, and please feel welcome to lift a glass to the dearly departed."

A quiver of discomfort ran through the group, none of whom were much older than the kid who'd spoken, and all of whom had clearly bought tickets in hopes of meeting McConal. At the same time, though, they were obviously afraid of angering or somehow displeasing Sean Byrne, until one of them—not the original twit—blurted, "We'll take the refunds so," and all at once the group of them were in a terrible hurry to get off the stage.

Byrne pinched the bridge of his nose as a handler went to deal with their refunds. "That's the third group of young gombeens who've pulled out because their hero is dead. It's hundreds of euro down the drain."

"I can invite my listeners to come use the tickets," Hannah offered. "They'll pay full price, and I'll stay so they can talk to me."

"With all due respect, love, I think I'll let the attendees here know some tickets have come open," Byrne said. "I'd rather have tasters who weren't inclined to vote for a favorite based on their internet browsing habits. McConal's fans are no loss there, at least. Here now, Erin, are you all right, love?" McConal's manager, leaning heavily on Niamh's slight form, returned to the stage tables with her makeup in surprisingly good condition for a woman who'd just been sobbing.

She stiffened under Byrnes's question and Niamh offered the festival manager a smile. "She'll be all right, I'd say. This is all too much, though, and it's worse knowing there's nothing to be done but keep moving forward."

Erin said, "Like a shark," in a bitterly heartbroken tone, and Megan couldn't help wondering if that was how she thought of herself.

As if she'd heard the thought, Erin turned the bitter look on Megan herself. "And what are you here for? To claim your granda had nothing to do with any of it anyway?"

Megan said, "uncle," automatically, even though she knew it wasn't important. "I don't think he did, no, but—"

"No, you'd always believe the man over the woman's story, wouldn't you. It's the way of the world." Erin Ryan stomped to the back of the stage again, leaving Megan at a loss.

To her surprise, and almost to her irritation, Hannah Flanagan came to the rescue, murmuring, "Erin's gotten a lot of guff, being a woman manager in a male-dominated industry. Even when Aibhilín Ní Gallachóir did the retrospective on her a few years back, it didn't get her the respect she hoped for. Because it was Aibhilín, they were accused of favoritism and playing 'the woman card,' rather than Erin being seen for her merits. Since then she's been prickly about anybody, especially women, taking a man's side over her own."

Megan grimaced. Aibhilín Ní Gallachóir was a groundbreaking sportscaster in Irish television, and had spent years fighting to be taken seriously. While Megan's personal interactions with her had left her mostly annoyed with the sportscaster, she couldn't deny the woman's place in the fight for equal rights in Ireland. "Right. I suppose anything I said would be protesting too much." She sighed and looked up at the younger woman. Hannah had a couple inches on her by nature, and was wearing three-inch platform heels that left her close to towering over Megan. "What'd she tell *you*?"

A smile twitched the corner of Hannah's mouth. "You can hear it on the podcast. I promise you'll come off better on it if you have a wee little chat with me on record, too."

Megan felt her mouth thin. "I'll take my chances."

The girl shrugged and turned away with a flip of her hair. Megan went to Niamh's side and the actress murmured, "Erin Ryan didn't believe for a minute that Angus and Maggie were having an affair, but I'd say she has enough rage in her to be the killer herself."

"Really? She slapped Rabbie, but I assumed it was the moment. You think it was more than that?"

Niamh nodded. "She's bubbling with the fury. I wonder if she was losing control of McConal. A client like that, with twenty years of managing him behind them? If he was looking elsewhere for representation . . . well, managers forget that they work for the client, not the other way around."

"To the degree that it's a killing offense?"

"Angus McConal was worth millions year on year, darling. I assume Erin's got other clients, but have you ever heard of them?" Niamh shrugged gracefully. "You wouldn't usually kill the fatted calf, but if he's out of the way, then you're left with the rights to his image and his tragic story. A savvy manager can milk that for years."

Megan shook her head. "I wouldn't want to live like that. As a commodity."

Niamh gave her a wry, sparkling smile. "It has its moments. And to be fair like, I wouldn't want to live with bodies falling dead at my feet every few months, and you manage that." She hesitated, then cautiously asked, "How's Jelena?"

"I don't know." All at once, Megan was very aware she hadn't had much sleep. The people milling through the market square suddenly looked surreal, slightly disjointed and at different depths, like Megan's perception had gone off the rails. "She's decided I'm an instrument of fate and can't help getting involved in these things."

"Is that . . . good?"

"I don't know. I don't think being an instrument of fate makes it any easier to deal with bodies popping up all around me. Or dropping dead, I guess." Megan shook her head again, then went to sit at the tasting table. The whiskey was already poured, a blind taste test for the group of gobshites who had rushed away. Pencils and paper sat in front of each row of drinks, with places to mark down opinions on each whiskey. The Peoples' Choice Award didn't carry anything like the prestige or financial value of the all-around winner, but it certainly didn't hurt.

Megan looked around. No one seemed to be paying her any particular attention, so she picked up one of the little tumblers of whiskey and had a sip. Niamh, grinning, sat in the next chair and tried the first tumbler there, then wheezed. "Woo, that'll set the auld nose hairs on fire, won't it?"

"I can't believe that's a contender." Megan's eyes were watering as she put the shot glass back down, and for a moment she thought there were too many glasses in front of her. She wiped her eyes, looked again, and laughed hoarsely, because she couldn't do anything else after that whiskey had stripped the phlegm from her throat. "Maybe it's not. There are seven glasses. One must be a ringer of some kind. Okay." She marked down her first impressions as *jet fuel* and *a shock to the system*, which were not, she reckoned, official whiskey-tasting terms, but would get the point across.

The second was a gentle walk in the breeze, compared to the first. Megan marked it as such, then leaned over to read Niamh's assessments, which were much more formal. "Do you actually know how to do this?"

"I had a stage role as the daughter of a distillery owner when I was about fourteen," Niamh said. "The director said he wanted Method actors, but I think he just liked to drink. We spent a lot of time at the Jameson distillery."

Megan's puritanical-American streak rose. "When you were *fourteen*?"

"Well, me ma or da was always there," Niamh said. "It wasn't like I got to drink anything. Or much, anyway. But I did learn a lot, from listening."

"Oh. Okay." They went through the other four whiskeys, two of which were very nice, another one of which tasted like lighter fluid, and the last of which was middling but not unpleasant. The instructions told them to go back through for a second taste, now that first impressions had been noted down, and Megan thought the first one was actually worse on another try. "Usually seven sips of whiskey would kill my taste buds. This must be really incredibly bad if I can still tell it's bad."

"You're not taking big sips, though," Niamh pointed out. "I wouldn't say I've drunk a full shot's worth, yet. So it won't affect you as badly. That said, it's appalling."

Megan giggled, which wasn't particularly dignified or mature. "I need to remember I've only had a little sleep, and not get drunk on the tasting menu."

"Did you eat breakfast?"

"Ages ago. Maybe we should go over to Milano's after we've finished these." The pizza restaurant was less than a short block away. Megan thought she could navigate that far, even after however many sips of whiskey were in her near future.

"You're really trying to get me in one of those *Stars: They're Just Like Us!* photo spreads, aren't you?" Niamh had taken several more notes and tapped the second whiskey. "This one's too good. I don't trust it."

"Maybe that just means it's Harbourmaster. Wait, shouldn't you be able to recognize your own whiskey?"

Niamh leaned over and whispered, "I really only drink whiskey in Irish coffee," in a sotto voce that would do a six-year-old proud. Megan thought it probably carried to the far corners of the Meeting House Square, and wasn't sure whether Niamh had done that on purpose or not. They finished their flights, after which Megan tried to figure out how much they'd drunk.

Enough to not be able to figure out how much they'd drunk. A couple of shots' worth, probably, although she hadn't finished the truly awful ones, and really, two shots shouldn't be enough to have her wobbling. She was wobbling anyway and giggling like a loon, as she and Niamh worked their way toward the edge of the stage. Just before she started down the steps, a thought struck her and she turned to Niamh, whose eyes were owlish with concern at Megan's expression. "What?"

"Did we do what we came up here to do?"

Niamh rolled her eyes like she was trying to look into her own skull for the answer. After a moment's thought, she said, "Yes," definitively and then, considerably less definitively, "Probably. I think so. Yes. Maybe?"

Megan took it as an overall positive and nodded, then shook her head. It all made her dizzy. "I should not have drunk two shots on virtually no food and less sleep. If I fall down the stairs and break my neck, give all my money to Rafael."

Niamh blinked at her. "Rafael? Your friend in America? Not Jelena?"

That struck Megan as a minefield of potential disaster, but she squinted, thought about it, and said, "Yes. Raf is trying to have a kid. Jelena isn't. Money is good for kids."

"I think you better write a will when you've sobered up," Niamh said sternly.

"Good idea." Megan, concentrating on every downward step and then on the slightly uneven market floor, didn't look up until she ran directly into the broad chest of Carmen's security detail, Ramon Sanchez.

CHAPTER 10

Ramon caught her by the shoulders so she wouldn't fall over as Megan blurted, "Shoot! Sorry! I'm not drunk!" before cringing at that last. The bodyguard's thick eyebrows rose a little and embarrassment sank through Megan's belly like a stone. "I don't know why I said that."

"Because you're drunk?" Ramon hazarded and Megan cringed again.

"I'm really not, but I'm less sober than I should be, too. It's Niamh's fault."

"Here now!"

Megan watched Ramon's gaze go beyond her to discover a bona fide movie star in her wake, and was impressed that this discovery didn't engender more than a flicker of surprise in his eyes. But then, he was Carmen de la Fuente's head of security. He probably met almost as many movie stars as Niamh herself did. He said, "Señorita O'Sullivan," politely and cautiously let go of Megan's shoulders, as if uncertain whether she would remain on her feet.

She wasn't nearly that drunk, or even that tipsy. Three hours of sleep, two shots of whiskey, and one small meal hours earlier just wasn't a great combination. "Are you here for the celebrity tasting?"

A smile twitched the corner of Ramon's mouth. "Are we tasting celebrities?"

Niamh, in a mutter, said, "This celebrity chooses not to be tasted, thank you," and Megan pulled a hand over her own face.

"The stage tasting. Where people might get to interact with celebrities. It made sense in my head!"

"It did make sense," Ramon assured her. "But it was also funny. And yes, although Señorita de la Fuente isn't a celebrity. Still, sometimes being rich is close enough."

"Meghaaaan!" Carmen appeared, trilling as always, and embraced Megan. "Tell me, have you solved the case of Angus McConal's murder yet?" Her piercing voice, which seemed to know no volume other than "top," drew attention. Megan cast Niamh an apologetic look, because drawing attention tended to leave her the center of it, but this time somebody said, "Jaysus, it's herself, the murder driver!"

Alarm crawled up Megan's face in the form of heat. She'd ended up on television a couple of times because of the murder driver thing, but the last time had been months ago, and she didn't expect to be recognized on the street. There were abruptly a dozen or more people around her, voices eager and phones out. Megan caught a glimpse of Niamh's stunned expression as she was actually elbowed out of the way and had a terrible, overwhelming worry that Niamh would be offended that somebody else was suddenly the mob's focus.

The fear dissolved almost instantly. Nobody in their right mind could be upset that they weren't the one being jostled and yelled at and photographed without permission. She planted her feet, trying to stabilize herself, confident she could run the mob off before it got out of control, but Ramon stepped between her and the crowd. "Ms. Malone is not available for pictures or commentary at this time."

He didn't shout, but the note of authority in his voice carried and a handful of the . . . fans? Megan didn't know what to call them. Whatever they were, some of them broke away immediately, looking sheepish. Others were more determined, but another broadly built man in event-labeled gear appeared, increasing the breadth of the human wall between Megan and her unexpected admirers. She cast a frantic look around, only reassured when she realized Carmen and Niamh were also both on her side of the security guys.

"But you are the murder driver," one of the dispersing crowd said to her, past Ramon's broad presence. "Are you investigating Angus McConal's death?"

Megan took a breath to answer, but a pressure squished her foot. She looked down to discover Niamh's shoe very firmly on her own, and raised her eyes to meet the star's warning expression. "Never," Niamh said, hardly louder than a breath, "answer their questions without a publicist's clear-ance."

"I don't have a publicist!"

"I'm sure mine will help you out in a pinch."

By then the swarm of people had broken apart. Megan's stomach churned as she wondered how much longer it would have taken for the group to disperse if she'd been even a little bit more well-known, much less as famous as Niamh. "How do you do this?"

"Reluctantly, sometimes. Are ye well?"

Megan nodded and Niamh squeezed her arm in reassurance. "Let's go get that pizza."

"Ramon Sanchez?" Erin Ryan's outraged voice snapped over their heads. Megan, Niamh, and Carmen all twisted to see Erin at the edge of the stage, spots of color high in her cheeks. "What the hell are you doing here? You're not allowed within fifty meters of my cl—"

Her color changed as she all too visibly remem-bered that Angus McConal was dead, and her out-rage nearly dissolved. She grasped for it, though, holding on to anger so grief wouldn't overwhelm her, and stalked down the stage steps to square off in front of Carmen's bodyguard. "You lying, dop-ing snake, here to laugh in the face of Angus's death, are ye? Have you no shame? No kindness in your heart? Are you happy now, is that it? Well? Have you nothing to say for yourself? For shame," she snarled, not giving him the slightest chance to say anything for himself.

Megan exchanged brief, wide-eyed glances with both Carmen and Niamh, then edged a few steps away, trying to get around Ramon so she could see his expression. She could already see that the deep golden brown of his skin had gone ruddy, but his lips were a thin line, and his gaze was focused somewhere beyond Erin Ryan, not looking through her, but above her. Erin's ranting picked up both pace and volume and, unsurprisingly, a crowd began to gather again, drawn to the commotion.

The venue security guard, who stood comfortably over six feet and had the shoulders to match, stepped between Erin and Ramon and spoke with an Irish-flavored Eastern European accent. "Ma'am, I have to ask you to take a step back and lower your voice."

Erin's gaze snapped to him and, without changing pitch or tone, she said, "I don't know how they treat women in your country, laddie—"

Megan drew a sharp breath, genuinely startled. It wasn't that racism, or in this case, nationalism, didn't exist in Ireland, but most people—especially those in public positions like Erin's—usually didn't show their prejudices quite so obviously.

She was about to speak up in defense of the security guard when he said, "This is my country," with the placid confidence of a bull facing down a rabbit.

Erin came up short, staring at him in what appeared to be genuine confusion, then tried again. "Look, laddie, I don't know how they do things in your country—"

"This is my country."

The sports manager, who certainly should have known better, swayed and stared and, for the third time, said, "Well, however they treat women in your country—"

And was met, once more, with the security guard's mild, "This is my country."

Whether it was anger, grief, bigotry, or all of those things combined, Erin Ryan evidently couldn't get past her need to define him as *other*. After a few more flushed-faced seconds, she turned and stalked away, leaving Megan's little group to let out a collective breath. Megan said, "That was incredibly well done," to the security guard—his name tag, when he turned toward them, read Karolis—and the big man gave her a brief smile.

"When they start with 'go back to your country' kinds of things, it's almost always easy to derail them just by saying I'm already here." His glance darted to Niamh for a heartbeat, and she—of Afro-Caribbean lineage, as well as white Irish—twisted her mouth in recognition. Karolis nodded a little, then turned his attention to Ramon. "Are you all right?"

"Sí, yes. She mistook me for someone else." Ramon shrugged, making light of it. "Who knew there was another Spaniard as handsome as I am out there?"

Megan, Niamh, and Carmen all said, "Antonio Banderas," at the same time. Ramon pursed his mouth, obviously trying to decide if he should be offended that they'd all immediately thought of another handsome Spaniard, or pleased he ranked with Antonio Banderas.

"What the hell is going on over here?" Detective Dervla Reese pushed her way through the crowd to join them, her jaw set with understandable irritation. There had been a constant kerfuffle of action since Megan had set foot on the ground beside the stage, and it had all passed quickly enough that Dervla had probably just barely had the time to cross the square and get to them before speaking.

All of them, including Karolis, exchanged somewhat guilty glances, as if nobody wanted to confess to the police officer what they'd been up to. Not, Megan thought, that any of them had actually done anything wrong, but *never talk to the police* flared in her mind like a warning.

Which, of course, was wildly hypocritical of her. She talked to Paul all the time and Niamh was dating him. It still lingered in her mind. While she—and the rest of them—looked for a succinct answer to Reese's question, Hannah Flanagan stepped down from the stage, her phone out and no doubt recording, to say, "Erin Ryan accused this gentleman of being engaged in doping and implied there was a restraining order against him regarding Angus McConal. I'm Hannah Flanagan with the *Flanagan's Flight* podcast. It's a pleasure to meet you, Detective . . . ?"

Rather than answer, Reese gave Hannah's phone a contemplative examination. "Have you been recording today?"

Hannah, who, unlike the rest of the people who had been out late at the convention center the evening before, looked fresh and rose-faced, practically preened as she nodded. "I've been on for the whole festival so far. It's going to take loads of editing, but it'll be a brilliant podcast when I'm done."

"I'll be needing your phone, then," Reese said blandly.

"What?" Hannah blanched with horror and clutched her phone to her chest. "No!"

"I have reason to believe it contains evidence in relation to an ongoing investigation," Reese replied. "I'll be needing it."

Megan could all but hear the good sense in her own mind crying "Nooooo!" as she said, "Are you arresting Ms. Flanagan, Detective? If so, on what grounds?"

Dervla Reese's neck stiffened so much that Megan was sure it creaked as she turned her head toward her. "I'll invite you to stay out of this, Ms. Malone."

That would be the wise thing to do. Megan knew it. She certainly didn't want to give the guards any more reason to dislike her than they currently had, and she owed Hannah Flanagan absolutely nothing. In fact, she specifically believed that the police would eventually get a warrant, or whatever was necessary, to take possession of the phone, or at least Hannah's raw audio files.

Getting a legal warrant was one thing. Unilaterally demanding someone hand over their phone—especially when the someone was very young and not likely to buck perceived authority—was evidently something else, in Megan's mind. She put on a smile and said, "I don't think you have to give her the phone, Hannah. The guards can confiscate your belongings if they believe they pertain to evidence in an ongoing investigation, that's true, but only if you've been arrested."

"Really?" Hannah's watery blue eyes were enormous and she still clutched her phone to her chest. "I don't mind sharing the files, honestly I don't, but I don't want to give her my phone."

Dervla's ears slowly turned the same color as her hair. "Ms. Malone, you have been *specifically warned* about interfering in an investigation!"

Megan, trying very hard to employ the same mild tone Karolis had used, said, "I'm not interfering, Detective. I'm just informing an Irish citizen of her rights. Hannah, are you recording right now?"

"Yes?" Hannah's voice was small and she shot an incredibly guilty look at Niamh. The actress raised an eyebrow, but kept her mouth shut, and Megan could see the smirk she kept hidden behind the sunglasses she'd put back on.

"Do you back up your files to the cloud automatically?" Megan asked, still in the very mildest tone she could possibly manage.

Hannah's guilt fled into a brief bout of professionally injured pride. "Of course." The professional pride collapsed into remembered dismay and she muttered, "I didn't have the backups turned on once and I lost three shows' worth of files. Now I don't wait to be connected to Wi-Fi, I just pay for the data plan."

Megan spread her hands and watched Detective Reese's expression grow even tighter as she realized that, for the second time in an hour, Megan had her over a barrel. If Dervla insisted on confiscating the phone after being recorded in a conversation where Hannah was warned she didn't have to hand over her phone, no matter what else happened, it would look very bad for the police detective. Genuine anger bunched Reese's jaw muscles.

"If you'd be so good as to provide me with copies of those files, Ms. Flanagan."

Hannah, with confidence born of a flickered gaze toward Megan, said, "I'll have the family solicitor contact you, Detective," and Megan thought Dervla's head would actually explode.

She gave Megan an utterly furious glare, snarled, "That'll be grand then," and stomped away in a genuine fury.

The moment she was out of earshot, Niamh breathed, "*Jaysus*, though, Megan, Paul's going to have your head," and Hannah collapsed, leaning against the stage's side for support.

Her eyes positively shone with relief, though. "Thank you so much, Ms. Malone. This phone is my life. I'd die if I had to give it to the guards."

"Well, you can pay me back by never recording me." Megan made a snipping motion at the phone and Hannah hastily turned the recording app off. "And also by never assuming the police have your best interests at heart."

"Ah sure and we're not in America, are we."

Megan lifted her eyebrows. "Not two minutes ago a cop here was trying to illegally take your phone off you, or have you forgotten?"

A faint frown marred Hannah's childish face. Megan, sighing, left her to the difficult thoughts she was no doubt having, and finally tried to focus on Erin Ryan's accusation. "What was that about, Ramon? Oh." She blinked over her shoulder toward where Reese had gone. "Know what, in a minute she's going to stop being quite so mad at me and realize she didn't follow up on what Hannah told her about Erin Ryan."

"Either that or she's going to go talk to Erin," Niamh suggested. "But we might want to not be here when she comes back. Pizza," she said longingly. "I still want that pizza."

"I haven't talked to the Murphys or . . ." Megan paused. "Or Hannah Flanagan or the people behind Midnight Sunrise whiskey. Right. I'll come back for the Murphys. Let's go get food."

CHAPTER 11

Carmen happily trilled her way out of the Meeting House Square and down the street, leading a merry band of . . . well, mostly women. Ramon was the only man there, in fact, and he looked very much as if he'd rather be somewhere else. Niamh convinced the restaurant to seat them in a downstairs corner where she would be less likely to be noticed, and the five of them trooped down the spiral staircase to a windowless, but pleasant dining area. Megan, reminded of the river right below their feet, as well as the one a stone's throw away, stomped on the floor a couple of times to make sure they wouldn't fall through. Hannah gave her a peculiar look and, slightly embarrassed, Megan mumbled, "I was saying hi to the Poddle."

Hannah looked at her feet, startled. "Oh! Is it really right beneath us?"

"Honestly, I'm not sure. I know it goes through

Temple Bar and along Dame Street to Dublin Castle, and that the Meeting House Square was an island in it back in the day, but..." Megan shrugged. "It could be anywhere. Everywhere. It's Schrödinger's river!"

"Close enough." Hannah thumped a foot on the floor, too, and scooted into the booth they'd been given. "All right, I'm not recording because Misses Murder Driver and Movie Star here won't have it, but what was that all about with Erin Ryan?"

Ramon said, "*No sé*. I don't know," with a dismissive shrug, then slowly looked around the table and allowed himself a chuckle. "Who am I, out to lunch with *cuatro mujeres mas lindas en Dublín*? Antonio Banderas could never!"

"I mean, Antonio totally could," Niamh said to her menu, then put it aside. "Salad on pizza. My fate is salad on pizza. Someone please order the garlic dough balls so I can indulge in one. Or the cheesy bread. *And* the cheesy bread!"

Megan, who had eaten out with Niamh often enough to know she was being theatrical, promised to order both the cheesy bread and dough balls for starters, and took out her phone to text Rabbie after deciding on a chicken Cobb salad for lunch. **Was McConal ever involved in any doping scandals?**

Rabbie, unaware she was trying to be discreet, immediately rang her back. Megan said, "It's Rabbie," to the table at large, told Niamh her order, and went upstairs where her lunchmates couldn't hear her and—at least as importantly—the reception was much better. "I take it the answer is yes."

"I never believed it," Rabbie said firmly. "The one thing I'll say about his father is the man had no use for drugs, performance-enhancing or otherwise. But there were accusations, back before Barcelona. Someone came forward claiming they'd seen him using and that his turnaround in Barcelona was the result of drug use. He was cleared of it all and the man who accused him was shamed, and I never heard anything else about it." He paused, clearly only belatedly wondering, "What makes you ask?"

"Do you remember the name of the accuser?"

"Jaysus, no, it was some Spaniard they reckoned had lost money on his fights. Erin Ryan went and got a restraining order against the man, but Angus himself invited the fellow to come say all of it to his face, and they'd see who was who and what was what. Megan, it's my mind I'm losing over all of this."

"Are you still hiding in the guest room?" At Rabbie's sound of guilty admission, Megan sniffed. "Get yourself out of there and go talk to Jelena for a few minutes. Having a conversation with a real person instead of staring at your phone will be good for you."

"You've got those bloody—" Rabbie cleared his throat. "*Charming* dogs. It's not that I don't like dogs, Megan, but they get all underfoot when an old man is just trying to make his way around a house. Ah, never mind, lass, I'm only talking to hear myself talk. I'll take my own self down to the tasting event for the chance to hear someone else talk, instead. It'll be grand so."

"Detective Reese is there. Don't talk to her without a lawyer."

Rabbie scoffed, "You paranoid Americans," and hung up, leaving Megan to mutter, "It's not paranoia if they're really out to get you," at a blank phone screen. Then she pulled up the search engine and asked it about Angus McConal, doping, and Ramon Sanchez.

She was not even slightly surprised when a picture of Carmen's bodyguard, much younger and with far more hair and considerably less muscle, came up in the hits.

Surprised or not, it took Megan several minutes to decide what to do with that information. She ended up going out on to the cobblestoned street, pacing a few steps up and down its uneven surface as she called Paul Bourke, who answered with a warning, or possibly despairing, tone. "If you're calling because somebody else is dead, Megan . . ."

"No, I'm calling because Detective Reese will probably find this out, too, but if she doesn't, I don't want to be accused of keeping things from the gardaí and I have your number and not hers."

There was a brief pause as Paul digested that, and then she heard him blow a breath out like he was preparing himself. "All right. Tell me what you've got."

"Carmen's bodyguard accused McConal of doping back early in his career, probably to try to get back money he'd lost on a fixed fight. He told me the part about the money last night, but the doping came up in a different conversation today—"

Paul made a noise on the other end of the line indicating he might murder Megan himself, for keeping that first bit of information to herself, but he didn't actually interrupt and she barreled on, afraid she'd lose her nerve if she lost momentum. "—and I checked online and he's the same guy. Which puts a whole different spin on him dumping McConal off the side of Carmen's yacht at that party a couple years ago, Paul."

The police detective was quiet so long Megan checked to be sure the connection was still open and almost missed him saying, "I'll update Dervla. I swear, Megan, part of me wants to strangle you and the other part is grateful you're on our side. Do you know where Sanchez is?"

"Downstairs at Milano's in Temple Bar with Niamh, Carmen, and Hannah Flanagan."

"For pity's sake, Megan!"

"Well, I didn't know it was going to get fraught, did I!"

"Go eat your pizza and act normal!" Paul hung up and Megan, having no better idea, went back into the restaurant to try to act normally.

"Meghaaan," Carmen said as she returned to the table, "Meghaaan, first you tell me not to talk to the podcaster and then you leave me with her for minutes at a time! Which am I to do? Talk or not talk? Especially when she is so pretty? I think she would dress up nicely as a princess, do you not? You are too young for me," she informed Hannah, who was blushing happily as she stole garlic dough balls off the plate that was nominally Megan's, "but I do not fall in love with *every* woman I dress. If I were more serious, I think I would be a fashion designer, sí? But there is so much pressure, and I like only to design things for my friends, like Meghan here."

"Wait, you designed that? My gold suit?"

Carmen blinked long eyelashes at her. "Of course, yes. I do not sew it, no, not so fast, but the shape of it? That is mine, meant to fit you. Here, you see?" She took her phone out, flipped through galleries at an astonishing speed, and after a few seconds showed Megan a series of sketches that ranged from a basic pencil outline to a full, if sketchy, painting of Megan in the gold suit. Even in the painting, the hems pooled beautifully around the model's feet, the way they did in real life, and the model's pose was so like Megan's own posture that she could see clearly how the suit really had been designed for her specifically.

"Carmen, that's amazing. I had no idea you were that talented. And these are your sketches?" Megan paged through some of the pieces before her own suit, recognizing not just other outfits from Carmen's "princesses" at that party, but the women who had worn them as their own models for the clothing. "You're an incredibly good artist!" A suspicion struck her and she started to smile at the other woman. "Carmen, did you design the Midnight Sunrise logo?"

"Design, no, not the logo, *diseño gráfico* is not my strength, but the painting, yes, I did that." Carmen looked so shyly pleased Megan wanted to hug her. "That is my contribution. Well, that and money." She rolled her eyes and the whole table laughed.

"I'd love to interview you about that," Hannah said hopefully and, at Megan's warning look, said,

"*After* the investigation is complete. Really, though, I could do a whole segment on the new whiskeys' labels, and a deep dive into some of the classic label stylings and how they've matured or modernized . . ." She got her phone and started taking notes with a stylus, writing faster than Megan had ever seen anybody do on a phone. "Off the record, Ms. Malone, who do you think did it?"

Megan grunted around a mouthful of mozzarella and tomato. Maybe if she kept feeding herself, Hannah would lose interest, although as the young woman lifted her head curiously, Megan realized everybody at the table was looking at her like she might have all the answers. "I really don't know," she said when she finished her bite. "I don't have enough information. The police might."

Emphasizing it was someone else's job to solve the case did absolutely nothing to diminish the interest around the table. Megan groaned. "Really, I don't. Everybody at this table involved in the competition in any way has some kind of motive. So do the Misters Murphy and Danny Keane. And that's just keeping to whiskey rivalry. I don't know anything about McConal's other business pursuits, or his love life, or any boxing-world conflicts, or . . ."

A drop of ice seemed to fall down her spine and she shivered, remembering Ramon's cautious question about whether she knew about the less savory elements attached to boxing. There was a whole *world* of trouble that Megan knew nothing about that could have been following Angus McConal. She shook her head, trying to pass off both knowledge and responsibility for getting that knowledge, but Hannah, brightly, said, "Sure and you must know he'd a reputation for fancying the married ladies."

"Must I?" Megan asked in a kind of despair and then, as if she couldn't stop herself, she added, "Anybody in particular?"

Carmen folded her hands in front of her chest and leaned in like she was going to share a secret. Everyone, even Ramon, leaned in, too, perking their ears. "You know Señorita O'Sullivan is not the only movie star who is a face of the new whiskeys, sí?" She used more Spanish in her conversation when Ramon was around, Megan noticed. As everyone nodded, her voice dropped even farther. "I heard that our man is not here this week because his wife had an affair with McConal, and that he broke the contract to be here rather than risk breaking Angus's neck." She sat back, satisfied as surprise ran across the faces of everyone else at the table. "I think he is not too sad today, don't you?"

Megan started with, "Surely his wife is too old for McConal?" but Niamh shook her head before the sentence was half out.

"She's older than McConal by a fair bit, but younger than her husband by more. I'd say it's a love match on his part, but . . ." Niamh shrugged and Megan grimaced.

"That's hard. So it seems like there might be a lot of people who aren't too sad today." She badly wanted to ask if anybody'd heard any rumors about McConal and his manager, but she didn't want to lead the conversation, or worse, put ideas into Hannah's head.

"If it's not about the whiskey," Hannah said thoughtfully as she stole another dough ball—

Megan should have ordered two plates of them—
"then why now? If it was mob activity, they'd have
gunned him down, yeah? And if it was another one
of his business ventures, they'd have to have gotten a pass to the festival opening to poison him—"

"See," Niamh said under her breath, "she called
it poisoning, too."

"—and surely somebody could check for that."

"The guards," Megan emphasized. "The *guards*
could check for that. And I'm sure they are."

"Why does she keep doing that?" Hannah asked
Niamh. "Acting like she doesn't want to solve it?"

Megan said, "It's not that I don't want it solved."

Niamh, who at least had a reliable handle on
discretion, said, "It *is* the guards' job, Hannah."

"I didn't say you didn't want it solved. I said why
are you acting like you don't want to solve it!"

"I don't care who solves it as long as it gets
solved!"

"Oh look," Carmen said, falsely bright as she
warned them of incoming staff. "*La comida*! The
food!"

The main meal arrived a heartbeat later, two of
the waitstaff carrying plates for everybody. The
way the second of them carefully barely looked at
Niamh suggested she'd volunteered to help so she
could see the movie star in the basement, and now
didn't want to be obvious about it. Niamh smiled
at her. "Thanks, love."

The girl turned beet red and almost curtsied before rushing back up the stairs. Ramon, who had
been very quiet since deflecting Hannah's questions, said, "You did that on purpose."

"She wanted to be noticed," Niamh said with an easy shrug. "Now she's got a little story to tell."

Carmen shook her head. "I am *muy* richer than you, but no one does that when they see me. I think I would be badly behaved."

Niamh laughed. "To be fair, an awful lot of people are. I think I came up slowly enough to not have it all go to me head, you know? Stage and a little television when I was a teenager and small parts in films," she leaned into the word, saying *fil-ums*, as many Irish people did, "or large parts in small films, until I went viral the night Megan met me."

Hannah breathed a laugh of surprise. "Wait, what? That's when you met?"

"I was her driver that night," Megan said with a smile. "I'd been in the country about five minutes, just long enough to get a job, and I drove this glamorous young woman to the film festival red carpet. I knew who she was when I picked her up, and I was a little starstruck, if you want to know the truth. But *everyone* knew who she was when she got back in the car."

Ramon looked at Niamh curiously. "What happened in between?"

"Oh, it's on YouTube, you should watch it," Hannah said enthusiastically. "A red carpet reporter questioned her Irishness because she's Afro-Caribbean and she shredded the bloke."

"I wasn't a main event on the red carpet," Niamh said with a faint smile. "Supporting actress, trailing in at the end of the line, all the interesting people well ahead of me, and they didn't want a nobody ranting at the cameras, so they cut away. But there were a dozen or more fans filming with their phones. I was modestly well-known in Ireland when I started down that red carpet. By the time I reached the theater doors, I was already trending. I had no idea. We went in to the awards show and when we came out, I was the only one anyone wanted to talk to. Megan was a lifesaver that night, honestly. She kept her head when I was overwhelmed."

"You were cool as a cucumber," Megan promised, which was true. Niamh hadn't broken down until she was safely in the car, behind mirrored windows that kept the paparazzi from photographing her panic. That was the part of the story they kept to themselves: Megan driving around the block, parking, and crawling into the back seat to hug the young woman whose life had changed forever because she'd stood up for herself in public.

"That's amazing." Hannah was almost as starry-eyed as the waitress had been. "Friendship forged in fire!"

Niamh laughed. "Something like that, yes. And in stealing garlic dough balls." She took the last one, making a production of eating it, and the whole table was laughing when the police came to arrest Ramon Sanchez on suspicion of murdering Angus McConal.

CHAPTER 12

Beneath Carmen's cries of, "*Qué*? No! Ramon! Say nothing! I will call my lawyers," Megan watched Hannah surreptitiously turn her phone's recording app on, and couldn't blame her. Guilt surged in Megan's own belly, souring the food she'd eaten, as Ramon turned a betrayed look on her, although that was the sum of his protests. The color had drained from his face, and she thought his shock was real. The only question was whether he was stunned at being accused, or at being caught.

Carmen went with him up the stairs, tears flooding her cheeks, and Hannah, after a slightly apologetic look toward Megan, scurried after them, her phone in one hand. Megan pushed her plate away, unable to eat anything more just then and strongly wishing she hadn't had any whiskey earlier.

Niamh pursed her lips. "You checked him against

that Spaniard early in McConal's career and called
Paul, didn't you?"

"I felt like I had to."

"Oh, no, I'm never scolding you for it. Dervla
would have followed up anyway, and she'd have
had your skin if you knew something and kept it
hidden. She's a fierce wan. All you did was tell
them where he was right now."

"And ruined lunch."

"But made for a hell of a story."

Megan, caught off guard, snorted a little laugh.
"Well, there's that. At least there's no reason for
anybody to associate me with his arrest. '*Murder
Driver Nabs Another One!*' Except the tabloids would
find a way to make a pun," she added. The Irish
gossip rags were willing to stretch the language beyond all acceptable parameters if they could
squeeze a pun out of a sensational situation.

"'*Murder Driver Ram-ons Another Case Through,*'"
Niamh suggested. "No, that's not very good. '*Mur-
der Driver Solves Case in One Fuel Swoop.*' '*Heart-
Braker: Murder Driver Gives Up Bodyguard.*'" She
took a breath to continue, but was drowned out by
Megan's pained howl.

"Is it in the water, is that it? You drink it up with
your mother's milk? My God, Niamh, you should
be ashamed of yourself!"

Niamh laughed. "But I'm not." She sobered a
little, glancing toward the stairs. "Think any of
them are coming back?"

"Oh, I don't know. It's hard to imagine Carmen
actually going to the police station, and I'm sure
they won't let Hannah. That girl's a real go-getter,"

she said with reluctant admiration. "I wonder if she'll keep podcasting or if she'll go into investigative reporting or something."

"The mean part of me wants to say that would be too much like real work, but I'd say she puts real work into her podcast—have you listened to it? It's good—so I'll try not to be a cow about it. I—oh, here comes Carmen. Pretend we weren't talking about her."

"We weren't!"

Carmen flung herself into the booth in a ripple of fabric, soft golds and reds and blacks flowing together and making Megan suddenly realize she was dressed in the colors of the Midnight Sunrise whiskey label. That was a nice, subtle touch for advertisement. "Ramon did not kill Angus McConal, Meghan!"

Megan sighed and pushed her food even farther away. "Ramon only told us half the truth about losing money on McConal all those years ago, Carmen. He's definitely the guy who tried to get McConal busted on doping charges. Look him up yourself."

Tears filled the Spanish woman's eyes again. "I did. But that is not the Ramon I know, Meghan. He is a good man. The evidence is, how do you say? Circumcised?"

"Circumstantial." Megan bit the inside of her cheek so she wouldn't smile. *"Circumcised es circunciso, 'circumstantial' es como evidencia circunstancial."*

"Oh!" Carmen clapped her fingers over her cheeks, color flooding through them. *"Lo siento,* my mistake."

Megan shook her head. "They're similar. Don't worry about it."

"Yes, but a bad mistake to make." Carmen's eyes were still wide.

"Not among friends," Niamh assured her, and Carmen looked skeptical, but her blush faded and after a moment she began to poke despondently at her lunch.

"I have called my lawyer. What else can I do? You must fix this." Carmen focused on Megan, sending a fresh wave of guilt through her. "Find the real killer, please. I know Ramon is new to you, he is sneaky to you, not someone you have seen to care about, but he is my friend, my employee for a long time, and I cannot lose him to this."

"Carmen." Megan sighed the name. "What if he's guilty?"

"No! I don't believe that. If he were going to murder Angus, he would have done it at my party. An accident, of course. But a better opportunity than the whiskey gala."

Ramon had even said as much, and truthfully, Megan was inclined to agree. "It doesn't look good, though."

"And so I tell you that you must find the real killer. If it is easy for the *policía* detective to say that Ramon is guilty, if there is proof enough to convince a jury, then she will make him guilty. *You* will find the truth. There is no promotion, no pay rise, no incentive for you to choose a convenient lie over what has really happened."

A thin smile touched Megan's mouth. "I thought rich people trusted the police."

Disdain spilled over Carmen's face. "The middle class trusts the police, Meghan. The wealthy pay to make problems go away. Sometimes they pay police, sí, so yes, sí, they trust that their money makes the police, mmm, not trustworthy, but . . ." She tapped a flawlessly shellacked nail on the table. "How do you say it."

"An honest politician stays bought," Niamh offered and Carmen pointed sharply at her.

"That, yes. They are not trustworthy. They are employees. Expected to perform a service."

Megan breathed, "That's cynical," although she knew it was all too true in many cases. "I'd like to think better of Dervla Reese than that."

"So would I," Carmen said, "but just in case, I have you."

Hannah came down the spiral stairs at a pace Megan wouldn't have risked, which made her feel old and slightly grumpy as the young woman rushed to throw herself into her chair at the table. "I got it all," she announced breathlessly. "This is going to be the most exciting *Flanagan's Flights* ever. Me socials are going mad with it, everybody's asking if I'm after being there for it all and I'm getting loads of lift on everything I post. I'm thinking of doing a whole breakaway series focused on the murder, only it'd be best if I was part of solving it. I can come along with ye, can't I, Ms. Malone? My fans know the murder driver will get the job done."

"Your fans?" Megan asked, dismayed. "Why are you talking to your fans about me? Oh, God, I forgot, you sicced them on the garage this morning. You need to call them off, Hannah. I'm not part of your social media empire. I thought I was the enemy."

The young woman waved her hand breezily. "That was last night, when you were getting in the way of me interviewing everyone. This is different. Now I'm at the scene of an arrest with Megan Malone herself."

"You really turn on a dime, don't you, kiddo?"

Hannah showed teeth with her smile. "It's the way of the world, *Megan*. Keep up or drop out."

"I think I'll drop out." Megan stood, picking up her lunch so they could box it. "I'll get lunch for everybody. You wouldn't be here if it wasn't for me."

Niamh said, "Don't be silly," and Carmen looked like she was about to, but that she then remembered Megan had gotten her bodyguard arrested and wasn't sure she wanted to be generous.

After a few seconds, though, she did say, "No, let me," but followed it with, "and I'll need you to drive me home."

"I took the Luas to city center, Carmen." At the rich woman's blank look, Megan grimaced. "The tram system. Because the garage was mobbed with Hannah's free speech activists. And also I wasn't working today, so why would I have a car?"

Carmen squinted suspiciously. "You always have a car."

"Because you hire me to have one!"

"So now I am hiring you!"

"I'm not at work!"

"Well—be at work!" Carmen almost stomped a petulant foot and Megan laughed, going back to where she started.

"I can't. Hannah's fans are mobbing the place. How did you get downtown, anyway? You and Ramon got here somehow."

Childish sullenness set Carmen's lower lip in a pout. "I am staying at the Westbury, but you cannot expect me to walk there on my *own*, Meghaaan, what if I am accosted?"

Megan stared at her incredulously. "The Westbury is barely a ten-minute walk away, Carmen. Even Niamh can get that far without being bothered, most days, and you might be rich but nobody knows who you are."

Genuine injury replaced Carmen's sullenness and Megan sighed with exasperation. "You know what I mean. Yes, people know your name, but they don't know your face. You're not going to get mugged or kidnapped in broad daylight, and since I've never met Ramon before, I know for a fact you go places without security, so don't be silly. You can just walk home."

"Yes. Silly. That is me. Too frivolous for anyone to take seriously." Carmen sniffled and left with the air of a woman who was going to say "I told you so" if she got mugged.

Niamh, sounding like she was trying not to laugh, said, "I guess she told you, didn't she."

Megan winced. "Apparently her girlfriend broke up with her recently because she's not a serious enough person. I think I hit her where it hurt, saying she was silly. I'll have to apologize."

"Apologize by finding the killer," Niamh said wryly. "Just make sure it's not Ramon Sanchez."

They went upstairs to find that Carmen had, in

fact, settled the bill, and Megan groaned. "Way to guilt-trip me, Señorita de la Fuente."

"If it makes you feel better, you can pay me back for it," Niamh offered. Megan stared at her, and the actress laughed her big, rich laugh. Heads turned, her eyes widened, and they scurried out of the restaurant back into Temple Bar before anybody managed to get up and ask for selfies. Hannah hurried after them as they ducked around the corner next to a gallery and huddled against its glass wall, beneath a low overhanging roof that arched from the ground up to above the doors. The whiskey tasting was still going strong a few meters away, and Niamh lifted her hand, showing off the stamp Diarmuid had given her earlier. "Should we go back in? Talk to the Murphys?"

"They seemed in grand form last night," Hannah reported. "Couldn't believe this had happened, all that, all the right things to say, but they weren't much bothered. I think the one doesn't care much for fighting sports. He had a bit of a 'what can you expect' air to him."

"You're Johnny-on-the-spot for all of this, aren't you." Megan gave the young woman a thin smile. "I don't suppose your ratings have been dipping and you were in need of a scandal."

Hannah Flanagan turned a shocking color of pink and straightened up so fast she smacked her head on the low roof. She sank into a crouch, then dropped onto her butt, fingers over her head as she moaned. Megan made a tiny motion of apology, maybe like she would stop the accident from happening, but obviously too late. "I'm so sorry."

Niamh crouched beside the girl, putting a comforting arm around her shoulder and pulling an empathetic face at Megan. After a long couple of minutes waiting for the pain to subside, Hannah whispered, "That *hurt*," and gave Megan a bitter look, like it was her fault. Then, still in the hoarse whisper, she said, "My ratings *are* down, and this will boost them like mad, but I didn't *kill* a man for the ratings, you sick cow. *Jaysus* that hurt."

Megan repeated, "I'm sorry. I was joking and I sure didn't mean for you to hit your head." Even she thought she sounded particularly Texan right then. "Did you mention to the guards that your ratings were down?"

Hannah, hands still pressing on the bump on her head, stared at Megan belligerently. "No, 'cause what's that got to do with the price of tea? I'm not going to just go handing over a motive, am I? Even if I had, I was never near the punch bowl all night long. Believe it or not, the smell of whiskey gives me a headache!"

Startled laughs broke from both Megan and Niamh, and Megan thought they probably both deserved the hard look they received for their amusement. As her laughter faded, though, Megan said, "Oh, that must be hard, growing up in a family with a distillery, then. The smell must be around all the time."

Hannah's face went pained, clearly not just because her head hurt. "You have no idea. I started the podcast because I thought if I had to be around it all the time, I might as well get something out of it. And then the podcast took off and now I'm stuck with it. But if I can do something amazing with this murder, then maybe I can go out with a bang."

Megan squatted next to the other two women, looping her arms around her knees. "How old were you when you started that podcast, Hannah?"

"Seventeen."

"Heh. When I was that age, I was signing up for the US military, because I thought it was the best way to take control of my life. I stayed in for twenty years," she said with a little lift of her eyebrows. "You want to know what the best piece of advice I ever heard in that whole twenty years was?"

Hannah, ornery again, said, "*No*," and then in the grouchy tone of the reluctantly interested, ". . . maybe. I guess. What?"

Niamh softly said, "I'm glad you asked, because I was going to have to if you didn't."

"A Master Sergeant—do you know what that is?"

Hannah shook her head and Megan grinned briefly. "They're one of the highest-ranked non-commissioned officers, the ones who worked their way up through the ranks instead of going to military academy or officer training. They've got their acts together," she said with a certain amount of respectful emphasis. "Not just theirs, but everybody else's, too. So if the Master Sergeant has something to tell you, you listen. And what this particular one told me was that the choices you make at seventeen, or twenty-five, or seventy, don't have to define who you remain for the rest of your life. There is *nothing* wrong with walking away from what you chose when you were younger, and doing something new."

"That," Niamh said, sounding surprised, "is *good* advice."

"But I've spent five *years* doing this," Hannah wailed. "All that time is wasted if I do something else."

"No time is wasted," Megan promised. "You've learned a million things in that time, met hundreds of people, taught total strangers, made people laugh, earned a lot of money, and even won some awards along the way. None of that is wasted. In fact, it's an amazing springboard to start something new from. But the thing is, even if you don't have an amazing springboard, it's okay to start something new anyway. Who you were doesn't have to be who you always are."

"Won't I be a failure if I quit?"

Megan groaned and sat all the way down. "Okay, I got this from social media, so don't think it's too cheesy, okay? But I saw a thing that said, Why do we think we have to do stuff forever for it to be a success? You've run a wildly popular podcast for five years. Why isn't that enough? Why do we think 'it's time to move on' equates to failure?"

Hannah finally pulled her hands off the top of her head and rubbed them across her eyes. "Because my family's been running a whiskey distillery for two hundred years, so anything less than forever is actually unthinkable?"

A small laugh escaped both Niamh and Megan, who ducked her head. "All right, yeah, fair point. But maybe you need to break that mold. For your own sake, if nothing else."

"Maybe." Hannah rubbed her face again. "How'd

this turn into an ancient crones give life lessons thing, anyway?"

Niamh said, "Ex*cuse* me!" with enough real outrage that Megan laughed.

"Don't worry. I'm the one dispensing advice, so presumably I'm the crone. Forty-three is ancient from your side of things, kiddo, but when you get here you'll be shocked how old you don't feel. In the meantime, heed your elders, for they are wise."

Hannah nodded. "I'll think about it. Thanks for, uh, I don't know. Being a busybody, I guess."

"I like to think of it as taking a healthy interest in the community around me." That, at least, got a smile out of Hannah. Megan scooted over beside her and, appetite restored, retrieved the leftover lunch from its takeaway box. "First we eat," she proposed. "Then we go back into the tasting event and I'll buy you a shot of . . . oh, well, I was going to say Ireland's finest new whiskey, but I assume if the smell gives you a headache, so does drinking it."

"Drinking whiskey gives everybody a headache," Hannah pointed out with a little grin. "Besides, would that be Harbourmaster or Flanagan's Blend?"

"I don't know," Megan said honestly. "The truth is, Keane Edge was really good. I'll be curious to see who I voted for in the blind taste test."

"As long as it wasn't that shite in the first glass," Hannah began, but the rest of her commentary was lost beneath a woman's anguished scream.

CHAPTER 13

The screams were unintelligible, but voices around them yelled for medical help. Megan stood fast enough to both dump her food and crack her own head on the low-hanging roof. She staggered, a flash of white blinding her before she pressed her hand on top of the bump, concluded she probably wasn't bleeding, and called, "I'm a field medic!" as she ran to scramble over the barriers that kept the unticketed masses out of the Meeting House Square.

People got out of her way, clearing a path to an end point she didn't recognize until she was there. Maggie Keane knelt beside her husband, who lay sprawled behind their booth table, blood trickling from his head. A woman pushed past her, going directly behind the table. "I'm a doctor."

Maggie Keane lifted a pale, tear-shocked face. "He fell. He hit his head. I don't know why. Help him, please help him."

"I'll try, ma'am." The doctor knelt as a man shouldered past Megan, muttering an apologetic, "I'm a nurse."

Megan stepped aside, although she said, "I was an army field medic, if you need backup," to the man as he followed the doctor behind the table.

He gave her a quick, acknowledging nod, but Megan was more than happy to let fully qualified professionals take her place. Field medics could do a lot in a bad situation, but at the end of the day, she had a four-month training course supporting her practical knowledge. Nurses and doctors had years of schooling behind theirs.

It didn't appear to take a lot of professionalism, though, to tell that Danny Keane was dead. The doctor raised her gaze to Maggie Keane and her expression said everything it needed to. Megan heard her gentle, "I'm sorry," but anything else she said was lost beneath Mrs. Keane's fresh cry of agony.

Detective Reese arrived on the scene just about then, and—rather unfairly, Megan thought—gave Megan a darkly warning glare as she stepped into the small space behind the booth. The doctor stood as Maggie Keane bent over her husband's body, wailing, and their conversation was lost, too. The nurse respectfully backed away, giving both the police officer and the grieving widow space. Megan sidled up to him and he cast her a brief look that turned into a wash of relief as he saw her—in some way, at least—as a fellow professional. "Probably a heart attack," he murmured. "He'd be the right age for it."

Megan nodded and didn't say she hoped so.

That would require explanation, and if the nurse wasn't the kind of person to leap to conclusions about two deaths in rapid succession, both associated with the whiskey festival, Megan wasn't going to take that leap for him. She said, "The poor widow," instead, that being the more socially correct kind of comment and the nurse, sad-eyed, nodded agreement.

A commotion stirred the mostly hushed crowd: news had spread fast, and the whole event had fallen almost silent, faces turned toward the site of the tragedy, phones lifted to get a glimpse of what couldn't be seen. Megan imagined social media was already ablaze with the events of the past few minutes. But Sean Byrne came through, muttering for people to lower their phones. Some did. More didn't and most of the people who had, lifted them again when he was past. The gray-blond woman Megan had seen him with before followed in his wake, her mouth and shoulders matched lines of tension. She was watching Byrne, though, not whatever had happened, and Megan wondered again who she was and whether her primary job was keeping Sean Byrne's temper in check.

Byrne's gaze flickered over the three people behind the Keane booth before landing unexpectedly on Megan with an air of recognition. "You. You're the murder driver. What the devil is going on here?"

Megan would have vastly preferred if he hadn't identified her as the murder driver, but sighed it away. "Daniel Keane just died. The third woman in there is a doctor who responded to Mrs. Keane's call for help. I assume you know Detective Reese."

Byrne swore and turned to the woman who'd followed him. "Patricia. Call PR and HR and get on top of this before it spirals out of control."

Patricia nodded, managing to not visibly convey the opinion that it was too late for that. She moved several steps away, still within vocal range of Mr. Byrne, and took her phone out. Byrne, now focused on Megan again, growled, "What the hell is going on with my whiskey festival?"

Megan shrugged and furious exasperation shot across Byrne's face. "I thought you were the murder driver! Figuring this kind of thing out is what you do!"

Nonplussed, Megan said, "What I do is drive cars, Mr. Byrne. I've just had some unfortunate incidents the past few years."

"You're the *murder driver*! And your very own uncle is caught up in this mess! Do something about it!"

"Mr. Byrne, it is *not my job*—"

The last thing Megan expected was for Dervla Reese to come to her rescue, but the detective, jaw tight with irritation, stepped out from behind the Keane Edge booth and said, "I assure you, Mr. Byrne, An Garda Síochána have the situation well in hand and require no assistance from amateur sleuths. Which, in Ms. Malone's defense, is a fact she was trying to impress upon you. Ms. Malone, I don't mean to be rude, but I believe it might be more helpful if you were . . . elsewhere."

An absolutely childish impulse to stand her

ground nearly burst from Megan's lips, but she held it back. "You're probably right, Detective. I'm sorry to have added to the excitement."

Dervla very briefly quirked a dubious eyebrow, then smoothed it away with an equally brief, professional smile. "I'm sure it wasn't your intention. Perhaps Garda Boyle could escort you to the gate."

Megan smiled thinly in return. "I can probably find my own way there."

"I insist." A skinny uniformed guard joined them at Reese's signal and Megan, irritated, allowed herself to be escorted from the Meeting House Square. Apparently the third time was the charm for Detective Reese. She'd been trying to throw Megan out all day and had finally succeeded. They passed the Sea Warrior Whiskey booth on her way out and Megan tried to make eye contact with the husbands, but square-jawed John was comforting an obviously distraught Jacob, and neither of them had any attention to spare for anyone else.

Niamh and Hannah, who hadn't vaulted the barriers to get back inside the square, *had* come around to the main gate, arriving just as Megan was politely ejected from the premises. Hannah, cheeks bright pink with ill-contained excitement, blurted, "What happened?" as soon as she was within earshot. Niamh, less overwrought but clearly interested, flickered her gaze toward the gate and lifted an eyebrow, conveying a world of meaning with the two subtle actions.

Megan said, "Danny Keane is dead," to Hannah and, "I don't know," to Niamh. "Detective Reese had me escorted out. I don't know if she'd let you stay or not."

"Me! I'll go!" Hannah ran for the gate, showing her stamped hand to the ticket-taker there. Diarmuid was apparently off-shift: this was a girl of about the same age, whose expression was a mask of uncertainty. She shook her head and said something uncomfortably, pointing toward the guards. Hannah pulled a rather magnificently cold gaze out and stared down the girl, who was certainly no older than Hannah herself. Her accent got very posh as she said, "Are you denying the press its freedom to be present at public events?"

The poor gatekeeper paled, blushed, shook her head furiously and finally, helplessly, stepped aside. Hannah sailed in like a woman three times her own age, brazen with confidence and Niamh, mildly, said, "I don't think freedom of the press works like that here."

"I'm not even sure it works like that in the States, but I *do* know that Americans hammer on about their rights and amendments so much there are definitely people in other countries who think those are universal laws."

"Well, that's embarrassing on a lot of levels. What happened to Danny Keane?"

"The nurse who responded to the emergency call said a heart attack, maybe, but . . ." Megan spread her hands.

Niamh nodded. "It wouldn't be impossible, but it doesn't seem likely, does it."

"No." Megan watched more gardaí go through the covered stairway that led to the Meeting House

Square from this side, the girl gatekeeper quailing as they hurried past. "I'd say the guards don't think so, either. They're going to interview everybody in that square."

"Hannah will regret going in, then," Niamh said with a brief smile. "At least they let you out."

"Well, Detective Reese knows I was there. Niamh . . ." Megan said the name as a filler, her thoughts starting to tumble into an order that she didn't like. "That's two of the competitors dead."

"Four left," Niamh said almost merrily, then followed Megan's line of thought and blanched. "Oh, bugger."

"It can't be one of the other competitors," Megan said slowly. "I mean, being the last man standing would be a little obvious. But what if it's someone with a grudge against Sean Byrne, or someone else involved in running the festival? Everybody with a whiskey in the competition could be a potential victim."

Niamh took half a step back, distancing herself from the very idea as she folded her arms in an unconscious act of self-protection. "And whoever it was must have just been here."

"Oh, God. Carmen. I sent her home alone." Megan jolted, almost breaking into a run, then stopped again as sharply, waiting for Niamh.

The film actress gestured her onward. "I can't run in these shoes. I'll go into the film institute building, call Paul, and sit quietly in the public eye until he's here to bring me home."

"You're a star, Niamh." Megan bolted and heard Niamh's quiet, wry laugh as she called, "Literally!" after her.

Carmen would have gone up the street Megan was already on, a straight shot—or as straight as medieval streets got—to Dame Street, less than a two minute walk from the restaurant they'd been at. It had been at least half an hour since they'd parted ways with the little Spanish woman, but Megan still ran like she might stop something terrible from happening to Carmen. Across Dame Street and past the convenience store locally known as the Gay Spar to stand indecisively at the Exchequer Street crosswalk for a few seconds, trying to decide if Carmen would have gone that way, or through the George's Street Arcade. Then she kicked herself into motion: it was too late anyway. It didn't matter which way *she* went, only that she got to Carmen's hotel and made sure the woman had arrived. If she hadn't, Megan could worry about what to do next, then. She darted through the Arcade and a few minutes later skidded into the Westbury's intimidatingly posh foyer.

Pale stone stairs, presumably marble, rose a few steps in front of the main doors, splitting to the left and right. The right said *reception*, so Megan went the other way out of curiosity, only to find herself at a sign that invited her to stand there and wait for someone to come pay attention to her. Apparently the riffraff were not allowed to just come seat themselves in the extensive first floor lounge, which was filled with peach and mint seating surrounding low tables that gleamed under light from oversized windows. It was, Megan thought, totally gorgeous.

She swung around to the right, past a display that she couldn't remember, two seconds later, whether it was sculpture or flowers, but it was definitely arty, and went up to the reception desk, where she received a disapproving look from the well-coiffed young man behind the desk. His "May I help you?" suggested that the answer was absolutely "no."

Megan breathlessly said, "I'm Carmen de la Fuente's driver, with Leprechaun Limos. Could you ring her room and tell her I'm here?" Orla would kill her for proclaiming herself a representative of the company while dressed in jeans and a sweaty overcoat, but Megan felt it was more important that she hadn't actually *lied.*

The young man's lip curled very slightly as he examined Megan, then lifted the phone as if her sweat and breathlessness had contaminated it from the other side of the desk. After a few rings, with the same disdain in his voice as was on his lips, he said, "Ms. de la Fuente is not answering. Perhaps she has," and his pause suggested *"more self-respect than to be driven by someone like you,"* but what he finished with was, "other plans she failed to inform you of."

Megan bared her teeth in what she hoped passed for a smile. "Would you mind telling me her room number?"

His expression grew even more dismissive. "Ma'am, we do not give out room numbers to random passersby, particularly for our most exclusive guests in our finest spaces."

"Right. No. Of course not. Thanks for your time," Megan peeled the fake smile off her face, went to the door, and looked up the Westbury online.

There was, according to their site, a presidential suite in a secluded wing of the hotel. If Carmen counted as an exclusive guest in their finest space, Megan bet that was her room. There was apparently a private lift from the car park, but she was sure that would require a room key of some kind, so sneaking through the hotel trying to find the secluded wing was probably a slightly better bet.

Or calling her boss and asking her to call Carmen, or to give Megan Carmen's number. Those would probably be even easier options than brazening her way past hotel security—which would have been almost effortless if she'd been in uniform, but she wasn't—and hoping to find her way to the right wing.

Orla picked up on the third ring. "I thought you said you weren't working today."

"I'm not! I was hoping you could call Carmen de la Fuente, or give me her number."

A judicious silence met the request before Orla said, "So it's over with you and Jelena, is it?"

"What? No! What?!"

"Well, she fancies you, does Carmen. I thought if yer wan had finally had enough of your nonsense—"

"Good grief, Orla, no! I'm just checking in on Carmen. Things are a bit mental at the whiskey tasting!"

"Somebody else is never dead," Orla said in horror and then, when Megan didn't respond, said, "*Carmen de la Fuente isn't dead, is she, Megan Malone?*"

"Well, I hope not, but it would help if you'd call her!"

"Holy sweet virgin Mary, Mother of Jesus, Blessed Lady of—"

"I'm at the Westbury," Megan interrupted. "If she picks up and she's here, can you have her call the front desk and have me sent up, please?"

Orla, still invoking the Blessed Virgin, hung up. Megan jittered back and forth across the lobby until the young man behind the desk exhaled all the disapproval in the world and said, "Ms. Malone?" like a rat had died in his mouth. "Security will escort you to the presidential suite."

Relief melted Megan's knees to the tensile strength of ice cream. They wouldn't bother bringing her to the suite if Carmen wasn't there. She gave the youth behind the counter a watery smile and wobbled her way after security, who led her to an area she'd never even suspected existed, then rapped on the suite's door like they didn't want her plebeian knuckles touching even the outside of their rarefied rooms.

A little to Megan's surprise, Carmen herself opened the door and even offered an acknowledging nod to the security men before her flat gaze landed on Megan. For the first time in Megan's acquaintance with her, she wasn't wearing shoes. Megan, who didn't tower over anybody, towered over her, not quite head and shoulders, but close. She blurted, "Oh, thank God," and stepped past the security men to hug Carmen.

One of the security guys put a hand on Megan's shoulder, but Carmen, audibly surprised, said, "It's fine," and broke the hug herself, stepping back. "What is wrong, Meghan? Five minutes ago you sent me away like a child, and now you come to bother me and hug me?"

"Danny Keane just died and I was afraid something might happen to you, too."

Carmen's jaw dropped. After a heartbeat, she waved the security team away, gesturing Megan into her room, and closed the door behind her. "What happened?"

"I don't . . . it could have just been a heart attack or an accident but . . . this place is amazing." A slightly overwhelmed giggle ran through the words as Megan glanced around. A glossy-topped table would sit eight; most of the furniture was leather and there was, for heaven's sake, a fireplace. The bed, of course, was in a separate room, so Megan couldn't check it out, but she did ask, "Is the bed comfortable?"

"Very."

"Good," Megan said, wide-eyed. "The whole room looks like it should be." She sat down on the front edge of a couch, feeling entirely too grubby for the cream leather, and momentarily put her face in her hands. "You're okay."

"Sí, yes, I am." After a moment Carmen came to sit beside her and carefully put a hand on Megan's knee. "You were worried for me."

"Terrified." Megan's voice broke on the word and she looked up with a fractured smile. "I'm probably borrowing trouble, but with two competitors dead I just had the horrible thought you were all targets and I'd sent you home alone and I just—" She dragged in a shaking breath. "I was scared for you."

"Ah, *pobrecita*." Carmen tugged Megan into a second hug, very gently. "But you were right, I could walk ten minutes alone in safety. No one knows or cares who I am."

"I didn't mean it like that, Carmen. And even if I had, right now I'm afraid I might have been wrong. You have other security, right? Someone who can stay with you?"

"Yes, of course. The large men at the door were not hotel employees, Meghan. But if Daniel Keane is dead, then surely Ramon is no longer a suspect? He was with *la policía* when Keane died?"

"I . . ." Megan straightened to take that information in, trying to work her way through the implications. "I don't know. I guess it depends on whether he's got a connection to Keane, and whether Keane really did have a heart attack, and . . . probably a thousand other things, too."

"Probably not more than three or four *otras cosas*." Carmen made a face. "Other things. I am forgetting to use my English."

Megan shrugged a little. *"Está bien. Hablo español."*

Carmen's jaw dropped. "You speak Spanish and all the time I have been killing myself to speak English with you? Sí, of course you know Spanish, you said to me the difference between *circunciso y circunstancial*!"

"Los padres de mi mejor amigo son mexicanos," Megan said with another shrug. Her best friend's parents weren't Tex-Mex, but Mexican immigrants to Texas. "Rafael grew up speaking Spanish at home and I hated not understanding, so I learned. You've never spoken it when I was driving you, so I

didn't, but you use it a lot more with Ramon around, so I did."

A laugh burbled from the tiny Spanish woman. "So you have always been nosy."

Megan smiled sheepishly. "Yeah." Her phone rang, startling her, and she muttered, "Oh, no, now what," as she took it from her pocket. Jelena's picture came up and Megan, worried, answered with, "Is everything okay, bejb?"

"I don't know," Jelena replied tensely. "Can you tell me why you're trending on social media?"

CHAPTER 14

Me? What? I'm trending?" Megan put the phone on speaker and flipped to another app to check the local trends. #MurderDriver was there, all right, and when she clicked the hashtag, there were even pictures of her at the Meeting House Square, with Sean Byrne raging at her. "Oh my God. Danny Keane died at the whiskey tasting this afternoon, and Sean Byrne gave out to me for not solving the murder already. He called me the murder driver in front of everybody. I didn't think about it. Oh, no. I'm sorry, Jelena."

Jelena's voice rose and broke: "Danny Keane *died*?"

Megan put the phone on the coffee table and sank her face into her hands. "Less than an hour ago. I don't know what happened. Hopefully it was a heart attack."

"*Hopefully*—" The word came out on a high, shattering laugh before Jelena's speech collapsed into rapid-fire Polish, much too quick and colloquial for Megan to understand, but she was fairly certain the gist of it was "How is this my life, that I should *hope* somebody just died of a heart attack instead of being murdered?" It took a long minute for Jelena to switch back to English and when she did, her voice remained too high, broken with stress and misery. "I can't do this, Megan. I can't do this. This is your fate, I can accept that, the dead call to you to be their voice, but I can't do it anymore. I'm sorry. Please give me some time before you come home so I can get some things together and find somewhere to stay tonight."

"Jelena, what—no! No? Please?" Megan jerked to her feet, tears stinging her nose and tightening her throat. She picked up the phone, turning the speaker off again, and put it to her ear, as if that would stop Carmen from knowing exactly what was going on. "Please, Yella? Can we talk about this?"

"We talk about it every time." Jelena's voice broke again. "Every time. You promise it won't happen again and I say all right, I understand, just this one more time, and it's not your fault, Megan. It's not your fault that fate has touched you and I love you, but I can't live like this. It will never end. I don't want to be the murder driver's wife. I just want to live quietly."

Megan's heart twisted until her breath left her body. "Wife?"

Jelena gave the most awful laugh Megan had ever heard, like someone cut it from her throat, and said, "Girlfriend" bitterly. "If things had been different . . . but they're not, Megan, and they never will be. I'm sorry. I love you. Goodbye." She hung up.

Cold glass pressed against Megan's forearms somehow, tears pooling on its clear surface. She didn't know how or when she'd ended up on her knees, leaning against the coffee table. A terrible sound, almost as awful as Jelena's laugh, rose in her throat in thin, keening waves, then broke into jagged sobs before it started again. Every time she tried to stop it, her throat clogged, leaving her unable to breathe. She thought it would hurt less if she could just stop breathing, but her body wouldn't let her, forcing the breath and the hideous wailing even when she tried to stop it.

Carmen, very gently and without saying anything, knelt beside Megan, put her arms around her, and held on when Megan turned into the embrace to cling and cry helplessly.

When the worst of the first of it had passed, Carmen rose, still silently, and first got Megan a huge glass of water, which she drank without speaking, and then a second, much smaller tumbler of whiskey from the suite's bar. Megan grimaced and took it, although she didn't sip it yet. Not until Carmen sat beside her again and delicately, as if knowing the question would cause pain, said, "You think she won't change her mind."

Another horrible sob, disguising itself as a laugh, broke from Megan's chest. Her whole face felt swollen. She had never been able to cry prettily. "No. She won't. And I can't even blame her. She's never liked the whole—" She gestured broadly, nearly spilling the whiskey. Carmen reached out and moved it to safety, then rose and got another glass of water, and a carafe to refill it with as Megan croaked, "The whole murder driver thing. Which is only sane of her. It was always too much. She just kept holding on, hoping it really would stop. But Daniel Keane didn't really die of a heart attack. You and me and her and the guards all know it even if the medical examiners don't yet, and—"

Fresh tears, more exhausted than raw, choked her again. "And it's never going to stop, or at least not soon enough for Jelena. And I . . ."

She hated where that sentence went, so didn't finish it. After a long moment, though, Carmen did, as kindly as it could be. "You like solving the murders more than you like Jelena."

"How can I be that terrible of a person?" Megan wailed. This time when she took the whiskey, she drank it, one fiery shot that cleared her throat for new sobs. "What's *wrong* with me?"

"Nothing." Carmen sounded tired and old. "I am not a serious enough person and you, mi amiga, you are maybe too serious."

"Or too much of an adrenaline junkie, some kind of stupid thrill-seeker who gets off on being involved with *murders*. That's not *normal*, Carmen—"

"No, it's not. But what is normal, Meghan? Normal is a story we are told, with princesses and happy endings, with . . . how do you Americans say, white picking fences?"

"Picket." Megan's smile felt fractured. "White picket fences."

"Sí, yes, picket. And a man and a woman and two children and a dog. How many people have 'normal' according to that story? Some, of course. But as many—more—don't. Normal is only a story. Messy life is the real normal and it is not the same for anyone. Your normal is to drive a limousine and tolerate a rich woman who flutters about and dresses you in gold, and to discover and solve murders."

"And Jelena can't live with that normal, and I can't leave it alone." Megan put the whiskey glass aside and turned to bury her face in her arms against the couch seat. "This isn't what I wanted."

"So will you go try to convince her to stay?"

After a long minute, Megan said, "No," into the cushions. "Because that's not what she wants."

"And you are sure?"

"She's been telling me all along." Grief rose in Megan's chest again, swelling until she couldn't breathe. "I just thought maybe . . . maybe it could work somehow, anyway."

Carmen sighed and put her hand on top of Megan's head. "Yes. That's the story we all tell ourselves. I'm sorry, Meghan. I truly am." She paused a moment. "Would you like to get very, very drunk?"

Megan laughed hoarsely. "Maybe? That was pretty good whiskey. Oh." She lifted her head, vision blurry with tears and exhaustion. "Was that yours? Midnight Sunrise?"

"It was." A little flash of pleasure brightened Carmen's eyes momentarily. "I'm glad you thought it was nice."

"Not as good as Harbourmaster," Megan said loyally, if not necessarily accurately. She'd have to taste them all together, knowing what she was trying, to really be sure, but the comment made Carmen smile, which made Megan's breathing a little easier for a heartbeat or two. Then she sagged back down into the couch cushion, eyes closing. "Should I go talk to her?"

Carmen shrugged. "She asked you not to. But sometimes people ask you to do a thing, or not to do it, as a test, to see if you care enough to break the rule, or also maybe to see if you care so little that you break the rule. Is Jelena the kind of woman to test you like that?"

"I don't think so. I hope not. It's not good either way, is it?" Megan sounded thick and dull even to her own ears, more than talking into a pillow could account for. "I can't read her mind. All I can really do is what she asks me to do, and assume that's what she really wants."

"So you have your answer."

"Yeah. I'd take another shot of that whiskey," she said after a minute. "I don't know if I want to get drunk, but a little numb might not suck."

Carmen brought the tumbler to the bar and filled it, but came back with the bottle, too. "Just in case."

"Just in case." Megan took a sip of the whiskey this time instead of just tossing it back, then coughed as her phone rang and hope shot through her with a fiercer burn than the alcohol. Paul's number came up, though, not Jelena's, and it took a few seconds to convince herself to answer with, "I know I'm usually the one calling about dead bodies, but I already know Daniel Keane is dead."

"I know. Niamh called me and I'm on my way to pick her up. Did you find Carmen? Are you all right?"

A whole new sob rose in Megan's throat. It took everything she had to say, "I found Carmen. She's fine," more or less steadily.

Evidently it wasn't steady enough, because concern came into Paul's voice. "What's wrong?"

"Nothing." Not even Megan believed the cracked rigidity she spoke with could possibly sound like nothing was wrong. "Nothing, it's fine, it's just—it's just that Jelena just broke up with me."

"*What?* Oh my God, Megan. What happened?"

"Daniel Keane's dead and I'm trending on social media because I was there. It was the camel-breaking straw." She told him what had happened, every word coming out more unsteadily than the previous one, until her voice broke hopelessly on the last few. Tears rolled down her cheeks again and she was too wrung out to even brush them away.

"Oh my God. I'm sorry, Megan. Do you want me to go see her? Talk to her?"

"Yes, but—" Megan's voice shattered again and she gulped a couple of heart-wrenching sobs before managing, "But not to try to convince her she's wrong. She isn't. Just make sure she's okay? And h—he—help her get her st—u—uhff if she needs help? And . . ." She gave up trying to speak and after a moment, Carmen took the phone from her.

"Hello, Detective Bourke. This is Carmen de la Fuente. Megan is here with me, so she is not alone. No," she said acerbically. "She is not okay. But she will be. We are going to get drunk." The acid left her voice there and she smiled briefly, first at the phone, then at Megan. "I have an extensive bar. I think we cannot drink our way through it before you get here."

"But Jelena might need his help," Megan rasped.

Carmen was quiet a moment, listening to Paul, then lifted her eyebrows. "He says he will call her, to ask if she needs help, but he and Niamh will come here first, to check on you and maybe to drink."

Paul spoke again, audible but incomprehensible to Megan, and Carmen smiled. "He says not to drink. I say we will see. Also he asks if you know where Rabbie is, Megan."

New tears sprang to Megan's eyes. "No, and I didn't even think to call him. I'm the worst!"

"He says he will call him, too," Carmen reported. "That you have enough to deal with. And also that he has spoken already with Detective Reese and told her of your fear that someone is targeting the competition entrants." She paused, listening, then said, "He says too that he kept your name out of it."

Megan blurted a sad, wet laugh and put her head on the couch again. "Probably a good idea. I'm sorry," she wailed. "I'm not handling this very well."

Carmen's eyebrows went even higher and she handed the phone back to Megan. Paul said, "You just got dumped, Megan. You're allowed to not handle things well for a while."

"But I'm *forty-three*!"

"Heartbreak is not the sole provenance of teens

and drama queens, *cuisle*. Stick with Carmen. I'm just about to the IFI and I'll get Niamh and we'll come over." He paused. "Where are you?"

"The presidential suite at the Westbury."

He paused again, an audible break before responding. "I didn't even know they had a presidential suite."

Carmen, loudly enough for Paul to hear, said, "I will tell security to expect you."

"They'd probably let Niamh in anyway," Megan said as Paul hung up, and Carmen smiled briefly.

"Well, no, not while I'm here, but yes, I'm sure if she wanted to rent it, they would be very eager to have her. The, um, how do you say it, *oficioso* young man at the desk downstairs? *El oficioco joven de abajo temblaría*," she said in the tone of a woman looking for a translation to the English.

"Officious, yeah." Megan actually couldn't stop a quick, but real, laugh. "He would. He'd quiver in his shoes. Maybe you shouldn't warn him."

"Quiver! *Oficioso* is close to *officious*, but I could not think of quiver." Carmen gave her a wicked grin. "If we are to not tell him we must go downstairs to watch him quiver, and if we are to do that, you must wash your face. Your eyes are puffy."

"My whole head feels puffy." Megan got up awkwardly and made her way to the bathroom, where she stopped and laughed. "I think this is bigger than our whole house. *My* whole house," she added miserably, remembering. "I guess it's going to seem a lot bigger with just me in it." She got a washcloth and ran cold water over it, then pressed her face into it, which felt nice enough that she wondered if she could just stay there forever. The bath was probably big enough to live in by itself. Of course, the dogs would betray her and sleep with Carmen on the enormous comfortable bed.

Not that the officious young man downstairs would let the dogs in to his precious hotel. Megan was sure he would if she was as rich as Carmen, but that wasn't in the cards, so she just finished washing her face before risking a glance at herself in the mirror.

Her eyes were tired and sad, but not as swollen as they still felt. Even if they didn't go downstairs, this was a more presentable face for when Niamh and Paul arrived, although Megan figured she'd probably burst into tears on them, too. She left the bathroom to finish the second shot of whiskey Carmen had poured for her, then sat wearily on the couch. "Maybe we should just try to get everybody who's left out of the competitors into your suite here and wait to see what happens next."

Humor sparkled in Carmen's eyes. "A locked door mystery, sí? Is that what you call them?"

"Oh. Hah. I was just thinking of trying to keep everybody safe behind a wall of security, but yeah, I guess it could be. If someone died we'd know it was someone in the room. But I don't think the hotel would be very happy if we brought everybody in so a murder could be committed on the premises."

"For me they would do anything," Carmen said with a sniff.

"Probably, but would they let you stay here again? Murders make hotels uncomfortable." Megan sighed. "Murders make most people with any sense uncomfortable."

"And then there's you."

"Yeah. I guess so." Getting drunk was starting to sound like a good idea, although in Megan's experience, it didn't help and arguably made things worse, since later she always still had the same problems but then also had a hangover on top of them. And she'd only had about three hours of sleep, so the hangover would almost certainly be epic. "Do you have any enemies? People who hate you enough that killing others as a smoke screen would be worth the effort?"

Carmen blinked dark eyes at her, then slowly shook her head. "Not personally, I don't think. I am very, very rich, and people hate me for that, but it is a . . . a one-percent hatred, not a hatred of *me*, I think. Ah," she added as the phone rang. "I forgot to call down to say Niamh and Detective Bourke were visiting. That is probably our officious young man asking if they can come up. I hope they let Ramon go soon," she added more softly as she went to answer the phone. "I would like this thing solved, and swiftly."

"Ideally before anybody else dies, or anybody else's heart gets broken." Megan stared into her whiskey tumbler while Carmen arranged for Paul and Niamh to be escorted up to the suite, and thought she was doing all right up until the moment Niamh swept in and hugged her. Then, mortifyingly, tears sprang to her eyes again and she wailed, "The dogs are going to miss her so much," into Niamh's shoulder.

"Ah, there now, chicken." Niamh patted Megan's hair and hugged her tighter. "They'll be all right so. Don't you worry, pet. Now, look, love, it's not that

I mean to distract you, but you need to pull yourself together for two minutes, all right?"

"Why?" A dreadful combination of selfish despair and gut-twisting alarm ran hot and cold through Megan. She sat back, wiping her eyes and snuffling like a child, to see Niamh's worried gaze dart to Paul, then back to Megan herself.

"It's probably nothing," Niamh promised. "He's probably in the loo or something, but Megan, nobody can get ahold of your Uncle Rabbie."

CHAPTER 15

He was going to the tasting," Megan whispered. "Last I talked to him, that was the plan. But he was at our house, I'll—" Her stomach lurched and brought not just a whiskey-tasting burp with it, but a wave of sorrow she struggled to push back down. "I'll call Jelena and ask if he's still there."

"Ah, love, I can do that," Niamh said in genuine distress.

Uncertainty boiled in Megan's gut. "He's my uncle, I should be the one to call . . . No, I should," she said more decisively, then lost all her conviction. "Shouldn't I? I should," she said again, and this time got her phone to make the call before she lost her nerve.

To her surprise and relief, Jelena actually answered, although she opened with a terse, "Megan, I don't want to talk about this right now, it's hard enough already," in a voice that sounded like she'd been crying as much as Megan had.

Megan's stomach churned again as a horrid, desperate hope lanced through her. Maybe if it was hard, it wouldn't last. But maybe it was just hard. "No, I know, I'm sorry I'm calling, it's just— is Rabbie still there? He's not answering his phone."

"What? No, he left at least an hour ago. Why— oh, no." Worry spiked in Jelena's voice. "Do you think he's okay?"

"I hope he's just not hearing his phone," Megan whispered. "But with two competitors dead, I don't know what to think. I'm sorry for bothering you. Thank you. I—I'll let you know if we find him."

"Megan—" Jelena sighed hugely. "Yes, please do text me. Goodbye." She hung up again and Megan bit her lower lip until it hurt enough that she thought she wouldn't cry.

"He's not there," she told the others through a scratchy throat. "I can . . . I should go back to the Meeting House Square and see if he made it there. Or check . . . check the Luas? He'd have taken the Luas to town. There's no trend saying there are disruptions, just that it's—" Her voice broke on a tiny laugh as she checked social media for trends and updates. "Just that it's free. Oh, Dublin, never stop."

Paul, blankly, said, "The Luas isn't free," and Megan smiled weakly at him.

"No, it's not, but did you miss the whole thing— it was years back now—where a reporter said he'd always wanted to start a disinformation campaign about the Luas being free, and Irish social media ran away with it?" At Paul's blank look she concluded, "You're not online nearly enough."

"You're online too much," he told her and Niamh laughed.

"I'm not online *that* much and *I* caught the whole free Luas thing!"

"You," he said to Niamh, "have secret accounts so you can follow people you like without getting harassed and are online way more than you admit. And there's a hundred euro fine if you're caught riding the Luas without paying for a ticket!"

"You're such a cop," Niamh said fondly, and kissed him before turning back to Megan. "Paul should go look for Rabbie in Temple Bar. For one thing, you got thrown out already, and—"

"What? What'd you do to get thrown out?"

"I existed," Megan said miserably.

Paul's eyebrows quirked up, but he ended with an accepting shrug and nod. "Fair, that'd be enough for half the guards I know, and Dervla's one of them. I'll go," he agreed. "You three sit tight."

"There's no reason for me to," Megan protested. "I'm not really part of any of the whiskey teams. I could go check on . . ." She trailed off, because everybody she might check on was probably still at the Meeting House Square, and Detective Reese wasn't going to let her back in. "All right, *fine.* We'll sit here and drink Carmen's whiskey while you go do the legwork. Fine!" She narrowly avoided adding *See if I care!*, but clearly her tone said it anyway, because Paul gave her a rather dry look as he kissed Niamh's cheek and hurried back out the door again.

Carmen wordlessly got another whiskey tumbler and poured Niamh a healthy measure, as well as topping off her own and Megan's glasses. Niamh quirked her eyebrows in thanks, took a sip, and twitched her eyebrows higher. "That's nice."

"It's Carmen's whiskey," Megan said thickly. "Midnight Sunrise. I don't think I should have any more. I'll cry. Or fall asleep."

"Ah, love." Niamh sat beside Megan and pulled her into a hug. "I'm sorry, my petal."

Megan said, "Me too," miserably into Niamh's shoulder, then moaned like she already had a hangover when her phone rang. "If that's Orla, I'm drowning myself in your swimming pool, Carmen."

"I have only a bathtub," the little rich woman said prissily enough to make Megan's chest heave with a silent laugh, even if it didn't get farther than that.

"Close enough." She lifted her phone, then nearly fumbled it trying to answer the call. "It's Rabbie! Rabbie! Where are you? Are you okay?"

"I'm at the tasting, like I said I'd be." Rabbie sounded shaken. "Did you know Danny Keane's dead, Megan?"

Megan's bones melted with relief. The phone actually did slip from her fingers, but Niamh caught it, pressed *speaker* after silently confirming it was okay to do so, and put the phone on the coffee table. Megan, so far sunken into the couch cushions she thought she might be mistaken for one of them, croaked, "I did, yes. We've been trying to get ahold of you. We're afraid someone's targeting the contestants. Paul Bourke is on his way to you. Don't go anywhere with anybody except him or drink or eat anything anybody gives you."

"I've a finger of whiskey in me own hand!" Rabbie replied, obviously outraged. "You wouldn't have it go to waste, would you?"

"I'd rather it went to waste than you went to your grave," Megan snapped and her uncle, shifting from outrage to surprised dismay, said, "Jaysus, Megan."

Her perfunctory, "Sorry," barely made it past the hiss of the *s* before she gave up on it. "I just want you to be really careful. We could be totally overreacting, but I'd rather you were safe."

"Fair enough, lass." Rabbie sighed dramatically and she heard him offer his whiskey to a passerby. There was startled agreement on his end of the line before he said, "There, now it's not a problem."

"Unless it was poisoned and you just handed it off to some poor unsuspecting sod."

"*Jaysus*, Megan! What's gotten into you? Besides, if someone's poisoning people with kiwi and other small flightless birds—"

Megan snorted a laugh hard enough to make her throat hurt. Rabbie, who had evidently gotten over his earlier embarrassment about not knowing there were different kinds of kiwi, sounded immensely pleased with himself as he went on. "—then if it was meant for me it'd be something I was allergic to and what are the odds that I handed the drink off to someone with the same allergy? Not that I have any. Is that what Danny Keane died of?" he asked more soberly. "Poisoning? Or allergies?"

"I don't know yet. Probably nobody does. The doctor on the scene thought it was probably a heart attack, but the odds of that seem incredibly low." Megan reached for her whiskey glass, then thought better of it and poured herself water from the carafe Carmen had set out earlier. "I just want everybody to be safe. Are the Murphys and Hannah Flanagan still there?"

Rabbie said, "Em," thoughtfully. "I'll have a look around and ring you back in a minute or two."

"Okay, but just—be careful. Call Paul. Tell him where you are." Megan hung up, drank her water, and oozed back to mostly lying flat on the couch. "I may not be in any fit condition to do anything else today. I may," she said, slightly more strenuously, "be slightly inebriated."

"That was the idea," Carmen said as placidly as Megan had ever heard her speak. "Drowning our sorrows in *uisce beatha*."

Niamh gave a startled shout of laughter and applauded as Carmen developed an ever-so-slightly smug smile. "That was as Irish as I've ever heard," Niamh said approvingly. "Not a trace of the Spanish in it. Have you been practicing?"

Carmen actually dimpled and wriggled her shoulders with pride, making Megan giggle quietly. "It's the only thing I can say in Irish," she warned Niamh. "But at least I say it well."

" 'Water of life,' " Megan said to the ceiling, translating the Irish phrase for 'whiskey' into English.

"Right now I think it might be the water of sleep. How do you say that, *uisce* . . . sleep." She had slightly more Irish than Carmen, but only slightly. "I should probably take some Irish classes."

"You already speak Spanish, some Polish, and are studying Yoruba," Niamh said fondly. "You probably don't need to pick up Irish, too."

"Sure I do. Up the Irish, stand up against the oppressors who killed our language, all of that." Megan's phone rang and she answered it with her eyes closed, relieved that something had stopped her before she went on a mild alcohol-fueled rant about disappearing languages. "Rabbie? Are you okay?"

"I'm grand," her uncle promised. "Your young wan, the Flanagan girl, she's here annoying the bejayzus out of the detective, but themselves are gone, the husbands. Sean Byrne said they left in a hurry, as soon as the guards were done talking to them. I can't say as I blame them. It's an eerie air here now, Megan. Like everyone's expecting to be haunted by ghosts. Ah, there's himself, good man, Paul!" The last was a shout, and Megan could hear her uncle waving vigorously. "All right, now I'm safe and sound with your detective, Megan. Are you happy now?"

"I am. Tell him thanks." Megan hung up and nearly rang Jelena, whose name was under Rabbie's in the recent calls list. Then her heart missed a beat and sent a pain through her throat that she tried to swallow away. Instead of calling, she sent a text saying Rabbie had been found and held her breath a few more painful seconds, hoping Jelena would respond and everything would magically be all right.

Jelena didn't respond and things were not magically all right. Megan draped her elbow over her eyes, letting her phone drop onto the couch beside her ear, and told herself to get it together. Instead, tears began leaking into her elbow and toward her ears, and although she didn't think she'd made any sound, Niamh said, "Aw, honey," and hugged Megan's knee, which was the closest thing to her.

"It's fine. I'm fine. I don't know why I'm not fine." Megan rolled toward the back of the couch and Niamh squished up against her legs like pressure equalled a hug.

"Because you've been together like three years," she said. "You've been living together since you moved out of that place Orla owned—that's what, eighteen months? And you've been dating almost as long as Paul and I have been. You're allowed to be upset over that ending, Megan. I'd be more worried if you weren't."

"I just want to talk to her," Megan wailed into the back of the couch. "I want to make it better, but I don't think I can. This has been a problem literally the entire time we've known each other. Literally! Why am I surprised? Why am I . . ." She ran out of words and choked another sob into the couch, then flinched as her phone rang right under her ear. "God, now what!"

She sat up in time to see Niamh and Carmen exchanging what she figured were probably actually sympathetic glances, but felt judgy, because she was full of judginess for herself. To make matters worse, she didn't know the phone number calling her and she hated answering unknown calls. She did anyway, snarling, "This better not be spam," as her greeting.

"Oh," a startled male voice replied. "Em, no? It's Jacob Murphy, of Sea Warrior Whiskey? The Misters Murphy?"

"Oh." Megan took a shuddering breath, trying to calm herself. "I'm sorry. What can I do for you, Mr. Murphy?"

"Sorry for ringing out of the blue," Jake said. "The guards said we ought to be careful and I'm wondering if you have any idea what's going on."

"How did you get my number?"

"I called Leprechaun Limos."

Megan groaned and made a note to . . . well, she probably shouldn't even think the phrase *kill Orla* under the circumstances. "I really don't know what's going on, Mr. Murphy. I can't even legitimately say everyone's in danger, although I admit I'm feeling a little paranoid."

"I think we're all feeling a little paranoid," Jacob Murphy replied sharply. "Two of the competitors are dead and that can't be a coincidence."

Megan, feeling contrarian, said, "Well, it could be, but it probably isn't. Look, I don't know, go somewhere safe, sit tight, and don't eat or drink anything you haven't prepared yourself? I don't know what to tell you, Mr. Murphy."

There was a brief commotion, as if Jake Murphy had partially covered the phone's mouthpiece while talking to someone else, before he said, "We've just watched a police detective escorting

Rabbie Lynch away. Why isn't he taking us with him?"

"Because the detective is a family friend, not on duty, and doing me a favor?"

"Preferential treatment for the straights," Jake muttered. "Isn't that always the way."

Megan opened her mouth, emitted a cracked sound, and closed it again to try to find her voice. "I'm sorry," she managed on a second try. "Who are 'the straights' here?"

"You and your uncle, obviously."

"Well, as far as I know, you're right about Rabbie, but my girlfriend just dumped me so you can—" Megan took a sharp breath, heavily edited her language, and finished with, "—take that into consideration."

"Oh. Oh, shite, I'm sorry, I didn't know—"

"Yeah, no kidding." Megan, not feeling particularly proud of herself while also reveling in her rudeness, hung up without saying anything else.

Neither Niamh nor Carmen were making the slightest effort to pretend they hadn't been listening. Both women, in fact, had wide eyes and pursed mouths that suggested a combination of humor and admiration. "That was very restrained," Niamh said with apparent sincerity. "More restrained than I would have been."

"You would have eviscerated him on the red carpet." Megan reached for her water glass, got to the whiskey tumbler first and had a sip of that, even if it was against her better judgment. "I'm going to feel slightly guilty if they end up dead."

"Then I suppose you'd better find out who done it. I mean, you don't have to justify yourself to Jelena anymore. Too soon?" Niamh grimaced politely as Megan gave her a dagger look, but didn't seem to have much actual regret to offer up. "I won't tell you she wasn't good enough for you, love, but maybe it was never going to work."

"Still too soon," Megan said into her whiskey. Even if Niamh was right and realistically, she probably was, it was still too soon.

Niamh nodded, then picked up her own phone as it buzzed. "Paul says he'll be here in a few minutes with Rabbie. What's the plan from then?"

Megan said a sullen "I don't know," to her tumbler, then deliberately put it down and picked up the water instead. "I guess I go talk to, I don't know, friends of the Misters Murphy, to see if they have any deep dark grudges against any of the competitors, or Sean Byrne, or anybody else that the killer could be striking out against."

"Everyone has grudges against Sean Byrne," Carmen said with amusement. Her eyebrows floated gently upward as Megan and Niamh both glanced at her. "You must know that. He is not a well-liked man, even among other rich people. All the bullying and posturing, the bragging about his companies. I think many people would be happy to stab his back."

Megan's voice rose. "Would *you?*"

"Mmmn." The noncommittal sound did very little to reassure Megan, although after a few seconds of consideration, Carmen shrugged. "No, I think even our finances do not run in the same circles closely enough to feel he's wronged me. But I don't like him, either. He must always be the big fish, yes? Men like him are tiresome." After a judicious pause, she added, "Women, too, but they are often not as obvious. Sean likes pushing people around."

"Yeah. I saw him at the gala last night, and I guess he tried pushing me around at the tasting this afternoon. 'Go solve the mystery, Megan, isn't that your job?' Ugh. No," she added more sharply, mostly to herself. "I have to get up. I have to go do *something*, so I'm not wallowing."

"You're allowed to wallow, Megan!" Niamh sounded more than a little exasperated.

"Not until I'm sure everyone's safe, okay? I really am going to just send everybody here to hang out with you, Carmen. This is probably the most secure location I have immediate access to."

"I'll order snacks." Carmen rose to do that. Megan thought maybe having everything else fall apart around her was helping distract the tiny Spaniard from her own breakup. Embracing chaos was probably better than sinking into a couch and eating ice cream for a month, which was what Megan wanted to do at the moment. Although she'd pay for it forever at the gym, if she did.

A groan rumbled through her chest. "The gym."

Niamh shook her head. "What about it?"

"Jelena and I have been going to the same gym at the same time for years now. It's how we met. I'm going to have to change gyms."

"Why should *you* have to change gyms? Why can't she?"

"I don't know. Because."

"Ah. An unassailable defense," Niamh murmured.

Megan glared at her, but then her phone rang

again and she answered with a sigh. "Megan Malone's Moaning Misery at your service."

Paul Bourke said, "Em," then chuckled, although it ended in an apologetic sound. "Look, I'm dropping Rabbie off in a minute and I'll ring Jelena to see if she needs help, but I just saw Jacob and John Murphy rushing off toward the Sionnach Rua Whiskey Shop up at College Green and I thought someone might want to . . ." He trailed off like he was only just hearing himself, and Megan could all but hear the shrug that preceded his, "Well, find out why."

"And you're not asking Detective Reese because . . . ?" Megan didn't want to be smiling, but a trace of humor tugged at the corners of her mouth as Paul replied in a chastened tone.

"Because there's nothing illegal about a whiskey development team visiting a whiskey shop, but I heard John Murphy's tone and he didn't sound any too broken up about Keane's death when he said they were on the way to the shop. It's probably nothing," Paul emphasized.

The smile won, pulling across Megan's face. "But it's the kind of nothing I can pop in to eavesdrop on?"

"Something like that."

Megan let the whole darn grin develop. "I'm on my way."

CHAPTER 16

The walk from Carmen's hotel to Sionnach Rua—the Red Fox—whiskey shop was a ten minute dawdle down Grafton Street. Megan didn't dawdle, but did detour for a huge cup of Belgian chocolate and honeycomb flavored gelatos. She shoveled the ice cream into her mouth tragically as she hurried her way through weekend shoppers on Dublin's high street.

Sionnach Rua sat more or less across from Trinity College, its vast plate glass windows looking toward the old college's southwest face. The shop glowed with dark, mysterious warmth from the inside, golden liquids glimmering as the sun or the soft internal light caught them, and felt like a surprisingly welcoming spot. Megan had only ever been inside a couple of times and, to her embarrassment, had never done the catacomb tour or been in the whiskey museum next door. Generally she regarded being able to tell clients what tourist attractions were worth it as part of her job, but somehow she'd never actually done the museum. Maybe she would pop in and do it after listening to whatever the Misters Murphy were in a hurry to talk about.

Megan paused at the museum's door, reading about the tours, and winced. For one thing, they ended at six, which it nearly was already, and more importantly, they included up to four tastings. She probably didn't need any more alcohol today. She took her phone out to text Jelena to ask if she wanted to schedule a tour, remembered, and slunk into the Sionnach Rua feeling like someone had punched her in the gut. Again.

The shop smelled good, at least, a tinge of tobacco and whiskey in the air, and its interior was really quite beautiful. There were four or five people in it, enough to be busy without being overwhelming, and the Misters Murphy were two of them. Both were in conversation with an older man at a small counter near the other end of the shop. Megan thought Jacob's shoulders were tight, but John looked relaxed and comfortable as he leaned against the bar.

A bearded man in his twenties gave Megan a brief, welcoming smile as she took a deep, slow breath upon entering. "Looking for anything in particular today?"

"I don't know. Something good for a breakup, I guess."

"Oooh." He grimaced sympathetically. "Sorry to hear that."

"Me too."

"Come on over and we'll have a look at what we've got on the wall, and maybe have a taste or two. We'll find something for you."

The last thing she wanted was more whiskey, but it got her closer to the Murphys. Megan sluffed her way to the tasting counter—glass, with half a dozen whiskeys you could make your own blend from, if you wanted—and made sure to lean so that her back was mostly toward the husbands as they chatted with the older whiskey seller.

"Now." Her young man—his name tag, partially hidden behind his lapel, told her that his name ended in *ac.* Off the top of her head she could only think of one boy's name that ended with *ac,* and decided to think of him as Cormac until given a reason not to. "Is it a bitter or a sorrowful breakup?"

"It's my own fault," she said and for once, even she thought she sounded Irish. "Sorrowful, I guess. I couldn't, or wouldn't, change."

Cormac made another sympathetic sound. "And would your taste in whiskeys run to the raw or the smooth?"

"Smooth. And usually on the rocks."

"Right then." Corman turned away to examine the wall of whiskeys and Megan perked her ears, trying to hear the conversation going on a few feet away.

"—advantage of a terrible situation," John Murphy was saying in a low voice. "But then again there's no point in pretending it's not an opportunity, is there? I'm thinking we could rebrand, change Sea Warrior Whiskey to Survivor's Whiskey, and—"

"John," Jacob said in an agonized, if quiet, voice. "That's only dreadful altogether."

"Theatrical, though." The third voice had to be the whiskey seller. Megan dared a quick look over her shoulder, assuring herself it was the older man who'd spoken, and turned her visible attention back to Cormac while holding her breath like it would help her hear better. "Drama is good for sales. But you'd be better off with a second whiskey— one of your younger ones, maybe—named Survivor. The drama will peak and fade and you're looking to establish a long-running brand."

His voice went unexpectedly cold. "At least, I trust you are. I've no time for dalliances. This is a serious business."

"No, no, of course we are," John murmured reassuringly. "We wouldn't be here talking with you if we weren't. But I thought if we could get ahead of the traditional media picking up on the story, we might parlay it into something positive for our brand. Maybe not Survivor, on second thought. Maybe that's too macabre. We could bring that in later. Right now it could be an homage. Keen Warrior Whiskey."

Megan snuck another glance over her shoulder. The man they were talking to looked mildly impressed. "Introduce some confusion into the brand name," he said with a note of interest. "Have people saying what was it, Keane Edge or Keen Warrior that had the man die. Not a bad idea. And then there'd be the Sea Warrior Whiskey beside it to bring it home."

"John, we shouldn't," Jacob said in a low, miserable voice. "A fair competition is one thing. Profiting off Danny's death, that's something else."

"Well, I didn't hear you complaining when Angus McConal dropped dead, did I?" John muttered. "Or being upset that he died with the Harbourmaster recipe on him, for that matter. You don't mind *those* waters being muddied, do you?"

"We could just stay above the fray," Jacob said unhappily. "Three of our competitors are tangled up in death or disarray, with that recipe being found on him. We could take the high road."

"The high road never made any money." The third man sniffed dismissively and Megan realized Cormac had been trying to show her a bottle of whiskey for at least thirty seconds.

"Sorry. I was . . ." She couldn't come up with an excuse, but the young man offered another sympathetic smile.

"Thinking about your ex, I'd guess. That's all right, miss. Now, I wouldn't want to be too much on the nose, but there *is* Writers' Tears, and it's a soft enough whiskey with a name to suit the situation, if you don't mind me saying so." Cormac handed her the bottle and Megan, through the combination of upset and trying to listen to the Murphys, found herself coughing a small laugh.

"I don't know. I'm not a writer."

"Ah, no, you can assume someone who is has shed them, and the broken heart of an artist has been distilled into a drink to soothe your soul."

Another small laugh shook Megan's chest. "You're pretty good at this, aren't you?"

"That's what they tell me." Cormac winked, but

by then Megan's too-American accent had drawn
the Murphys' attention, and Jacob came over to
frown apologetically at her.

"I'm glad to run into you, Ms. Malone. I really
am sorry about earlier. And about your breakup."

Megan, wisely or not, said, "I'll take it," to Cormac and, with a sigh, turned to Jacob. His skin was
flushed and his gaze flickered around the room,
clearly stressed. She wanted a conversation with
him, so she tried not to sound grudging as she
said, "Apology accepted. Will they be carrying your
whiskey here, if you win the competition?"

He smiled thinly. "Everybody will be, but John's
hoping we can strike a better bargain. This was always going to be a tense competition because so
much is on the line for everyone, but at this point
I just wish we'd never even started down this road.
It seemed like a wonderful idea, five years ago,
but . . ." He shook his head.

"Five years, is that all? I know some of the competitors have been working on their whiskeys for a
couple of decades."

"But they only have to age three years, so five is
enough if you get it right out of the . . ." Jacob
Murphy's eyebrows flickered down and he rubbed
his forehead. "Gate. That phrase ends with *gate*,
doesn't it? Not barrel. I've been too involved with
whiskey for too long, if I can't remember common
idioms."

"I don't know. Getting it right out of the barrel
seems appropriate, under the circumstances. Mr.
Murphy," Megan added as John came to join them.
"Fancy meeting you here."

"At this point I'm surprised all of us who are alive aren't here drinking ourselves to death," John Murphy replied a bit grimly. "Since things went sour at the actual tasting."

"Whiskey sour?" Megan got such a reproving look from both men that she coughed on another laugh. Jelena would have given her the same look.

Her humor, thin as it was, fled, and she sighed. Finding out that the Murphys were plotting to capitalize on the deaths wasn't nothing, but she didn't think Jacob, at least, had the stomach for committing murder in the name of financial success. John seemed a bit more ruthless, but unless he had access to more information about Danny Keane than Megan imagined, he was probably just a cold-hearted businessman, not a killer. "Was there any update on Keane's death after I got thrown out?"

They both looked startled, though Jacob's indrawn breath to comment was interrupted by Cormac coming back with Megan's bottle of whiskey and the card machine. She paid, took the bag, and tipped her head toward the door, inviting the Murphys with her. As soon as they were in motion, Jacob said, "You got thrown out?"

"On my ear." Megan thought that was overselling it, but Uncle Rabbie had told her to never let truth get in the way of a good story. "The guards don't like me very much, and Detective Reese was looking for an excuse to get rid of me all day. Sean Byrne giving out to me was what she needed."

"We heard that," John said. "I think the whole square did. I wondered what it was about."

"He wanted to know why I hadn't figured out who killed McConal yet, and how it was I'd let Danny Keane die on site. More or less."

"I told you it was because she was the murder driver," Jacob said to his husband and then, back to Megan, "So Detective Reese had *you* thrown out?"

"She didn't want me investigating. Not that I was trying to, but . . ." Megan rolled her eyes, then shivered. A wind had come up while she was in the shop, and now it ran straight down Grafton Street and through her like a cold knife. "There was supposed to be an event tonight, wasn't there? Is that still on, do you know?"

"We could step in and ask." John gestured to the whiskey museum and when Megan blinked in confusion, smiled. "It was just meant to be a private gathering of the competitors, distributors, and their hundred closest friends."

"Sponsors, you mean," Jacob said dryly.

John shrugged. "Sure so. Elbow-rubbing, you know? The whiskey museum was hosting." He held the door, ushering his husband and Megan into an old alley now lined with whiskey barrel tops featuring many of the kinds of whiskey made in Ireland. At the end of the alley a surprisingly steep and narrow stairway led upward. Megan, feeling faintly as if she was on an adventure, climbed them to be greeted by a smiling woman in her thirties.

"Welcome to the Irish Whiskey Museum. Are you here for the tour?"

"No, I'm afraid not, although I was thinking earlier today that I really needed to do it. We're with the festival. These are John and Jacob Murphy, of

Sea Warrior Whiskey? And we were wondering if the event tonight is still on."

Barely disguised bewilderment crossed the woman's pleasant face. "As far as I know, yes. Why wouldn't it be? We're setting up upstairs."

Apparently Sean Byrne wasn't going to let a few tragedies get in the way of making a buck. Megan hesitated, unsure whether she should explain, but Jacob Murphy, who evidently had the restraint of a toddler in a candy shop, blurted, "Danny Keane of Keane Edge Whiskey dropped dead this afternoon, after Angus McConal was murdered last night at the gala."

"Oh my God!" Genuine horror whitened the woman's cheeks as she clapped her hands over them. "I hadn't heard! My God! Was it murder?"

"Of course it was," Jacob said with enormous conviction. "What are the odds that two competitors would die, one murdered and one of natural causes, within twenty-four hours of each other?"

"Oh my God," the woman said again. "Please excuse me. I have to talk to my manager and the owner. At the very least we're going to have to see if we can increase security, and there's only two hours to do it in. Oh my *God*." She whirled away, leaving Megan and the Murphys alone and bemused.

After a moment, John said, "They're never going to cancel it on this short of notice," like he was trying to convince himself.

"I don't think so," Megan agreed. "It's late Saturday afternoon already. Even if they cancelled it immediately, Mr. Byrne would have to let everyone know, and even if he's got every single attendee's number to call or text, not everybody would see it. Although I guess they could just lock the doors and put an *event cancelled* sign up. That's what I would do, if I were Mr. Byrne. For the safety of my competitors, if nothing else."

"He wouldn't." John was nearly as pale as the museum employee had been. "This meet and greet is critical to the competitors' long-term success."

"Who cares about that, if people are dying? If cancelling keeps somebody safe—maybe one of us safe, John!—then they should cancel it!"

John Murphy waved an impatient hand. "No one is coming after us, Jake. Angus McConal wasn't well-liked and everybody knows Danny was having financial trouble. He probably took out a loan from the wrong people and got himself killed for not being able to repay it."

Megan's forehead crinkled. "You think a loan shark murdered him by faking a heart attack in a public square?"

"All right, when you put it like that it seems unlikely." John shrugged. "Still, why would anyone come after us?"

"You're gay," Megan pointed out. "Hate crimes. Not that that seems in keeping with the deaths so far, but if the targets are competitors, then that's the only common denominator that matters. Or do you know any reason somebody would just want to kill Danny Keane?"

"I'd have thought his wife would be more likely. She's a hard one, is Maggie Keane," Jacob said with an uncomfortable shift of his shoulders.

John waved it off. "Sure and I'd think you'd

want to kill Erin Ryan, not Angus McConal, myself, but what do I know?"

"Why, what'd Erin do?" The suggestion in less than ten seconds that two women would have made better targets than the men who'd died made Megan suspect the Murphys were operating on internalized misogyny, but she was certain saying as much wouldn't win her any points. Or, more importantly, earn her any gossip.

"Well, McConal was the cash cow, wasn't he? Killing the golden goose is an eedjit's move. It'd be smarter to take the manager out and move in on collecting her percentage."

"Not that we have any interest in managing a boxer," Jacob put in hastily. Megan thought he was more aware of how they sounded than John was, or cared more. "John's speaking theoretically."

"Of course. So you know the Keanes?"

"Danny Keane got us into the whiskey-making business," John said. "I hadn't known anything about it, but I got interested because there was a while there when he wanted—"

He kept speaking, but for a moment Megan's ears filled with the rush of blood. Keane had told her he'd sunk a decade's worth of his family's finances into Keane Edge. If the Murphys had followed in his footsteps with more financial security and a whiskey ready at the same time his was, she was astonished one or both of *them* wasn't dead. "Sorry," she said, shaking herself. "I think I've drunk too much whiskey today. I missed the last bit of what you said?"

John was still talking, already deep in some obscure detail of whiskey production, but Jacob said,

"He asked us to invest, but John said it was a bad risk. Of course, he wasn't happy when we went into the business ourselves."

"I don't see what that's got to do with anything, though." John drew himself up, suddenly defensive. "That was a long time ago, water under the bridge."

"*Uisce beatha* under the bridge," Megan said with a faint smile, and both men, their defensiveness defused, chortled. "Look, tell you what, I've got Jacob's number and you lads have been at the tasting all day. I'd bet you need dinner under your belts before we all get together for more whiskey. I'll call around and see if anybody's got the story on whether the meet and greet is on tonight, and ring you with the news."

"Oh, that's brilliant of you." Jacob seized on the offer with a smile. "I'm starving of the hunger, now that you mention it. Would you say Shanahan's has seating at this hour, or do you think we need reservations?" he asked, his attention now fully on his husband.

"I think if we ring and make reservations we'll have a seat when we get there. *Go raibh maith agat,* Megan, we'll talk to you later." John tucked his arm through Jacob's and they headed back up Grafton Street toward the steakhouse on St. Stephen's Green.

Megan waved cheerily, then strode the other way, getting herself all the way around the corner before she staggered over to lean on the wall of a tourist information building and think.

Daniel Keane had asked the Murphys to invest. Angus McConal had died with the Harbourmaster recipe on him. Megan could see a through line there, one where the Murphys had stolen Keane's recipe to start with, killed Angus and planted the recipe as a red herring, and then murdered Danny Keane to make sure he'd never figure it out.

She wasn't positive. Not yet, anyway. For one thing, someone still had to have leaked the Harbourmaster recipe. But John Murphy seemed like a cold-blooded fish, and Jacob came across as a slightly worried man inclined to follow his husband's lead. If she could find a link that tied them to the Harbourmaster recipe, Megan thought they were a more solid lead than Ramon Sanchez.

Feeling better than she had all day, Megan took her phone out and rang Rabbie. "So give me all the goss about the Murphy husbands."

CHAPTER 17

Rabbie, disappointingly, told her to come back to the hotel for the gossip, as they were currently eating the best dinner he'd had in his life and he wouldn't be sparing a minute from it to talk to her on the phone. Megan agreed with a smile and then, because thinking of Ramon had put her in mind of it, rang her friend Rafael in San Francisco. She hadn't talked to him or his wife Sarah in weeks. She wasn't surprised to get voice mail—it wasn't even ten AM there, and Sarah worked late nights while Raf worked all the time—but her voice still broke a little with disappointment as she left a message.

"Hey, Raf, it's me. Um, well, there's been another murder, two actually, or at least probably two, and Jelena broke up with me because of them and I can't even blame her—" The words came out incredibly fast because Megan's throat tightened up and blurting them was the only way to get through it. "—and anyway that's kind of all I know but I guess it's, you know, plenty, so um, text me when you can call, huh? I'd like to talk to you two."

She sniffled and hung up. She had never met Rafael's wife in person, but they'd talked enough on the phone and video chats to make Megan feel close to her, and she wanted to share the whole mess with Sarah as much as Rafael. But they might not get in touch until tomorrow or even the next day, given the eight-hour time difference and their unpredictable schedules, so Megan sucked it up—almost literally, taking a deep breath to steady herself—and marched back to Carmen's hotel.

The officious young man at the desk just looked weary when he saw her this time and waved her on. Megan wound her way through the hotel to the secure wing, knocking on the door to be surprised, again, that Carmen answered it herself. "I apparently keep expecting you to have a butler, or something."

"Usually Ramon would answer the door, from that side." Carmen's forehead wrinkled prettily as she stepped aside to let Megan in. "I hope he's all right. When will they let him go, Meghan? He cannot be the killer, if Danny Keane is dead, too."

The hotel was warm after the chilly November evening, and Carmen's room felt positively cozy, with low, indirect lighting glowing around the gathering of people at the coffee table. It also smelled amazing. Megan took a moment to breathe deeply, appreciating the scent of good food before answering. "That assumes there's only one killer."

Sheer dismay wiped all the light from Carmen's eyes. "Do you think there's more than one?"

"I really don't know." Megan's stomach rumbled and she edged toward the coffee table, which was laden with what appeared to be everything on the hotel's menu. There were actually several filets, as if the four people currently in the room—Carmen, Niamh, Rabbie, and now Megan—might each need one along with spatchcock chicken, a mushroom risotto that looked mouthwateringly delicious, four different kinds of salad, a brioche that smelled like heaven itself, and a huge stack of sides, mostly vegetables done to visible perfection. "I *should* have brought the Murphys back here. They went for steaks anyway."

"We can't gossip about them if they're here. Dessert is on the bar," Niamh said between bites. "I don't know how we're going to eat it all but I'm going to try. Thank you, Carmen."

Rabbie, sitting with a plate of steak and an air of holy communion, murmured, "If we're all to be murdered at least it's a worthy last meal. Sit down, lass, you've not had a bite to eat yet."

Since Megan had just arrived, she assumed he was talking to Carmen, whose smile regained some of its lightness. "Ah, Señor Lynch, gracias. No one has called me anything like 'lass' in a long time."

"Sure and you can't be more than half my age," Rabbie replied expansively. "What else should I call you but lass?"

Carmen's unexpected laugh pealed across the room. "I should have met your uncle a long time ago," she said to Megan. "He has a kind soul."

"He does." Megan sat to try a bite of the brioche,

dipping it into a creamy sauce that made her whimper. "Oh my God. That's amazing. What is it?"

"Cauliflower velouté," Carmen said carelessly as she joined the others at the coffee table. Megan didn't even know what a velouté was—presumably the sauce—but thought she could probably live on it, given the chance. "What did you learn from the Murphys, Meghan?"

"John's a shark," Megan said. "Or that's the impression I got. I actually came back here to get Rabbie's local knowledge on them."

Her uncle preened as everyone's attention turned to him. Megan almost laughed: he was genuinely happiest when he could spin stories for an interested audience, and everyone in the room was currently a willing captive to his tale. "Well, what I know is that Jacob Murphy and Danny Keane were schoolmates back in the day, and it was long enough ago now that you'd have gotten more than a side-eye for suggesting they were more than mates, if you know what I mean."

There was a brief silence in which no one did know what he meant, and an eruption of sound a heartbeat later when all three of the women listening understood at once. Gossipy enthusiasm went to war with a twist of dismay just beneath Megan's breastbone. "You mean they dated?"

Rabbie made a face. "Is it dating when neither of them would so much as admit it? I don't know what you'd call it. Desperately afraid of being caught, I'd say, and most people wouldn't have seen it for what it probably was, but I knew Jake's older sister and she kept a weather eye out for trouble for the lads, back when. The only reason I know about it is she mentioned it once, when she got the invite to the wedding. To Danny and Maggie's, I mean, and she was surprised. Not that she thought Danny and Jacob would end up together, but that Danny'd decided to marry a woman."

"Well, bisexuality is a thing," Megan muttered. Maybe her bisexual disaster theory held some water after all.

Rabbie shrugged at her. "So it is, but even now people forget that, don't they? And to be fair, I don't think she liked Maggie very much, but then, not many people do. She's a hard one, is Maggie Keane."

"That's what Jacob said, too. What's the story?" Megan leaned forward, listening intently, then noticed there was more food in front of her. It would probably be impolite not to eat it, since Carmen had ordered it up for everybody.

The steak was even better than the brioche. Megan thought she might weep with it as a bite practically melted on her tongue. It took a moment to bring herself back to what Rabbie was saying, his tone thoughtful. "I'd say Maggie Keane had big dreams for her life, and none of it worked out the way she thought it would. She's a pretty woman and thought she would parlay that into a career. Modeling, acting, something, and maybe she would have, but her mam died young and she took over the raising of her brothers and sisters while her father worked and drank. I think she imagined marrying Danny Keane was her way out. He was a promising young man."

"I hate that phrase." Niamh put her cutlery down and scowled at her plate. "Promising. What if you don't want to be promising? What if you just want to live a life, without people expecting something great of you?" She looked up, jaw tense as she shook her head. "If you're promising, you either have to live up to your promise or you're a disappointment. That's a hell of a burden to put on anybody, but especially a kid. It's not like they don't get that disappointment is looming, if they're promising."

Rabbie studied her a moment. "They called you promising."

"So I know what I'm talking about. Living up to that promise is a lot of work and *God*, don't I feel it when a bad review comes in, or a film does poorly, or even if I forget somebody's name on the press circuit. 'She was so promising.'" Niamh's lip curled. "I get that it's well-meant, but it's a cruel thing to do to a child. Or anyone."

"Danny said their whole lives were riding on him winning this competition," Megan said into the little silence that followed. "I wonder if he saw it as his last chance to live up to his promise. Did John Murphy know about his relationship with Jacob?"

"He'd never kill him over a teenage romance," Rabbie protested, but Megan wobbled a hand with uncertainty.

"He asked the Murphys to invest in Keane Edge. After that is when John got interested in making whiskey himself."

Rabbie said, "Oh," and then, "oh," again, a frown pinching his eyebrows. "That's not on."

Megan nodded. "It isn't, is it? I wonder now if he asked Jacob, more than the pair of them. Have they any connections to you or your team, Rabbie?"

"It's a small country," her uncle said dismissively. "We're all connected in one way or another. Why do you ask?"

"I'm wondering if anyone on your team could have given them the Harbourmaster recipe."

"Ooh," Carmen said, wide-eyed, as bewilderment slid over Rabbie's face. "Ooh, I see, Meghaaan. You think Angus's death is a cover? That Danny was the real target?"

The fact that she drawled her name made Megan smile. For the moment, at least, she was the vivacious woman Megan was most familiar with. "It seems possible, and if there was an old relationship then that makes it seem a little more possible. But none of it holds together without knowing who leaked the Harbourmaster recipe. Not this theory, not Ramon, nothing."

"Well." Rabbie sat back and pointed dramatically at Niamh. "It wasn't yourself, because you've never seen it, and I trust you all know it wasn't *me*. Now, it couldn't have been the marketing team—"

"They don't have access to the recipe?" Megan asked.

Rabbie paused. "Well, I suppose they might, at that. All right, then, there's Mick and Seamus and Brian and Hugh and Patrick and—what?" Rabbie broke off, staring at Megan as she began to giggle.

"I'm sorry, it's just like you're listing the entries from *A Dozen and One Names for Your Irish Baby*."

Carmen, dubious but hopeful, said, "Is that a real baby name book?"

Megan, still giggling, shook her head. "No, unfortunately not, but when you go through a family tree and you find your mother Mary and her grandmother Mary and her two sisters-in-law named Mary and their mother and grandmother Mary and three of them have Maureen as a second name, and it's the same way on your father's side except they're all Barry and Peter, it starts to feel like there should be. Sorry, sorry, Rabbie, go ahead, I'm sorry." She put another bite of steak in her mouth and pretended her eyes weren't watering as she tried not to laugh around it.

"You're having a difficult day," Rabbie said with a sniff. "I'll allow a bit of nonsense."

Megan, who had briefly forgotten she was having a difficult day, sobered fast enough that guilt flickered across Rabbie's face. "Most of the lads have been in this since the beginning. I can't imagine them giving the recipe away. You met Willow, the young wan who's heading up our marketing, at the opening gala last night, and I'd say she's as sound as sound could be. Who else is there?"

"Okay, see, there's a name that doesn't come from the Dozen Names book," Megan said with a brief smile, then nodded. "I saw her again today at the tasting. She was shoring up Erin Ryan for a little while there."

"Sure and they go way back. Well. As far back as a young creature like that can go. Erin hired her straight out of university to do some promotional work for McConal's brand and to get her a leg up as a marketing specialist. I remember how nervous she was for their first big—ah," Rabbie said as the silence around him went from intrigued to exchanging glances. "Ah, I see now how that could be an exploitable connection. But that's to Erin Ryan, not the Murphys." He broke off, considering what he'd said, then shook his head at Megan. "I don't see how you do it, lass. All of this sleuthing, putting it together. I can talk all the gossip in the world but I'd never see how one thing links to another."

"It's like doing a puzzle. I just keep trying pieces until they start to fit together. And sometimes people tell me things they wouldn't mention to the police, which helps. Like, how long ago did Willow and Erin work together? How many people know that? There's no particular reason it would come up, talking to the police."

"Oh, it must've been five years ago? Maybe seven? Angus was pivoting from purely boxing by then, trying to become a . . . what do you young ones call it?"

"An influencer," Niamh said without hesitation, which was good, because Megan hadn't known what he meant.

Rabbie pointed at her, though. "That's it. An influencer. Erin Ryan's a little too old-school for that, so she brought Willow on for a six-month contract to raise Angus's profile beyond boxing. I'd say it worked. He's out there with the whiskey and sports drink contracts and—or he was." The old man's face fell as he remembered and it took him a moment to recover. "Anyway, Willow went on to other work. She came on with us about ten months ago, when we started getting ready to really make a push for promotion, win or lose this competition. We've got her for another two months, and then she's off to the next thing, whatever that may be."

"Do you think she could feel enough obligation toward Erin Ryan to sell Harbourmaster out?" Megan hoped not, but Willow was the only solid connection they had between Harbourmaster and McConal's whiskey, Fighting Chance. "Is there anybody else on the team who could have had motivation?"

"Money is always motivation," Carmen said. "Perhaps you are overthinking it, Meghan. Perhaps there is someone who simply accepted money to give the killer the recipe so it could be put on Angus's body. Perhaps they did not sell the recipe, but sold a distraction in the form of a recipe. Does anyone on your team need money, Señor Lynch?"

Rabbie spread his hands, taking in not just the suite, but the meal laid out in front of them. "By your standards, lass, I'd say we all do. The guards would find that, though, wouldn't they? If one of us had more money than could be accounted for?"

Niamh murmured, "What was the name of the horse, Bertie?" and all of the Irish people in the room, including Megan, laughed. Carmen's eyebrows rose quizzically and Niamh said, "There was a lot of financial scandal around Bertie Ahern while he was Taoiseach. Hundreds of thousands of quid that he came by without any explanation. He claimed it was from winnings on the races, but he would never tell anyone what horse he'd won on."

"Oh, yes. I have met Señor Ahern. A charming scoundrel, yes?"

"The Teflon Taoiseach," Megan agreed. "But yes,

I'd think the guards would find it if one of your team had more money than they could explain, or paid off debts or something. And unless I put together an actual TV-style detective club with a grifter and a hacker, I'm never going to find *that* out my own self, so I'll leave it to them."

Niamh brightened. "I could play the grifter!"

"You'd have to *be* the grifter, Niamh, and I don't think 'international film star' is a particularly sneaky cover for somebody whose job is making people think she's somebody else."

"Ah, sure, be that way then."

Megan's phone rang, startling her, and she answered it to Jacob Murphy's, "We didn't hear from you, but we did hear from Sean Byrne. The meet and greet is still on, if your uncle doesn't know."

"Let me check." Megan pressed the phone against her shoulder, although she didn't think it really muffled her voice as she said, "Did you get a text or a call from Sean Byrne, Rabbie, Carmen? There's supposed to be a marketing meeting at the Whiskey Museum tonight and apparently it's still on."

Both Carmen and Rabbie looked for their phones, with Carmen finding hers first and nodding. "There is a message, sí. Do you think it's wise to go?"

Megan pursed her lips, then said, into her own phone, "He got the message, yes, thanks. We'll probably see you there," before hanging up and contemplating her friends. "I think we should go."

"Are you mental?" Rabbie asked in genuine surprise. "There's somebody murthering competitors, Megan!"

He went so Irish on the word *murder* that Megan
smiled despite the topic. "Don't eat or drink anything, I guess. The thing is, I don't know if the
guards will be there, but *we* will be. Every possible
victim, every potential suspect. If we want to get to
the bottom of this mess, I think tonight is the time
to do it."

CHAPTER 18

About two hours later, Paul Bourke, on Niamh's arm as they went into the Whiskey Museum, muttered, "This may be the only time in my life that being a movie star's boyfriend will be helpful to my career, not that I'm here in any sort of professional capacity."

"No," Megan said in an equally low voice, "but since the organizers decided no guards were allowed in, you're our ringer. I wouldn't have made that call."

"So you've said about four times," Paul replied. "Neither would any of us, but Sean Byrne thinks he's a law unto himself, and it's a private party. He can keep us out."

"Them out," Niamh said with a sparkling smile. "Tonight you're just eye candy, not a detective."

Paul brushed his knuckles over the front of his coat, primping and fluttering as Niamh laughed and Megan smiled. No one was nearly as dressed up as they'd been for the gala last night, but he looked sharp in a dark blue skinny suit with pin-stripes and Niamh, who rarely looked less than fabulous, wore a slinky gold dress that flowed and glimmered like whiskey itself.

Megan had gone back to her house to change and feed the dogs, and it was just as well Rabbie had gone with her. Even with only a couple of hours to pack up, Jelena had taken an awful lot of herself away. Throw blankets that she'd brought with her from Poland were already gone, the back of the couch looking empty and dull without their bright, blocky colors. Their bedroom didn't look ransacked, but the wardrobe door stood open, making it clear that Jelena's clothes were gone, and when Megan half-heartedly opened a dresser drawer, she had to close it again immediately be-cause its light weight and bare interior made a fist tighten around her heart.

Bulkier items were still there, like the pillows that matched the throw blankets, but that only made the blankets' absence more obvious. Jelena's big stand mixer, bright red and chrome, had been set aside with other kitchen implements that belonged to her, rather than to Megan or the household. She hadn't put a ceramic mug that was technically Megan's but that she used all the time with her things, and Megan, with shaking hands, added it to her stuff in case she decided she wanted it.

The dogs had wound around Megan's ankles, whining with uncertainty and confusion. If Rabbie hadn't been with her, Megan would have just sat down on the kitchen floor to cry on them for the rest of the night. Rabbie had let her indulge for a while, then came out to the kitchen, dressed in a dapper gray suit that gave him the air of an elder statesman, and murmured, "That's enough, now, love. It's not that I'd deny you your mourning, but if I'm putting me neck on the line at this party tonight I want my niece the murder driver on hand to keep me alive."

He smiled at Megan's warbled laugh and when she rose, gave her a hug. "She was a lovely girl, was Jelena, but take it from an old man who's had his heart broken a time or two himself. This wasn't the life for her, and so you weren't the woman for her. It's nothing you did wrong, *a cuisle mo chroí.* Now go wash your face and put on something pretty so you can solve a murder tonight."

Megan had given another thin, high warbling laugh. "People keep telling me to wash my face today. I'm beginning to feel like I'm eight. And I don't think I have to look nice to solve a murder."

"No," Rabbie had replied with a note of genial steel, "but it'll make her think again when your picture's in the paper tomorrow and she's wondering what she's lost."

Pettiness and spite could work wonders even on a broken heart. Megan had gone to wash up and dress well enough to make an ex regret her choices. Even Niamh had wolf-whistled when she arrived at the museum in dark green wide-legged trousers with suspenders—braces, in Ireland; suspenders were garters—over a white blouse, and finished off with a long wool coat that matched the trousers well enough that they'd been an excuse to buy each other. Megan had never worn the outfit before and felt a rush of silly relief and pleasure at Niamh's reaction.

"I'm buying you a hat to go with that coat," Niamh said as they went into the museum. "In fact, we'll go to the millinery and have one dyed to match. A bolero, I think. Fedoras are so passé."

"I don't even know what a bolero is. There are still millineries?"

"Flat topped hat with a wide, round brim. Spanish cowboy hats. And of course there are still millineries. There are at least four in Dublin that I know about, and I'm sure that's not all of them. It's not even that expensive to have a hat made."

"I had no idea." They were upstairs at the door to the event room by then, having shrugged their coats off and handed them over to a coat check person on the ground floor. Megan's trouser hems brushed the floor with the two-inch heels she wore, but she hadn't wanted to wear a higher, less blocky pair of shoes. She could run in these ones, if she needed to.

They'd arrived fashionably late by American standards and early by Irish ones. Even so, a few dozen people were already there and at least a handful of them had already visibly partaken of the whiskey available for tasting. Megan hadn't considered the possibility that half the guests would be inebriated by ten PM, and wondered if that would make investigating more or less difficult.

"Remember," Paul said at her ear, "it'll be my head if I'm caught investigating, so I'm only here to ring Dervla if it comes to it. Good luck."

"Oh, don't be silly. You're also here to look pretty."

Paul laughed. "What a disappointment I'll be, then." He and Niamh broke away as someone waved at her and Rabbie, hanging back at Megan's side a moment, let go a mournful sigh.

"All this drink to tipple, and I daren't even taste it until you're sure no one's going to kill me with it."

Megan made a face. "I've already drunk more today than I usually do in three months—possibly three years—and on only three hours of sleep. I wouldn't have another drink if you paid me to, right now."

"I bet you would," Rabbie said philosophically. "It's just a matter of finding the price."

Considering that she'd be paying rent on her own from now on, Megan thought the price might be lower than her standards would like to imagine, but since no one was likely to pay her to drink tonight, it didn't matter. She did make her way to the bar, where she asked for a glass of tap water and, with a twinge of paranoia, watched like a hawk as the bartender filled it. "Not that I know what I'm being paranoid about," she said to the glass when he handed it to her. "I'm not allergic to anything."

Of course, she didn't know that Danny Keane had died from an allergic reaction, either. She had no idea if an allergic reaction could present as a heart attack, although a quick glance through search results on her phone suggested it wasn't impossible. But it was one thing to murder a celebrity with a known allergy. Megan thought having the personal knowledge to take an ordinary citizen out the same way was something else.

The obvious person to have that knowledge was Maggie Keane, who, unsurprisingly, wasn't there. The Murphys had arrived, though. Megan thought she'd corner Jacob later and ask if he knew whether Danny Keane had been allergic to anything.

Nearly everyone she recognized from either the gala or the tasting that afternoon filtered in over the next half hour or so. Many more people she didn't know also came in, and she assumed they were mostly the marketing and promotional consultants that John Murphy had been so eager to meet. The Sionnach Rua's proprietor, whom the Murphys had been speaking to earlier in the day, was there, and Megan told herself it was probably her imagination suggesting the glances he and John Murphy exchanged were sly.

Erin Ryan was now dressed in harsh black instead of the sparkling but mournful navy from earlier. Hannah Flanagan looked pretty in a baby blue dress with a soft lace ruffle along the single-shouldered neckline. Megan thought she was going for elegant, and that she might have succeeded in a stronger color. She felt a reluctant wash of fondness for the young woman, and hoped Hannah would never give up her obviously beloved baby blues for colors other people might take more seriously. Maturity would get her where she wanted to go in its own time, pastels or not.

Even though this gathering was nominally of people accustomed to working with the high-powered, wealthy, or famous, a cluster still formed around Niamh and by proxy, Paul and Rabbie. That was exactly why Megan had suggested Niamh come on to the Harbourmaster team, but watching the film star pull everyone into her orbit made Megan think she'd underestimated Niamh's value as a draw. Rabbie clasped hands and patted shoulders comfortably, obviously in his element, while Paul remained a pleasant but mostly silent partner in the entire affair. He was far more relaxed than he'd been early in their relationship, but he still clearly had no desire for the limelight himself.

A thread of Megan's thoughts carried on down that line, momentarily wondering what it would be like to be in that kind of relationship. Then she hit a wall of truth: she *had* been in that kind of relationship, up until that afternoon. The scale was different, and she knew Jelena and Paul had talked about being with someone whose recognition-factor eclipsed the norm, but Niamh was *famous*. Megan was just . . . more famous than most people.

And even that had been too much. At least, when combined with an ongoing series of murders and amateur investigations. Megan sighed and shook her shoulders, bringing herself back to the event and watching cards being exchanged among the different little groups. The Sionnach Rua's proprietor stood with the Murphys, where instead of cards, several of the younger marketing people lifted their phones to offer codes to scan. Every time someone did that, the whiskey proprietor looked so pained that Megan started rooting for codes over cards.

"Please tell me you're here trying to figure out who's killing our competitors," a woman's voice said softly beside Megan. The woman who worked for Sean Byrne—Patricia someone—stopped beside her, asking for a drink from the bartender with an absence that suggested she was doing it for show. She wore a soft gray gown, dressier than many of the people at the event, but achieving the understated elegance that Hannah had been going for and hadn't quite reached. Her eyes were tired, almost bruised-looking. "Sorry. Patricia Dillon. Trish. We haven't formally met."

Megan said, "Megan Malone," although Patricia clearly knew who she was. "You're Mr. Byrne's . . . ?"

"Keeper," Trish said with a brief, wry smile that played up the weariness in her gaze. She had astonishing cheekbones and eyes just a few shades bluer than her gown. "Sean is one of those men who doesn't like people handing him things. Or answering phones. Or a great many other things. I'd say he couldn't find his pants in the morning without me, but I do have limits."

Megan struggled not to laugh, as she was quite certain Trish Dillon meant "pants" in the Irish vernacular way, which was to say, underwear. Instead she made herself use her best neutral voice, the one preferred by clients who expected a chauffeur to be a blank slate with no opinions or thoughts of her own. "He seems like a complicated employer."

Trish flashed her another brief smile, a spark momentarily brightening her eyes. "I see you've met people like that." She sobered quickly, though, nodding at the crowd. "Anybody you like for it?"

"Did Mr. Byrne send you to sound me out?" Megan smiled crookedly and shook her head. "Honestly, I wish he'd let Detective Reese attend. This is her kind of job, not mine."

"No one's going to do business with a guard hanging over their shoulders," Trish said with a dismissive shrug. "And you've a reputation."

"Which your boss announced at a shout to four hundred people this afternoon, after which my girlfriend broke up with me. I'm not feeling super-sympathetic to his plight, if you want to know the truth." Megan knew she was drawing a correlation that didn't exactly exist, but it wasn't a lie, either, and Trish's face slackened with dismay.

"Oh, no. Oh, God, I'm so sorry. Sean doesn't—"

"See other people as people, just things that do or don't get him what he wants?" Megan arched her eyebrows. "So tell me about your relationships with the contestants."

"Em—uh—we—" Trish stuttered her way through the sounds, obviously taken aback, then gathered herself. "Em, Rabbie Lynch is the only one he's got what I'd call a relationship with. They're close enough to of an age, and Sean's done businesses through the ports his whole career. They've known each other forty years, at least. I'd say he's Sean's favorite to win, but this isn't a game of favorites."

"Is it not?" Megan turned her attention to Sean Byrne, whose height made him stand out among the older men. The marketing and publicity people, especially the younger men, were as tall or taller than he, but his gray head distinguished him, too. "I'd think it would be easy enough for the festival manager to make sure his favorite won. But to be fair, I think the integrity of the thing is actually important to him." She didn't think any such thing, but it let her ask, "Who would you favor?"

"Ah." Trish drew the sound out like she was really thinking about it. "I'd love to see Midnight Sunrise win. I knew Carmen when we were girls. Boarding school together, you know. Not the same year, but."

Megan tried to keep her eyebrows under control as she searched for the tiny Spaniard in the room. Either Patricia Dillon was aging very badly, and up close she certainly didn't seem to be, or Megan needed to upwardly revise her estimate of Carmen's age by *several* years. She'd thought Carmen was younger than she was. "I didn't know that. Are you still friends?"

"We say hello if we're in the same spaces, but her business and Sean's don't often cross paths. I know your uncle better." She smiled again at Megan, then pursed her lips as she glanced toward the Murphys. "I've barely met the husbands. Just last night, at the gala. They've got a good product, or they wouldn't have gotten this far. Now, Angus McConal, Sean liked him." Trish took a deep breath, steadying herself, and Megan couldn't blame her. The deaths were enough to rattle anybody. After a moment, the PA went on with, "He likes fighters, he likes his rags-to-riches story. He didn't think much of Danny Keane," she admitted. "He thought he was a worrier, that he didn't have enough money to be risking what he had on a whiskey brand."

"So he only likes certain kinds of rags-to-riches stories." Megan didn't add, "the kind with a manly man fronting it," but she would put money on Sean Byrne seeing himself as a scrappy fighter, even though he'd been born rich. "What about Hannah Flanagan?"

Trish glanced the girl's way with a trace of dismissal in her gaze. "No one takes her seriously. She's twenty-two and her family is supporting her in this whim before she gets married and has some babies to carry on the family business."

Megan's eyes popped and she drank the rest of her water fast so she wouldn't say anything injudicious. Then, in as measured a voice as she could manage, she said, "So Sean's not rooting for her, then?"

The other woman shrugged. "No, but no one needs to root for her, do they? With all that history and money behind her? She'll be just fine."

"I'm sure she will be." Megan asked for another glass of water and smiled politely. "Well, I'm afraid I'm not any closer to figuring it out, but you've given me something to think about, anyway. Thanks for your insights. I assume you gave them to the police, too," she added, and wasn't at all surprised by the faintly startled expression that crossed Trish's face.

"I suppose I told them Sean had professional relationships with the contestants. I wouldn't have said wee little Hannah was waiting to get married, no."

"No, of course not," Megan murmured. "I'll let you know if I have any revelations this evening. Thank you, Ms. Dillon." She made her escape with no intention of sharing any revelations, but with every intention of asking her uncle whether Sean Byrne would have stacked the deck for him.

CHAPTER 19

Hannah descended on Megan almost as soon as she stepped away from the bar, her enthusiasm suggesting she'd been waiting for a chance to talk. "Did you know Erin Ryan and Maggie Keane are friends? I was just talking to Ms. Ryan about—well, I was interviewing her, obviously, and she said she would be leaving early because she didn't want to leave Maggie alone too long. Do you think it means anything?"

"Maybe that the whiskey community is a lot more incestuous than I ever imagined."

Poor Hannah blushed nearly purple, making Megan consider her choice of words too late. "Sorry. I mean everyone seems to know each other in some capacity or another."

"Yes. Right. It's true, my parents know everyone here."

"I assume you do, too. I mean, you've had everybody on your podcast, right?"

Hannah, still blushing, shook her head. "I didn't want to get to know my competition before the festival. I was afraid it might make me feel bad if I liked them and I won. Some of them have spent their whole life savings on this, and I'm . . ."

"Rich," Megan finished helpfully. "It changes the playing field, doesn't it? You'll be fine, one way or another. Danny Keane, not so much." She winced. "You know what I mean. Did Erin say anything about his death?"

"They still think it was a heart attack, but they're doing an autopsy because he was young." Hannah, twenty-two, made air quotes around the word because Keane had been in his forties and paunchy: from Hannah's perspective, that probably made him decrepit. "And because he died so publicly and because of Angus's death. Oh, God, that was terrible. Let me try again. They still think it was a heart attack, but they're doing an autopsy due to his age, the public nature of his death, and its temporal proximity to Angus McConal's murder."

Megan gaped at the young woman in bewilderment, then bit off a laugh. " 'Temporal proximity?' What did you—why did you—oh, no, you're recording, aren't you. I told you not to record me!"

"I forgot to turn it off!" Hannah touched something in the ruffly neckline of her dress, and Megan realized she had a microphone hidden in the fluff. "There, it's off now. But yes, that's why I had to say it again, all those 'becauses,' that was terrible. I sounded four years of age."

"I don't know if I'm impressed or horrified that you can hear and edit yourself on the fly like that. Look, I'd like to talk to Erin, so if she's leaving early, if you don't mind . . ." Megan sidled a step away and Hannah waved.

"Grand so, I'll talk to you later." She turned the microphone back on as Megan left, and Megan reminded herself to be careful what she said around the young podcaster. She also wondered if Hannah was warning people that she was recording, or if she even had to. Megan had no idea what Irish law said about recording other people without their permission, but she bet Hannah knew. Niamh probably did, too, for that matter.

Without meaning to, Megan caught Jacob Murphy's eye as she worked her way through the gathering toward Erin Ryan. She smiled automatically and he edged out of the conversation he was in and came over to her like a man who'd been offered a lifeline. "You look like you're working the crowd."

"So far I haven't come up with any answers. But look, since I've got you, Mr. Murphy, can I ask you an odd question?"

Brief amusement quirked the corner of Jacob's mouth. "Will it help make sense of all this . . ." He moved a hand restlessly, like he couldn't decide on what word to use.

"I hope so. Maybe."

"Then go ahead."

Megan found she had to brace herself to ask, "Do you know if Danny Keane had any allergies?"

Startled, haggard lines settled deep into Jacob's

face for a moment, and he cast an uncomfortable glance toward his husband. "Not that I knew about, no."

Megan followed the quick look and tried to keep her voice gentle. "Does he know you and Danny were close when you were younger?"

Fresh surprise, less harsh, wiped away the haggard lines as Jacob blinked back toward her. "How on earth did you know that?"

"Uncle Rabbie knows everything about everyone in Ireland," Megan said wryly.

To her relief, Jacob chuckled softly. "Of course. He's a man with a finger in every pie. If this were a popularity contest, he'd walk away with it. Which is enough reason to sabotage him, I guess. Although I can't imagine Sean would, and he's the only one who had access to all the recipes."

Hairs stood on the back of Megan's neck. "What do you mean, he's got access?"

"As part of the expert tasting panel tomorrow. They do blind tastings and record what they think went into the whiskeys, everything from the mash to the blend, if it's a blend, and the barrels and the aging. At the end of the event their interpretations are set against the actual recipes, and the guest expert whose guesses are closest on all the whiskeys gets a cash prize. It's part of the fun of it all."

"You mean Sean Byrne has the Harbourmaster recipe?"

"Sure, and everyone else's. Oh." Jacob Murphy came to the same conclusion Megan had, just a few beats later. "He could have given it to McConal."

Megan pressed her fingertips against her eyelids, glad she hadn't worn much in the way of makeup to wipe off. "Did anybody mention this to the police? Surely someone must have mentioned this to the police." Although she would have expected Sean Byrne to have been taken in for a talking-to, if the guards knew he had access to the recipes.

Of course, for all she knew, Sean Byrne *had* been taken in for a talking-to. Megan might have to go back around to Trish and ask. Right now, though, Jacob shrugged. "It didn't come up when we spoke with the detective, but it didn't get around until the public tasting this afternoon that Angus had died with a recipe on his body."

But the police had known. They *had* to have asked Byrne about it, probably at the interviews the night before. Megan held her breath a minute, trying to make sure she had the timeline right. It seemed like it had been much longer than twenty-four hours, but in fact, Angus McConal had died barely a day ago. It was just that Megan had been awake for nearly all of the time since, and had had both too much whiskey and a lot of emotional turmoil in those waking hours. She said, "I'm getting too old for this all-night nonsense," and Jacob laughed.

"We all are. I envy Ms. Flanagan. She looks fresh as a daisy."

"Wretched child," Megan said without meaning it, then risked a careful, "Are you doing all right, Jacob? I don't know how close you were with Mr. Keane, lately."

Weariness crossed Jacob's face, and he passed his hand over his eyes like he could throw the exhaustion away. "I was devastated this afternoon. John took me away from the public tasting as quickly as he could, but . . . well, you saw us at the Sionnach Rua. His idea of comfort is distracting with business. I'd have rather gone home, or even seen if I could be any use to poor Maggie. But Danny and I hadn't been close in a long time. I was at his wedding, but even then, we'd grown apart. We came back in contact five or six years ago, and I'd have helped him financially if I could have, but John thought if we were sinking money into whiskey, it should be our own brand. I don't think Dan resented it, but I'd say Maggie did."

"I'm getting the impression that Mrs. Keane resented a lot."

Jacob sighed. "Life didn't work out the way Maggie expected it to. I don't suppose it does for any of us, but she's never been a happy woman, not as long as I've known her."

Megan, wholly uncertain if it mattered, asked, "Did she know about your relationship with Danny?"

"She doesn't seem to loathe me, so I'd guess not. It was a long time ago, Ms. Malone. We were teenagers and terrified of the world finding us out. It'd be hard to even call it a relationship, although there was a while when he meant the world to me. But I went to university, and he went another way. It's all just a memory now." Jacob sighed and passed his fingertips over his eyes again. "All of it now, I suppose. It's not that I won't miss him, but it might be the idea of him I miss more than the man, if that makes sense?"

"It does." Megan patted his arm and offered a smile. "I'm sorry to abandon you, but I need to talk to a few other people."

"Are you sleuthing?"

"Well, Mr. Byrne shut the police out, but everybody's in one room, so I thought I'd see what I could learn. In the event I come up with anything critical, I'll let you know." That was at least the second time she'd told someone she would keep them in the loop, although Megan didn't have any intention of doing that at all. The only person in the room who needed to be notified of anything was Paul, so he could pass on whatever she'd learned to the authorities.

Erin Ryan was still half a room away, but before Megan got near her, Willow Hartley, the Harbourmaster marketing manager, stepped out of the crowd and angled toward the bar, nearly running into Megan as she did so. "Oh, shite, sorry, Ms. Malone. It's mental in here, isn't it? Worse than the convention center last night, even though there aren't nearly as many people. But there's not as much space, either, is there? How are you keeping?"

"Grand so." "Grand" in Irish terms covered a host of sins, the way "fine" could in American English. "I'm glad to have caught you, Willow. I wanted to ask you something about Erin Ryan."

To her astonishment, without warning, tears filled Willow's eyes and she nearly collapsed against Megan, weeping. "I couldn't do it! She asked and asked, she said I owed her, but I couldn't do it, I swear!"

Megan's heart nearly leaped from her chest as she caught Willow's weeping form. "What? What did she ask? Come here, sweetheart." She led Willow out of the main room under the curious and judging gazes of the event attendees. If the whole case cracked open that easily, in the shape of a crying girl confessing all, Megan would be both thrilled and faintly disappointed. As a member of the staff went by, Megan said, "Excuse me, is there somewhere quiet we could go?" and saw the young man's expression of uncertainty give away to sympathy.

"Why don't you go down to the gift shop? Everyone is in the event rooms, so you can have a moment's peace there."

"Thanks very much." Megan brought Willow downstairs, where they ended up sitting behind the gift shop's register desk, which at least had chairs. Megan waited patiently for Willow to regain some degree of composure, and when the girl's breathing had steadied out, said, "All right, honey, why don't you tell me what Erin Ryan asked that's got you so upset?"

Willow's eyes welled up again immediately. "I said no!"

"I'm sure you did," Megan murmured as soothingly as she could. "To what?"

"She wanted me to come back and work for them again!" Willow wailed.

Megan sat back, startled. "She what?"

"After all the horrible business with Angus, she had the nerve to ask me to come back! She said I owed her for hiring me when I was right out of university! As if I didn't pay enough for that!" Willow's tears turned to a snarl and Megan blinked, feeling like a bus had knocked her over.

This was *not* the easy crack in the case she'd

hoped for, anyway. "You mean she didn't ask you for the Harbourmaster recipe?"

"What? No. Oh." Willow's emotions were as mercurial as a child's, astonished dismay now widening her eyes. "Oh. Maybe that's what she was going to do. I can't imagine why else—well, no, that's not true. I *am* good at my job."

Megan held her hands up, stopping the rush of words, then put her arm around Willow's shoulder again. "Okay, start at the beginning. Tell me what she wanted."

"I did a great job raising Angus's profile from boxer to influencer," Willow whispered. "Inside of six months he went from a household name, to be sure, but not a daily one, you know? 'Ah, Angus McConal, he's the lad that won the gold, isn't he, well done Angus,' that sort of thing, to 'Ah, Angus McConal, sure and he's doing well for himself, isn't he, parlaying that gold medal into a media empire, did yis see how he was on the talk shows promoting his . . .'" She made a sharp, impatient gesture. "Shoes. Energy drink. New movie. Whatever. All of it. I did that. Erin and the rest of her team, they could handle keeping his *incidents* quiet, but making more of him than he was? That was me. Oh, and he loved me for it, he did. I was the gold of the morning sunrise, so I was. We dated for a while. Until he broke my cheekbone because he *thought* I fancied another fellow."

"Oh." Megan's stomach dropped. "Oh, shoot. Those people whose privacy you were protecting yesterday. At least one of them was you."

"Erin convinced me not to go to the guards. She

paid for the surgery to fix it when it couldn't be done quickly through the public system—"

Megan's gut churned ever harder at that. Cheekbone fractures mostly healed on their own, because like ribs and a few other locations, it was just difficult to bandage them. If Willow had needed reconstructive surgery, Angus had hit her *hard*. The girl was still talking, her voice low and fast: "—and she got me to sign an NDA that paid off the rest of my contract and let me go early. I shouldn't have done it, I should have gone public, but I was so hurt and scared and—"

"You did the right thing," Megan said gently. "You did the right thing for yourself at the time, Willow. You got yourself out of the situation in the way that worked best for you then, and sometimes that's all that matters. Maybe that's *always* all that matters. You protected yourself. That's enough, honey. You don't owe anybody any other explanation. Okay? I mean that."

Willow nodded, hardly more than a tremor against Megan's shoulder. "So I was fecking gobsmacked when she asked me to come back. She said they needed my marketing skills, that their whiskey promotion wasn't going as well as they wanted, that Angus's reputation was starting to get out of hand and she knew I could turn it around and that a brand like Harbourmaster with Rabbie Lynch's charm and connections behind it didn't need my talent, but she did. And Angus missed me, she said! As if I could give a single damn what that bastard thought about me, not that I believe it for a minute, but that she had the nerve to even say it! Especially when I know she was raging that we even started seeing each other!"

"Because she didn't want people in the same company dating?"

A derisive laugh tore from Willow's throat. "Nah, mate, because she was in love with him."

CHAPTER 20

A noise lodged in Megan's throat as several protests tried to squeak out at once. She wasn't even sure which of them she wanted to start with: the age difference, the fact that Ryan had been McConal's manager; McConal's apparent tendency toward violence. All of it seemed like a disaster in the making.

Willow gave a sharp laugh and nodded. "That's what I thought, too. Some of the older people on his team said they used to be together, but they had to keep it quiet and Angus got to date because, you know, he was a young lad and the tabloids would go on if all he did was train like, yeah? Even so, there were some snaps of them that had the gossip rags speculating, but that's just what they do, so no one took it seriously. And after the gold medal he didn't want to be tied to an old lady, that's what they said, so he broke it off. They said she was barely able to talk him into staying on as her client. That was why they eventually hired me."

"But he was . . ." Megan took a moment to figure out the timeline and another moment to be glad she'd only been drinking water that evening. "You said you worked for her five or six years ago. He was in the Olympics more than a decade ago. She kept him on five or more years before bringing you on?"

"She had her hooks in him. C'mere now, she'd been his manager since he was seventeen."

Megan said, "Ew," and Willow gave her a tight smile.

"Nobody would ever say if they were hooking up before he turned eighteen, but I'd say they were. She's only six or seven years older than he is, which wouldn't be creepy if they started dating *now*, but when he was a teenager?" Willow shuddered, then shrugged. "Now I think she hired me partly because I was younger."

"You think she wanted him to fall for you?"

"I think she thought he'd be superficially interested, but that he'd come to his senses and realize he wanted an older woman with more experience." She shrugged again. "Except he fancied me, like proper fancied me for a while, and she was furious. Not that he fancied *me*. I know that now. It was that I made him look good. Me, I was an idiot and mad for him, even though all the signs were there that it was no good. He was jealous and controlling and forever telling Erin how bad I was to him so she'd coo and fuss." Willow made a throwaway gesture. "And even if he did fancy me, he was keeping Erin on the line, too, with that. I was twenty-three like, I didn't see it for the manipulation it was. He got to bang the hot young thing and keep his mother figure hopping for him, too. I didn't realize until later that he actually did just like older women, maybe because Erin got her claws in him early, maybe because they were so hot for a fit young lad like he was. But he worshiped his mam, too, so maybe it's just that he liked formidable women and got more of that with the lasses who were older than he was. I don't think he ever hit *her*."

Megan, hesitantly, said, "Erin, or his mother?"

"Either. I'm sure he never hurt his mam. But she died, you know. Not long before he got the gold. I think maybe it broke him." Willow sounded more empathetic than Megan would have thought possible toward a man who'd shattered her cheekbone. "It was after that he started having troubles. Started *being* trouble. But he talked about her like she'd been his guiding light. I think he was lost without her, and I think Erin wanted to take her place, but I'd say he never felt as much for her as she did for him."

"What a mess." Megan rubbed her forehead, then tried to drag herself away from gossip back toward the point. "So she wanted you to come work for her, for them, again, to promote Angus's whiskey?"

"Yeah. And I won't lie, part of me felt so guilty at leaving early after she got me the job back in the day that I thought about going back to work for her, even with everything that happened. But in the end I said no because that would be madness. And I'm glad I did, because he's dead now and I'd

have been likely for it if I was working for them."
Willow suddenly went pale. "Jaysus, am I likely for
it anyway? Now that you know all that?"

"I don't know," Megan said a little wearily. "Did
you kill him?"

Despite having just suggested that she might
have, Willow's eyes went round in genuine surprise and even injury. "No!"

Megan chuckled. "Then I guess you're not likely
for it. I mean, yes," she amended, unable to leave
it entirely alone. "You had motive, you were at the
gala so you had opportunity, and I'm guessing if
you dated you knew Angus was allergic to kiwi, so
you probably had the knowledge of how to do it.
But if you did, that would be an admirably long
time to wait for revenge."

"They say it's best served cold," Willow replied
morosely. "I didn't, though. I'd put it behind me,
honestly, until Erin called. The stupid thing is she
had a whole campaign planned. Good ideas like. I
don't know why she couldn't have just done them
herself, or hired someone else to. Why me?"

"Maybe she thought you owed her." Megan
stood and rolled her shoulders, trying to loosen
up a little. "I think I'll go ask her."

"What? Really?"

"Sure. I need to talk to her anyway, or—" A
chuckle rose in Megan's chest. "I want to. *Need* to
suggests I've got any business investigating."

"But you do, though. You're only the murder
driver."

"That isn't an actual thing, you know. It doesn't
give me any authority. Although at this point, I
don't know, maybe I should take a PI class or

something. I wonder if there are classes for that."
Megan nearly took her phone out to look it up,
then also nearly kicked herself. She had a job. She
did not need to add to An Garda Síochána's stress
by getting licensed as a private investigator.

"But you do it anyway. Can I come listen?"

"No. She'll probably be defensive anyway because I *am* the murder driver and everybody thinks
I'm at this thing tonight investigating—"

"Because you are."

Megan made a face. "Because I am, yes. And I
don't want to add the stress of an ex-employee
who left under difficult circumstances and then re-
fused another job to the mix."

"Ah, sure, that's brilliant. I wouldn't have thought
of that. She might not be defensive, though. You're
easy to talk to."

"So I'm told. Are you all right now? Can you go
back upstairs, or do you want to head out?"

"Oh, I'm going up. I don't want to miss it if you
solve a murder in front of everybody."

Megan grimaced again. "Don't hold your breath.
Hercule Poirot I am not. Mostly I seem to solve
them when the culprit is trying to add me to their
body count. And not in the fun way."

Willow blanched with faint horror and when
Megan's eyebrows rose in confusion, she said, "I
didn't know people your age knew there was a fun
kind of body count."

"Oh my *God*, how old do you think I *am*?"

"I wouldn't want to say," Willow said so primly
some of Megan's offense, which was mostly theatrical anyway, faded.

"Just wait until you're as old as I am, child. You'll

find out it's not that old at all. Except you can hurt your back by sleeping. That part's no fun. Do yoga," Megan advised. "Lots of yoga. Stay stretchy."

Willow gave her exactly the sort of tolerant, dismissive look she would have given herself fifteen years earlier, and hopped off the bench she sat on. "Let's go catch a baddie!"

"You are *so* much more confident than I am." Megan followed the young woman back upstairs, where they were met at the door by a once-more grim-faced Sean Byrne. Willow gave Megan a wide-eyed glance and skirted around the festival director, leaving Megan to say, "Mr. Byrne. What can I do for you?" in her best professionally neutral voice.

"I wanted to apologize for my outburst this afternoon," he said in the tone of a man who didn't want to do any such thing. "This has been a very stressful time, as I'm sure you can imagine."

"I don't even have to imagine," Megan replied with more sympathy than she meant to. "It's been madness for me, and I'm only peripherally involved. I'm sure you and Ms. Dillon must be going out of your minds with worry for your competitors."

Incomprehension flickered in Byrne's gaze for a heartbeat before he caught up to the narrative she was suggesting. "Yes, of course, very worried. Doing everything we can to keep the rest of the teams safe, of course."

"Which is why there's such a powerful police presence here tonight," Megan said as solemnly as she could.

A vein actually twitched in Byrne's temple. Megan

fought down the urge to giggle. "It's a closed-door event," Byrne said in what was obviously an attempt to sound civil, and came across more like a seething storm. "Ticketed, with a very limited membership of professionals vetted long before the festival launched. I'm confident of our security here tonight, that no one is in any danger, and that an active garda presence would have made the evening very uncomfortable for everyone. I'm sure you'll agree we've had enough discomfort the past twenty-four hours."

"Oh, absolutely. Look, Mr. Byrne, I really do appreciate the apology. It means a lot, coming from a man like you. Ah, come on," Megan said to the wariness creeping across his face. "You're an actual pillar of the community. Look at this festival. It's your personal project, but I can't even imagine how much money it brings in to the city and how much international attention it garners. Men like you don't often have to apologize, and actually do it even less, so I genuinely appreciate it."

She forbore to mention that everything about the apology, from his expression to his tone, had been grudging. The goal was to charm him a little, and like most people, he softened with the flattery. "Let me buy you a drink, Mr. Byrne, or at least, let's go sit down and we can pretend I'm buying a drink from the open bar, right? Honestly, I don't know how you've gotten through it. I'd be terrified for my own life, in your position. A powerful man like you, with competitors at his personal project being targeted? But I guess anybody who had it out for you would probably try to attack you financially, wouldn't they? Although I guess that could be what's going on here. I don't know what kind of hit you're taking with all this negative publicity."

"None at all." Sean Byrne wore a faint squint, as if he wasn't entirely certain how he'd ended up sitting at a table near the door, listening to an absolute load of nonsense pouring from Megan's lips. "There's no such thing as bad publicity, Ms. Malone. Everybody's talking about the festival. Ticket sales are up, there are orders flowing in for the winning whiskey, and sales are up for the last three years' worth of winners, too."

"Oh, wow. That's amazing. I hope nobody thinks it's motive to have thrown this whole thing in motion!" Megan tried to laugh like Carmen did, a bright little trill, and rather thought she pulled it off. Judging from the brief wash of horror across Byrne's face, either she was wrong, or the idea that the contestants' deaths could be seen as motive hadn't crossed his mind. Still trying to channel Carmen, she put her hand on his forearm, reassuringly. "Oh, don't worry, I'm sure nobody does think that. Although the whole thing where you have all the recipes and one of them was found on Angus's body, that's kind of a problem, isn't it?"

Byrne went white and pulled back. "How did you know that?"

Megan lost control of her Carmen-copied charm and let her smile go sharp. "Well, I'm the murder driver, aren't I? And you wanted me to solve this, so I've been investigating. How *did* Angus McConal end up with the Harbourmaster recipe on him, Mr. Byrne?"

"I don't *know*." The words didn't contain a single sibilant, but Byrne hissed them anyway. "The guards think I planted it, but why would I do that? Why would I kill one of my competitors?"

"You just said the publicity couldn't be bought," Megan pointed out. "Although I gather you liked Mr. McConal, so he doesn't seem like the most obvious target. Danny Keane, though . . ."

The big man blanched further, shaking his head. "You can't buy it, no, but I wouldn't have set it up, either. The sales will fade and we'll be left with this hanging over us for years. I need it sorted so it doesn't affect next year's festival. I'm altogether desperate for it to be a personal grudge, although what binds Angus McConal and Danny Keane together, I don't know."

"Do you think it could be Maggie Keane?"

Byrne's face went so blank it was nearly funny. "Maggie Keane?"

"Danny's wife. I've heard Angus fancied older women, although she can't be that much older than he is. Was."

"I . . ." Byrne appeared genuinely thunderstruck. "I've no idea. I wouldn't think they'd have ever met before the festival. They don't run in the same circles. Besides, if they were after having an affair, why kill Angus? I could see getting rid of Danny, but . . ."

Megan's breath caught as she remembered the increasingly silly suggestions she and Jelena had made to each other about motives. That had only been this *morning*. It felt like a hundred years ago. For a few seconds a wave of unhappiness washed out the rest of her thoughts. It must have shown on her face, because Sean Byrne, a man who came across as largely self-interested, went so far as to look concerned. "Ms. Malone?"

"Sorry. I'm fine, I just . . ." Megan had no interest in explaining her personal life to the festival director. "I chatted with your PA earlier. She said you and Rabbie were old friends, but do you know any of the others well? I don't think you're killing your contestants," she added with a smile that didn't go any farther than the corners of her mouth. "I'm just trying to figure out the connections. As I'm sure the police are."

Sean's gaze flickered toward Niamh and Paul, the latter of whom was laughing while Niamh looked pleased with herself. He certainly didn't have the air of someone trying to solve a crime, and Megan, a little dryly, said, "He's not on the job. Dervla Reese *really* should be here, Mr. Byrne."

"Detective Reese is waiting on Keane's autopsy report and would make everyone here nervous."

"Arguably, nervous is how you want a murderer to feel. They're probably more likely to make some kind of mistake that way, like standing up and saying, 'I did it! It was me! I can't live with the shame anymore!' "

Byrne's mouth flattened and Megan chortled. "All right, it's not likely, but it would make things easier, wouldn't it. Look, Mr. Byrne, mostly I'd just like to know if there's anything you think is askance. Something that hasn't felt right all festival, or something."

"You mean aside from two of my competitors dying?" Byrne fell silent a moment, gaze briefly distant like he was reviewing what he'd said so far, what he should say, and maybe even what he'd already told the guards. "Your uncle is the only one I know well. I'm acquainted with Hannah's parents, and with Ms. de la Fuente, but aside from the festival I don't really move in the whiskey circles."

"Why do you hold the festival, then? If you're not a whiskey man yourself?"

For the first time since she'd met him, a sparkle came into Sean Byrne's eyes, and Megan suddenly got the impression of a man who could charm the cows home from the field if he felt like it. His half smile was like a wink, warm and inviting. "Because I love the stuff, Ms. Malone. I don't want to make it, but I fecking love letting somebody else do the work so I can discover new whiskeys. This entire festival grew out of me fussing over a wee dram twenty years ago, I was that delighted with it. Friends started bringing me bottles from the world over and then with the resurgence starting here, I started getting the local stuff. After a bit I thought I could make something of it, and the next thing I knew, we had a festival."

His joy faded into a sigh. "And now we've got dead men. The truth is, I understand McConal. A lot of people didn't like him, and he was famous enough that killing him would make a stir, at least. But Keane makes no sense. The only reason anybody had heard of him at all was this competition. I don't see any value in killing him, if you'll forgive me the coldness of that."

"Maybe that was the point. He wasn't anybody, but now he's dead at the same time Angus Mc-Conal is. Maybe it's a way of tying his name to fame. Maybe to try making back the money he'd put into developing Keane Edge Whiskey." Megan frowned. "Which points the finger at his wife, doesn't it. Maggie Keane. The only person who isn't here tonight. Was she at the gala last night?"

"She was. I met her briefly. Pretty woman. Hard-looking."

"Jesus, that's what everybody says. I'd be ready to kill somebody myself if that was how I got talked about everywhere." Megan rose. "Somebody said Erin Ryan was her friend, and that she was leaving early to go see her. I think I'd better talk to Erin."

CHAPTER 21

Erin Ryan was gone.

Megan, having spent what felt like half the evening trying to get to the woman, spent another full fifteen minutes searching the building for her, like they were in a French farce and Erin simply kept stepping out of a room seconds before Megan arrived. She roped Paul and Niamh, and eventually Willow and Rabbie, into staking out the doorways, making sure Erin *wasn't* slipping out just ahead of her. Once certain Erin wasn't in the event rooms, the five of them went down to the gift shop. Megan wasn't entirely sure if they were planning to search it—for what, she wondered, Erin hiding in a replica whiskey barrel?—or just get their coats and go.

Willow poked around the little entrance hall apologetically, unsurprisingly not finding anything, and then, as if it was somehow her fault, said, "Well, she did say she was leaving early . . ."

"I know." Megan pushed at her hair, but it was up in its usual twist and couldn't be messed with unless she wanted the whole arrangement to come down. "It's just that I was either downstairs in the gift shop where I could see the front door, or sitting at the main door of the event rooms so long I would have thought I'd see her go."

"She probably went toilet and slipped out after. It's the best way to get out of an event that I've ever learned." Niamh had her coat on and an eager expression. "Are we going after her?"

"Are you talking about Ms. Ryan?" The kid at the coat check, who had barely looked up from his phone to give Niamh her coat, put the phone in his pocket and started taking everyone else's tickets for their coats. "She left about twenty minutes ago. I only noticed because she was the first to leave and she looked a wreck."

"Did she say where she was going?" Megan asked hopefully.

The kid gave her the look she deserved for such a bizarre question. "Sure now she said she was on her way to Ibiza for a house party, didn't she. C'mon along with me, Johnny, she said, but here I am, stuck behind the coat check desk, and me duty to eleven euro an hour outweighs the beach and the babes."

"All right, all right." Megan lifted her hands in surrender. "It was a stupid question."

"And here I thought the murder driver was

clever." The kid sniffed and went back to his phone, leaving Megan to stare at him briefly. She did not want to be casually recognized as the murder driver by random kids in Dublin. Or anywhere else, for that matter.

No wonder Jelena hadn't been able to take any more of it. Megan pressed her eyes closed, trying to bring her mind back to the topic at hand. "I don't know how we'd go after her. Or where. To Maggie Keane's house? That seems weird and stalker-ish. What if Erin doesn't go there? She's had a huge loss herself. She might just want to get away from the glad-handing." Megan's gaze skittered toward Willow, wondering if the young woman was right about *how* huge a loss Angus McConal had been to Erin Ryan. "And in case anybody forgot, I'm not actually a detective. I don't think I'm allowed to go pound on people's doors in the middle of the night and demand they talk to me."

"Well, you're not *not* allowed," Paul said thoughtfully. "Rabbie, do you know Maggie at all?"

"Of course I do." Megan's uncle sounded mildly affronted. "I knew her da better, to be sure. That was a sad story, that one. Herself died young, and he took to the drink when he wasn't mucking to keep a roof over their heads. Maggie's the oldest of five, and I'd say she did more than her share of raising her siblings."

"Someone else said that, too," Megan agreed. "But do you know her well enough to ring and check up on her?"

"I know everybody that well, if someone's got her number. Ah, no, here, I'll ring Sean and get it." Rabbie did just that, as the five of them trooped out to the street.

Megan regretted it as soon as they stepped outside. The rain had stopped, at least, but the wind was bitter and the night cold. "Oh, God, the dogs."

"They were out only a few hours ago, Megan," Paul said gently. "You don't have to go home yet."

"I don't know if I even want to. Of course, I have to at some point, but . . ."

"At least Rabbie will be with you," Niamh said equally gently. "You'll be all right, Megan."

"Of course she will," Rabbie said, coming back to them. "Sean's texting me Maggie's number. Jimmy Mac, listen to me, I sound like a young man, himself texting me herself's number. What am I coming to! Are we going to Maggie Keane's, then? Am I ringing her?"

"Ring her," Megan said decisively. "See how she's doing. If you think she's awake."

The four Irish-born all looked askance, and Megan sighed somewhat melodramatically. "Look, it's ten at night. You didn't call anybody after nine unless it was an emergency when I was growing up, and I know I've been here five years, but I still haven't gotten used to the idea that people start getting ready to go out for things at ten, instead of coming home then. I really am old," she said in despair to no one in particular. "But also, Mrs. Keane is a newly-bereaved widow and sleep might be her only comfort."

Rabbie, indignantly, said, "If you're old, what does that make me?"

"Sprightly," Megan retorted. "And more suited to the Irish lifestyle than your American niece."

He hmphed with satisfaction and without further consultation, rang Maggie Keane. Niamh whispered, "Let's walk, I'm freezing me arse off," as he did so, and without discussion, they headed for the pub less than two minutes away, although Willow giggled.

"Why did we leave the event where there's free whiskey to go to the pub where we have to pay for it?"

"Because we're *dumb*," Megan whispered back. Rabbie glared at all of them as they giggled while he began to speak into his phone.

"Maggie, love, it's Rabbie Lynch. I'm only calling to check up on you. I know it's late, so if you're well enough you needn't ring me back, but if you need an old man's shoulder to lean on, then call me at this number. I'm sorry for your loss, my dear." He hung up, announced, "She didn't answer," even though it was obvious, and frowned at the pub they'd just about reached. "Why don't we go back to the museum and drink for free there?"

A burst of laughter answered him and he glowered again. "What's so funny?"

"We were just asking ourselves that," Megan told him with a smile, although it faded. "She wasn't picking up, huh? Have you Erin Ryan's number?"

"Listen to her," Niamh said admiringly. "Asking like an Irishwoman."

"I remember the first time I accidentally sounded Irish," Megan said. "I was asking for a bottle of still water from a shop owner, and I still had my own accent, but I used such an Irish cadence that I surprised myself and forgot how to talk for a few seconds."

The next few seconds were filled with all four of the Irish-born trying to ask for a bottle of still water in American accents with Irish speech patterns. Megan stood in the midst of it making a Kermit face until they devolved into laughter around her and then she grinned, too. "I probably sounded as ridiculous as y'all just did."

"Y'all," Niamh drawled. "Spelled Y-O-U-G-H-A-L in Ireland."

"A fact which I will never get over," Megan informed her. She'd been to Youghal, a little town in Cork with a very nice lighthouse, and she still couldn't look at the name without thinking it should be said *you-gall*. "It's on me, though. Trying to apply English pronunciations to Irish words."

"In your defense, the British spent centuries making sure people did," Paul said. "Look, Megan, I know what I said, but I don't think the guards would look kindly on you showing up on Maggie Keane's doorstep at half ten at night, and I *know* they'd give out to me about it."

"If you did, or if I did?"

"If I let you." The police detective made a face as Megan raised an eyebrow at him. "Yeah, yeah, who am I to let you do anything; you're a woman of your own, but you know what I mean."

Megan muttered an agreement that Paul spoke over, following his own thoughts about her question. "They'd give out to me if I did, too, for that matter, as neither of us know the woman at all and my only excuse would be investigating, which isn't going to hold water this time. Erin Ryan is likely to be at the event tomorrow. You can talk to her then."

"Does anybody know when Angus's funeral is?"

"Monday, I'd say." Willow, shivering, spoke up. "Maybe Tuesday. They were quick about getting the autopsy report in because he died so unexpectedly, and I'd say they'll be as quick with Danny Keane. What," she said as the others stared at her. "I looked up how long these things usually take, because I wondered if being murdered delayed a funeral. It usually takes weeks for a coroner's report to be filed, but they can rush it if they want."

"At least the festival's over tomorrow," Rabbie said grimly. "Hopefully nobody else will die. But lads, if we're not going to Maggie's, I could do with a night's sleep, and so could all of you."

A wave of weariness hit Megan as soon as he said that. "Every once in a while I remember I only got about three hours of sleep and wonder why I'm still on my feet."

"Ah, it's grand so," Willow said. "I could go another few hours, I'd say. Want me to ring Erin?"

For a moment Megan balanced on a knife's edge between bewilderment and sort of wanting to kick the young woman in the shins. She was too tired for perky twentysomethings, and also apparently too tired to have realized that Willow had Erin Ryan's number. "Go on," she said a bit slowly. "See what's the story."

"Will I tell her I'm thinking to come to work for her after all?" Willow sounded eager enough to create intrigue that Megan smiled.

"Maybe just ring and say you noticed she left the party early and were hoping she was all right."

Willow had obviously hoped for something less mundane, but nodded and got her phone out, then froze. "Will she think I'm mental for ringing? Normal people text."

"Does she usually ring or text her own self?" Paul asked.

"Ring."

He flickered his fingers at her phone. "Ring, then."

"Right." Willow took a few steps away, then came back again like she wanted to make sure everyone heard her half of the conversation, at least. "Yeah, no, Erin, it's me Willow like. I noticed you left early and it's been a bloody awful couple of days so I thought I'd ring and see if you were okay. No," she said after a pause, with a sharp glance at Megan, "I won't be coming to work for you, but Jesus, Erin, that doesn't mean I'm not concerned. You're not alone, are you? I'd say you shouldn't be after the last day. Tell you what, I'll come over. No, I think I'd better. I'm sure, I am. All right. Bye bye bye byebyebye." She hung up, brisk and confident. "She's not at Maggie Keane's. I'm going to her apartment to keep her company, and I'll get her to the tasting tomorrow so you can talk to her, Megan. This is exciting! I'm helping solve a murder!" She clapped her hands together, then bounced off the direction they'd come from, toward Dame Street and the taxi ranks.

All four of the older adults stood looking after her for somewhat longer than was necessary, given the cold wind. Niamh, the youngest of them, said, "I sort of want to kill her," and the other three laughed.

"Look, will we go up to Dawson Street and get the Luas?" Megan asked. "You two can take the green line over to the red line, which is better than walking that far, and Rabbie and I can go home."

"I don't know. What's the shoe situation?" Paul examined Niamh's feet briefly, and she lifted one to waggle it for his admiration. She wore lower, blockier heels than she had the night before, more like the walkable ones Megan herself was in. "The Luas, then?" Paul asked and she nodded. The four of them bypassed the pub and walked up Nassau Street, around a construction site that felt like it had been there for a generation now, to wait at the light rail stop that sat between a bookstore and a record shop. Megan went to look in the bookstore window, despite it being on the wrong side of the street for their tram.

"Drowning your sorrow in books is probably better than ice cream," Niamh said at her elbow. "You doing okay, pet?"

"Not even slightly." Megan's reflection in the dark window looked nearly as fabulous as Niamh's, two well-dressed, well-coiffed women, one a little taller than the other, both tired, but on the surface, just fine. It amazed Megan how surfaces could be so wrong, sometimes. "I don't really want to go home. It was already too empty this evening, and for all I know Yella's been back to get more stuff. But I can't stay out all night. The dogs, for one thing. Also I don't have Willow's energy, oh my God."

Niamh made one brave attempt not to laugh, then chortled. "I'm not even that much older than she is, but God, your twenties! So much energy!"

"I don't usually feel old. Not enough sleep makes for a bad day."

In the reflection, she saw Niamh's gaze flicker toward her, but her friend had the kindness to not point out that being dumped also made for a bad day. "I'd say tomorrow will be better, but honestly, tomorrow will probably suck, too."

Megan laughed and wiped her eyes all at once. "I'm afraid you're right. But at least I'll have had enough sleep. And maybe the dogs can sleep on the bed with me."

"Oh, girl. That's a battle you'll lose for life if you give an inch now. Is it worth risking all future relationships over dogs in the bed?"

"Tonight it might be."

"Fair." Niamh put an arm around Megan's waist and hugged her. "Look, go home, sleep with the dogs, get a hot shower in the morning, and then once you've had a good night's sleep you can solve a couple of murders and embarrass An Garda Síochána again."

To her surprise, Megan laughed again. "And what does your boyfriend the garda think of that?"

"I'm fairly confident he has complete faith in both Detective Reese and you. It's just a matter of who gets there first." Niamh gave her a sly smile. "I've a hundred quid on you at Ladbrokes."

"You *don't*."

"I do! They started taking odds on you after Aibhilín Ní Gallachóir made you famous."

"Oh my God. Have you bet on me before?"

"Not only bet, but won." Niamh kissed her cheek as the Luas dinged in the distance. "All right. Home and to sleep with ye, my love. Tomorrow is a new day."

CHAPTER 22

Tomorrow was a new day that started horrifyingly early, as Megan, then the dogs, woke up just before her alarm would usually go off to send her and Jelena to the gym. Megan couldn't face the risk of seeing Jelena there, so she took the dogs for a long enough run that by the end of it they were lying down to stare at her reproachfully at every traffic light.

She made it up to them by crawling back under the duvet when she got home, and letting them climb onto the bed as she pulled the covers over her head. Dip wiggled his way through the pillows and licked her cheek as she hid, and Thong lay down in a warm lump against her abdomen, like she was putting herself between Megan and anything that might come at her. Megan didn't think she'd go back to sleep, but the dogs and their comforting snuffles helped her drowse off, and she woke up three hours later needing to pee but feeling a lot better.

Thong sat up when Megan did, giving her puppy dog eyes as she tilted her head to make sure Megan was okay. "I'm all right," Megan told her in a sleep-rough voice. "Look at you, manipulating me with your eyebrows. Wolves can't do that, you know that, right? That's all dog. Because humans are suckers." She tucked Thong into her lap for a little hug, then, as the Jack Russell stood on her bladder, yelped and put her aside to run to the bathroom. Both the dogs were sitting outside it when she emerged, their tails wagging in sync. "I forgot to feed you breakfast, didn't I?"

Two tails thumped harder. Megan croaked a laugh and went into the kitchen to get their food, with two clicky-toenailed shadows at her heels. They ate as she opened and closed cupboards and the fridge several times, as if something appealing to eat would appear if she kept looking. She even checked the freezer for ice cream, then, suspicious at not finding any, checked the recycling bin to find an empty pint carton in it. Jelena had evidently had it for dinner.

An indignant sense of self-righteous betrayal rose, completely at odds with an equally strong feeling of understanding. On one hand, at least she wasn't the only one wanting to take refuge in ice cream; on the other, *she'd* been the one who got dumped and it didn't seem fair that Jelena had eaten it. "I'm going to the bakery."

The dogs looked up from their breakfast briefly, exchanged glances, and gave Megan a look that clearly indicated they had no interest in joining her. She muttered, "Fair, I made you run a long way this morning. Just don't bother Rabbie," and grabbed her stuff on the way out the door.

The morning was relentlessly glorious after yesterday's cold evening. Megan resented the weather trying to make her feel better, although she supposed she would resent it making her feel worse even more. She muttered, "I have layers. Like an onion," and wished she'd brought the dogs so she had an excuse to be talking to herself. The bakery was busy for early on a Sunday, and she bought enough to feed three people for a week, not a single woman with a houseguest who would be leaving in the morning.

Her phone rang as she was paying. Megan stood at the register, swaying a little as she tried to guess who could be calling and about what. If someone else was dead . . .

If someone else was dead, she didn't want to take the call in the shop. She got out the door before taking her phone out, and nearly dropped it as her hands went cold. Jelena.

For a heartbeat or two hope so sharp it hurt cut through her, and she fumbled the phone again trying to answer. "Yella? Is everything okay?"

"Megan." Even in the one word, Jelena sounded as if things were far from okay. "Yes, I mean, no, but nothing is wrong the way you are asking. I thought I would come get the rest of my things, but I wanted to see if you were . . . if we needed to talk in person." Her voice cracked. "Do we need to see each other?"

"I don't know." Megan hadn't meant to sit down at the tables outside the bakery's storefront, but somehow she was sitting and holding her head like it weighed a thousand pounds. "Is there really anything else to say? I can apologize until the end of time, but it's not going to change the fact that this keeps happening and that I . . ." She sighed until she thought her whole body was empty of air. "Enjoy doing this. Trying to figure out what happened. Trying to help people. Trying to solve the mystery. I put your favorite cup with your things." Her voice broke as she blurted the admission, knowing she'd completely changed the subject but unable to stop herself. "You don't have to take it if you don't want it, but I thought . . . if you wanted it . . ."

"Thank you." An awful silence drew out before Jelena said, "I'm sorry, Megan. I know you want to help. I just . . ."

"No. I know. I understand. Want things to be normal. I'm not mad, Yella, just . . ." Megan's head hurt. She pinched the bridge of her nose, trying not to cry in public. "I just already miss you."

"Me too." Jelena sounded tight and unhappy. "I'll come over this afternoon to get my things. Some of the lads said they'd come help with the bigger stuff."

"I'm going to the last festival event at one," Megan whispered. "If you want to, you know. Avoid me."

Jelena wailed, "Megan," and Megan lost any hope of staving off tears.

"I'm sorry. That wasn't nice, or fair, or something, I just . . . I won't be home, okay? You can get your things and I'll talk to the landlord about taking your name off the lease and giving you a good recommendation and I'm sorry, Jelena. I'm sorry this is what I've chosen."

"I know. I'm sorry, too." Jelena hung up.

Megan said, "I hope you find happiness," to a dead line, then put her head down on the table and cried.

When she lifted her head, it was to find a very young woman at a table nearby, elbows on her knees and an expression of frank sympathy on her face. "Was he bad to you, love?"

A combination of tears and laughter snorted through Megan's nose, uninhibited and completely unstoppable. "She."

"Was she bad to you, then?" the girl said without missing a beat.

"No. Not at all. We just weren't compatible, in the end."

An even more sympathetic wince went across the girl's face. "That's hard. You've got friends to help you out?" At Megan's wet nod, the girl stood, came over, and actually hugged her. "You'll be okay, then. I'm sorry, but I hope you find happiness, too." She went on into the bakery, and Megan, red-faced and snotty, went home feeling like maybe the world wasn't a completely terrible place, thanks to the kindness of strangers.

Rabbie was up and conversing with the dogs as he made coffee when she arrived. "Terrible thing, waking up to no coffee," he told her in a querulous, old man voice, and Megan smirked.

"You live alone, Rabbie. You must wake up to no coffee every day. Also, don't you drink tea?"

"I do," he said expansively enough to suggest he was answering both the observation and the question. "But I thought all Americans made coffee in the morning, and I'm not above having a cup to be sociable."

"Well, thank you for making it. I brought pastries." And cake. And tarts. And brownies, and several other things Megan probably wouldn't eat, but had seemed like a good idea at the time. "Any news from anyone?"

"Maggie Keane rang to say thanks for checking in on her and she's doing well enough. The funeral's to be Wednesday, so I may stay on through then if you don't mind, Megan." He cast her a sideways glance to see if she accepted his excuse for staying, and Megan ended up smiling at him.

"That would be fine. It'd be nice to have you here a little longer."

Rabbie exhaled, satisfied that his subterfuge had worked. Not that Megan doubted he wanted to, and would, go to Danny Keane's funeral, but she thought most of the reason he intended to stay was to keep an eye on her for a few days. She thought of the girl at the bakery, and smiled again. She did have people to help her out, and was lucky for it. "I talked to Jelena. She's coming over to get the rest of her things while we're at the finals this afternoon."

"Do you want someone here while she does?" Rabbie was clearly being careful not to ask if *she* wanted to be there, and Megan's heart twisted with the gentleness he was trying to show.

"No, it's okay. I don't think she's going to make off with anything that isn't hers. Although the dogs might get worried if they start taking big stuff out. Maybe I'll ask Paul to come over. No, I'll text

Brian. He lives nearby." She did that, texting her American friend who ran a small press in Rathmines. "The coffee smells good. Thank you." They sat down to root through the bakery bags, and a few minutes later Brian replied that he'd come over, although Megan could feel his questions practically vibrating through the innocuous response.

She sent **There was another murder and we broke up. I'll tell you the details later** like that cleared everything up, and after what she felt was a judicious pause, Brian wrote **right** back, but nothing else. She sent a text to Jelena saying Brian would be over so the dogs wouldn't get in the way, and by the time she was done with that, she thought going back to hide in bed the rest of the day sounded about the right speed.

Instead, her phone rang for the second time that morning and for the second time, she had to brace herself to answer. This time it was Orla, voice crisp with demand. "Can you drive this afternoon?"

"I took the weekend off."

"I know, but it's Carmen." Her boss tried for a wheedling tone, which had a bit of a fingernails-on-chalkboard aspect to it. "She wants you to drive her to the final event this afternoon."

Megan groaned. "Tell her I'll come by her hotel and *walk* her to the bus and we can all take it to the Jameson's theater like normal people, but no, Orla, I will not arrange my weekend around her whim."

"She says you got her security man arrested and you owe her."

"Well, she's not wrong about the first part, but

there's no parking around Smock Alley Theatre, Orla. I'm not dropping her off so she can swan right in while I have to walk three blocks back in the rain."

"It's not raining."

"It's Ireland. It will be. Carmen can take a bus or a taxi like the rest of us do."

Orla, impatiently, said, "Carmen de la Fuente is worth half the national GDP of Ireland. She doesn't do anything like the rest of us do."

"Oh, she is not. I bet she's not even worth one percent of that." Megan didn't know what the Irish GDP was, or what Carmen was worth, but she was fairly certain one figured in the hundreds of billions, and the other in the hundreds of millions at the most, and if she was wrong, she didn't *want* to know. "Even if she was, I'm not driving her to an event I'm going to and would have to walk back from a car park from."

Orla sniffed. "On your head be it if she never hires us again."

"My world would crash to an end," Megan replied sourly. Orla hung up and Megan groaned again, this time loudly enough to concern the dogs, who wound around her ankles like they'd been taking lessons from cats. "Bad enough I don't have anything to wear. Worse if I have to wear my uniform to a do. And I can't even borrow anything from Jelena because she already took all her clothes." She dragged in a deep breath before tears started falling again, and rose. "I'm going to go find something to wear, and if necessary I'll call bloody Carmen and explain to her how to hire a cab."

"By calling the front desk at her fancy hotel and telling them to arrange one, I imagine," Rabbie said dryly.

Megan chuckled. "You're not wrong." She kissed him on top of the head as she went to find something to wear. She was still staring at her wardrobe when her phone rang for the third time, Paul's number coming up. She answered with, "Grand Central Station. Usually when I call you, there's a body, so what's the story?"

Paul's silence drew out long enough that Megan's stomach had already dropped before he said, "Erin Ryan is dead."

CHAPTER 23

"What?" Megan had heard Paul clearly enough. It just didn't make sense, in the way that unexpected news, especially unexpected death, never did. Paul had the decency not to repeat himself, and after a few seconds of white noise and blurred vision, Megan said, "When?"

"Sometime between Willow leaving us and this morning." Paul sounded grim, and Megan's thoughts, spiking in every direction, tripped ahead to the obvious conclusion.

"It wasn't—it couldn't have been Willow? No, Paul, Erin Ryan doesn't make sense. One of the Murphys, or Hannah or Carmen or Rabbie, but Erin doesn't make sense if they're decimating teams. They already killed Angus."

"That theory is obviously wrong. They're not trying to take somebody out from each team. There's something else connecting Danny Keane and Angus McConal. Something Erin must have known about."

"But Willow couldn't have." Megan sat on her bed, trying to remember how to think. "Could she? She couldn't have. She's just a kid."

"She's twenty-eight, Megan."

"And she had . . . oh, God, she had motive. For Erin and Angus, anyway." Megan sketched out what Willow had told her about her relationships with two of the three dead people, ending with, "but I don't know any connection to Danny at all."

"Jesus." A note of frustrated admiration rang through the word. "I'd say Dervla doesn't know a thing about any of that, and not because she's bad at her job."

Megan shook her head. "It was years ago and not something I would have brought up unless I thought I really had to. And Erin obviously didn't suspect Willow of anything, because she came after Rabbie, not Willow, at the opening gala. Oh my God. Is the final event even happening?"

"I don't see how it can. Three people are dead in three days. If I were the competitors I'd be locked in panic rooms until this was all over. What the hell is the link between Danny Keane and the McConal brand?" Paul's voice rose in frustration. "And if there isn't one, why is Erin Ryan dead?"

"I take it Detective Reese isn't keeping you up to date."

"The only reason I know Ryan is dead is that Sean Byrne was informed, and he's been ringing the other competitors. Niamh got the call a few minutes ago."

"He hasn't called Rabbie ye—" As she spoke,

her uncle appeared in her bedroom door, wild-eyed, and Megan breathed, "Never mind," into the phone before saying, "It's Paul. He told me. Are you okay?" to Rabbie.

"I'm better than Erin Ryan, aren't I? We never should have left the party last night without sorting this out, Megan! Erin might be alive if we hadn't!"

"Erin left before we did." That didn't make any sense, but Megan left it hanging there anyway. "The cops are going to be crawling all over everybody today. They're going to want us to come to the event this afternoon so they have everybody corralled. I thought it was Erin."

Paul said, "What?" in her ear and Rabbie looked like he needed a chair. Megan got up, flickering her fingers to send her uncle back into the common area, and they both sat in the living room as Megan said, "She was apparently in love with Angus. Willow believes they were together for a while, early in his career. I thought . . . I don't know. I thought maybe she was losing control of him and she'd rather have him dead than not hers. But there's no connection to Danny Keane there and now Erin's dead, so—she didn't kill herself, did she?"

"I hate not knowing the story," Paul said after a tight silence. "I don't know, Megan. I assume not, but . . ." He trailed off, then swore. "Dervla certainly won't tell me and I can't blame her for that, but Christ, I hate not knowing what's going on." The last words turned to a sharp laugh. "And now I understand why you keep poking around in these messes."

"*See?*" The word burst from Megan's chest with a

sense of justification so profound it bordered on tears. "These things keep happening in front of me and I promise it's not that I don't think the guards will do their jobs! It's just they've no reason to keep me in the loop and I hate not knowing so I try to find out so I don't lose my mind!"

"I'll ring Dervla and see if they're even going to allow the final event to go forward this afternoon," Paul muttered. "If they're not, we'll regroup and try to figure out how to move ahead with our investig—I am not after saying that."

"You did say it. And if they're going ahead with it, I'll see you at the event and we'll try to rattle everybody's cages there."

"You'll try. The boss will have my skin if she catches me asking a single question."

"Well, Dervla's going to arrest me for interfering with an ongoing investigation if I try, so . . ." Megan cracked a laugh. "Ah, well, we'll both be in trouble, won't we. Let me know what's the story." She hung up and dropped her head back to thump against the couch. "All right, Rabbie. You know everybody. What's the connection between Erin, Danny, and Angus?"

"The dirty old man in me wants to say sex," her uncle said without missing a beat. "I just wouldn't know who was having an affair with whom."

"Niamh thinks Maggie Keane's the type, and Angus liked older women, not that she's that much older. But that's spurious. There's no proof at all. I don't suppose Angus and Danny were hooking up."

Rabbie's eyebrows climbed. "Speaking of spurious? I've never heard a word that suggested Angus McConal enjoyed the company of men anywhere except in the boxing ring, and as good as people are at keeping things about themselves quiet, I'd known Angus since he was a lad. I don't think he fancied the fellas."

"Rats. It's the tidiest explanation I can think of."

"There's nothing tidy about this, lass."

"Well, you're not wrong about that." Megan sighed and glanced at her phone, like she might have missed Paul calling back. "Did Byrne say anything to you about the event this afternoon?"

"He doesn't want to call it off, but I reckon it's up to the guards. And to whether any of us will show up for it. Three people dead, Megan!"

"And we only know the cause of death for one. God, I'm going to *have* to get a PI's license if this keeps up. That way at least I might actually be privy to useful information like that."

"Danny Keane hasn't been dead twenty-four hours yet," Rabbie pointed out. "They might not have the official cause of death."

"Oh, I bet somebody knows. I don't suppose you're mates with the coroner?"

Rabbie looked shifty and Megan's eyes widened. "You are!"

"She'd never tell me a thing!"

"She might! Ring her!"

"On a Sunday morning?" Rabbie, as far as Megan knew, hadn't been to a church service except at Easter and Christmas in this century. His outrage seemed a little contrived.

"She's probably at work," Megan pointed out. "With Angus and Danny both dead inside a day of each other, and now Erin dead, I bet she's doing an autopsy right now."

"Then I couldn't interrupt her at work." Rabbie sounded positively sanctimonious.

Megan pointed at his phone. "Ring her. If she won't tell you, she won't tell you, but if she will . . . of course, the guards already know." She collapsed sideways into the couch and both dogs jumped up to make sure she was okay. "I'm not racing to figure it out before they do, am I?" she asked from beneath their warm, wiggling bodies. "I'm not making this some kind of mad competition, right?"

"I'd say you have some skin in the game," Rabbie said gently. "For one, it's people you know tangled up in the mess, but for another, Jelena ended things over this. Being the one to solve it might salve that wound, a little. I'll ring Nora, love. Maybe you deserve that much, at least."

"I don't know that I do." Megan stayed on the couch, hugging Thong while Dip licked her ear, as Rabbie went to the guest bedroom for a moment's privacy to call the coroner in. "Yeah," Megan said to the dogs in a low voice. "You two love me, at least, don't you."

Although the problem wasn't that Jelena didn't love her. Megan's life and the particular chaos it attracted was the trouble, and she could be devastated and understand that Yella's needs and expectations were completely reasonable all at the same time. She whispered, "Emotions suck," to Thong, and the small dog, trying to make her feel better, stuck her tongue up Megan's nose with an over-enthusiastic lick.

Megan gagged and laughed at the same time. "Gross. Gross. That was gross, missy. But thank you. Thank you for the kisses." She sat up just as

Rabbie returned, although the older man shook his head.

"She wasn't answering, love. I left a message asking her to ring me back, but we might be on our own. They'll have told Maggie, though, won't they? If she's at the event today . . ." He trailed off dubiously and Megan shrugged.

"I don't think she was happy about the whole project, but she might want to see it through for Danny, in case Keane Edge wins. I guess there's only one way to find out."

The final event of the whiskey competition, held at the Smock Alley Theatre, was the most somber affair Megan had ever attended outside of actual funerals. No one wanted to be there, least of all the panel of experts whose job it was to judge the competitors. There were three of them, two men and a woman, none of whom Megan knew at all. They were on their feet, standing near the back of a small stage, as if actively avoiding the table with flights of whiskeys already laid out.

There were folding chairs on the theater floor and auditorium seating above that. Megan assumed that most years, the higher seating was filled with onlookers and guests. Today they were empty, as was the rest of the building. The competitors were on the theater floor, huddled in groups that mostly ignored the folding chairs. Megan personally felt half convinced that at any moment one of those chairs might snap shut and swallow somebody, as if she'd stepped into a monster movie of some kind.

Nearly everyone wore black, even Carmen, whom Megan had never seen in anything other than bright colors. Hannah Flanagan, who normally wore pastels, was in deep lilac that felt appropriate enough for the situation. A couple in their forties, both of whom looked like Hannah, were presumably her parents; the woman wore mourning blue, far more flattering to her skin tones than black would have been, and the man, a dark dove-gray suit. Megan wondered if they'd come prepared with those clothes, or if they'd had to buy them. Rabbie'd needed to buy a new suit for himself, although the Murphy husbands looked tidy in black, as well-prepared as the Flanagans.

Trish Dillon sat to one side, entirely alone while Sean Byrne, in a badly fitted black suit, tended to his own affairs for once. The PA had aged visibly overnight, deep lines now showing around her mouth and across her forehead. Megan thought that with her pale skin, Trish could probably usually wear black with panache, but today she was so colorless that she could have been among the dead, herself. The high collar of her turtleneck framing her face with no relief didn't help, either.

"They were friends, Erin and Trish?" Megan murmured to Rabbie, who nodded.

"Erin must have been ten years younger, but they knew each other through Sean and Angus and the fights. Trish goes everywhere Sean does, and Erin went wherever Angus did. I'd say as the only two women in the room a lot of the time, they stood up for each other and the like."

"Did Erin have any family?"

"Not anymore." Rabbie left the sorrowful tone hanging.

Megan winced and nodded. Niamh and Paul arrived a little late, Niamh chic as usual in a black silhouette dress and Paul looking almost as terrible as Trish Dillion in his own black suit. Megan had never noticed how ghastly black looked on so many people before, although she glanced at the theater's house lights and thought maybe the shadows they cast weren't helping the situation.

Maggie Keane, though, looked almost as fantastic as Niamh. Not happy, but spectacular, with her hair swept up and her jawline defined, albeit with grief and rage. Her lace-sleeved dress's bodice suited her shape, and the asymmetrical skirt managed to be both demure enough for mourning, and flattering. Megan thought it had a revenge dress vibe, and wondered who, exactly, Maggie was getting revenge against.

Niamh and Paul joined Rabbie, Megan, and Carmen, who was the only representative of the Midnight Sunrise team, and clearly felt out of place in the somber gathering. She still air-kissed Niamh's cheeks and smiled at Paul, but Megan wished, for Carmen's sake, that anyone else had been able to join her. Even Ramon, although Megan wasn't sure if he'd even been released yet.

"Don't worry, Meghaaan," the little Spanish woman murmured. "My whiskey will not win. I am only here to see you solve the murders."

"I feel like you'd better be watching Detective Reese, then," Megan replied softly. Dervla Reese was one of the few people in attendance who wasn't in any kind of mourning colors. The detective garda stood to one side, arms folded across her chest and quiet intensity in her expression. If a gimlet gaze could extract a confession, everyone in the theater would be lining up to admit their sins.

And, of course, in just the few minutes that Megan had been watching, almost everyone in the theater had shot at least one uncomfortable look toward the guard. If nervousness was an indicator of guilt, the whole lot of them, probably including Megan, would be arrested by dinnertime.

"I'm going to go offer my condolences to Trish," she said in a low voice. "Rabbie, you know Maggie. Why don't you go check in on her?"

"And us?" Niamh asked hopefully.

Paul's face went long with apology. "We sit here being well-behaved mannequins, because if Dervla sees me near anybody but you, Nee, my head is going to roll."

"Aww." Niamh brightened. "Wait—what if I went and talked to Dervla? Maybe she'd let something slip!"

"My head," Paul reminded her again. "And there's no chance she'd let something slip, honestly. Not with you. Maybe with someone else, but she'd be on guard so."

Niamh muttered, "Ah, sure look," and pouted. Paul, clearly both guilty and amused, kissed her protruding lower lip, and she smiled into the kiss as Megan went to talk to Trish.

The PA looked very alone in her folding chair at one corner of the theater. Mrs. Keane had people coming and going around her, as if this was a wake already, but Megan supposed the loss of a husband was generally considered much more dramatic than the loss of a friend. She gestured at the chair beside Trish as she approached, and the older woman smiled briefly and echoed the motion, inviting Megan to sit. "Are you well?"

"I'm all right," Megan said, emphasizing the pronoun a little. "Are you? I don't mean to be rude, but you look shattered. Rabbie said you and Erin were friends. I'm so sorry for your loss."

"It's been the worst weekend of my life," Trish said tightly. "I can't even begin to tell you."

Megan glanced toward Byrne, who was on the stage now, talking with his judges. "Is he being difficult?"

Trish gave a bitter laugh. "Difficult is his easiest setting, love. He's in bits. Not that he cares one way or another that any of them are dead, but I know he meant to impress the Flanagans this weekend and this isn't what he had in mind."

"No, I imagine not. Why does he need to impress them?"

The other woman hesitated a moment, then shrugged. "He wants their legitimacy, I'd say. Not that I'd say," she added swiftly. "It wouldn't be my place, like."

"I didn't hear a word of it from you," Megan promised and Trish Dillion's eyes watered so brightly it made Megan think the poor woman never had anyone listen to *her*.

Trish closed her eyes, the tears thick enough in them to spill over. She brushed them away as if they didn't exist. "He'll never be a Flanagan," she murmured. "He'll never have the centuries of confidence behind his name. He bloody loves his whiskey and wants to be seen as the man in front of it all, like ushering a new whiskey to the world's attention is his domain, and his alone. And he does well enough at it, but for a man with all that money, I'd say he's got no confidence in himself. He feels like families like the Flanagans are laughing up their sleeve at him."

"Are they?"

The PA opened her eyes to give Megan a weary smile. "I'd say they don't even think of him if he's not in the room, and that's worse than being laughed at for a man like Sean. He's rich, but it's new enough money. He thinks old money sees him as crass."

Megan pressed her lips together hard, and a sharp smile cut lines around Trish's mouth. "Yes, well, I didn't say it."

"Neither did I!" Megan protested.

"No, you didn't. Anyway, he's desperate for influence, to be seen as a man of the world, however you'd want to say it, and he thinks Flanagan support would get him that, but I'll tell you for free that all of this dreadfulness isn't going to bring the Flanagans to his side."

"I suppose their daughter winning the competition would, though. Did you tell the guards about him trying to curry favor?"

Trish's gaze flickered down, her smile bitter again before her eyes came back up in surprise. "No, I don't suppose I did. It wouldn't go over well to paint my boss as a bootlicker, would it. And it seems obvious, doesn't it?"

"Well, I didn't know until just now," Megan pointed out. "Look, I don't want you to get in trouble with him. I can bring it to Detective Reese myself, just in case it's important."

Canniness flashed in Trish's expression, wiping away weary grief for the first time in their conversation. "You're balancing a fine line yourself, aren't you, Ms. Malone? Neck-deep in suspicious deaths and trying to find out what happened while not leaving the guards raging at you. I'd rather handle Sean than the whole Garda Síochána."

Megan made a face as she rose. "Yeah, me too; so if you ever want to trade jobs . . ." She left it hanging and angled her way through the sparse crowd toward Detective Reese. Rabbie, just leaving Maggie Keane's side, waved her down. Megan grimaced faintly, but Reese didn't know she was on the way, so she paused to murmur, "What's the story?" to her uncle.

"Megan." Rabbie's voice was low as he stepped up to her side. "They've just rung Maggie and I was there to hear them say that Danny Keane died of natural causes."

CHAPTER 24

"He what?" It took everything Megan had to keep her own voice quiet. "He just died?"

"He had a bad heart," Rabbie whispered. "Maggie was saying as much before they called. He's been on medication for years and the stress of it all killed him. She doesn't know whether she's coming or going with the grief, Megan. She was afraid it would do him in, and now it has."

Megan sat heavily in the nearest chair. Fortunately there were a lot of them, as the event wasn't anything like the celebration it was meant to be. "So he just *died?*" she said again, incredulously.

Rabbie sat beside her. "He just died. And I'm sorry for Maggie, I am, but what does that mean for your case?"

"It's not my case," Megan said fruitlessly, but added, "It means the only suspicious deaths are both tied to Fighting Chance Whiskey. Oh my God.

Where's Willow?" Her stomach dropped as she asked the question and she got to her feet again, looking for the young woman.

"Willow? Why?"

"She had a history with McConal and as far as I know, she was the last person to see Erin alive. She isn't here. Crap. I have to talk to Detective Reese or she'll pop my eyes out with an oyster spoon."

Rabbie, after a moment to absorb that image, said, "Ew," with great distasteful delicacy.

Megan laughed, quick and quiet, then got up and approached Detective Reese, whose stern expression became positively draconian. "What do you want?"

"My uncle was just with Mrs. Keane when she got the news that Danny Keane apparently did die of a heart attack."

Dervla's eyes bugged gratifyingly, although the expression did put Megan in mind of oyster spoons again. She bit her inner cheek so she wouldn't smile, and instead explained Willow's history with McConal and that she'd gone to see Erin the night before. Dervla's expression got stonier throughout, until she uttered a clipped, "Thank you," turned on her heel, and stalked out of the theater. A couple of guards followed her; a couple more didn't.

The door hadn't yet closed behind them when Paul and Niamh were at Megan's side, Carmen only a step beside them. "What? You got a break in the case?" Paul sounded as breathless as an ingenue, as if this was all an exciting divergence from his usual reality.

Megan explained it for the third time in a row

and sent Paul back on his heels with surprise. Then his face set into similarly grim lines to Dervla's. "She had means, motivation, and opportunity. This doesn't look good."

"It does if we want the case solved," Niamh said in a low voice. "But I like Willow. She doesn't seem like the murdering type. I know, I know, no one ever does, all those serial killers seemed like such nice young men, I know."

"Dervla will find her and find out," Paul said steadily. "It's not good that she isn't here, though."

"I forgot to tell her that Byrne is apparently trying to kiss up to Hannah's parents, but I guess that doesn't matter as much as I thought it might." Megan sighed. "I hope Detective Reese finds Willow soon and this can all be over. Including this tasting. Are they really going through with it?"

She nodded at the stage, where the experts were taking their seats. All three of them exchanged uncomfortable glances and eyed the flights of whiskey in front of them distrustfully. Megan had thought before that they didn't want to be there; now it appeared they were concerned for their lives, which, under the circumstances, seemed reasonable. Byrne, up on stage, made a show of greeting them, although he'd already done that while they were huddled at the back of the stage. Then he stepped forward to address the sparse crowd in solemn tones. "We've been beset by tragedy this weekend, so I thank you all for being here, especially Maggie Keane. Keane Edge is a fine product and I hope whatever else comes of the event this afternoon, that you'll find the success that your Danny hoped for."

Mrs. Keane's lip curled, a complete dismissal of his fine words. Megan thought that was fair enough. Byrne went on to introduce the other competitors and mentioned Hannah's parents as special guests. Megan was, as the Irish would say, scarlet for her: the poor girl looked mortified to have her parents on hand, as even the most dim-witted person there couldn't help but understand that having the actual Flanagan Whiskey family in the building brought a certain kind of pressure. Maybe whether the pressure was on Hannah to win, or on the judges to select her as a winner was something of a fine line, but either way, it was pressure.

"Megan." Rabbie bumped his shoulder against hers and offered her his phone, which must have been on *silent*, because it was live with a call. "It's Willow."

Megan's stomach lurched. She took the phone and rose as quietly as she could, moving to the back of the theater, murmuring, "Willow? Are you all right?"

"The head on me," Willow said at a cheerful enough volume that Megan winced and edged her way to the door. "I ran into some mates and we went out clubbing until half five. I didn't get to bed until seven and I only just woke up. I rang Rabbie to ask if there was any point in me turning up to the event, but he handed me straight to you. What's the story?"

By the time she'd finished explaining herself, Megan was just outside the theater doors, where she at least didn't feel she had to whisper. "Did you see Erin last night?"

"I went over, but Ms. Dillon was just getting out

of her car when I got there, so I thought she was probably fine and then a friend rang and I went out instead of visiting. Why?"

For the second time in as many minutes, Megan's stomach lurched. "Wait, what? Trish Dillon was at Erin Ryan's house last night?"

"Sure, they're friends like. I knew Ms. Dillon a little when I worked for Erin. Why?"

"I'll call you back." Megan hung up and returned to the theater, standing just inside the door to look over the little gathering. Her heart thudded with sick, heavy beats, making her feel more than a little nauseous.

Sean Byrne was still up on stage, pontificating. No one in the room appeared to be enjoying themselves. Hannah's father checked his watch and exchanged impatient glances with his wife. Whatever Byrne wanted from them, he wasn't greasing the wheel that would get it. Most other people were looking down, rather than watching the stage. Here and there a badly-hidden phone glowed in someone's lap. Megan was surprised there weren't more.

Now that the house lights were dimmed, though, Trish Dillon was watching Byrne with naked hatred in her gaze. Megan's stomach twisted again, making her wish she'd eaten something other than too many pastries and too much coffee that morning. She went around the back of the floor seating and came up to crouch at Trish's side, not knowing what she would say until it came out of her mouth. "Did you kill Erin Ryan?"

It lacked subtlety, but it was certainly effective. Trish screamed, as bloodcurdling and hopeless as

Maggie Keane's had been the day before, and surged to her feet. Megan fell backward in astonishment as Trish, still screaming, rushed the stage and threw herself at Sean Byrne. "It's your fault! It's all your fault! You did this to me! To us!"

Megan had rarely seen a tackle as well-executed as the one Trish took Byrne down with. She put her whole body weight into it, rushing him backward until he smashed into the experts table behind him. The table cracked under the impact and they both went to the floor, whiskey and glass flying everywhere, experts scrambling to get out of the way. Byrne was too stunned to fight back as Trish perched on top of him and pummeled him, shrieking incoherently. One of the male whiskey tasters tried pulling her off him, and she threw an elbow with such viciousness that he skittered back, barely dodging a crippling groin blow.

Megan was on her feet by then and vaulting onto the stage a heartbeat later, but the gardaí that Detective Reese had left behind were a little bit quicker. They got to Trish a step or two faster than Megan did and, with coordinated effort, grabbed her arms and lifted her, literally kicking and screaming, off the floored festival manager. Trish fought like a cat in a bag, her accusations ringing through the theater. "He killed my Angus, so he did! He killed him because that Flanagan girl's whiskey is pure shite, and Angus wouldn't play along with a plot to trade his whiskey for hers! Ask her parents, why don't you?"

"Mum? Dad?" Hannah stood, her voice thin and distressed. "Mummy?"

The elder Flanagans exchanged grim glances

again, and with what Megan thought was preplanned
agreement, declined to speak. Hannah, recognizing their silence for what it probably was, shrieked
and dropped into her seat again, hands barely
muffling her sobs as she hid her face.

"See? *See?*" Trish, still struggling and shouting,
kicked her feet in the Flanagans' direction, then
made a sincere effort to stomp on Sean Byrne,
who was being helped to his feet by the experts
team.

Megan raised her voice, looking for an answer
to the question she'd asked in the first place. "*Did
you kill Erin Ryan?*"

"*It was an accident!*" Trish's rage nearly tore her
from the gardaí's grasp. One of them, the skinny
kid who'd walked Megan out of the Meeting House
Square the day before, looked astonished at her
strength, and adjusted his grip. Trish shrieked, "It
was an accident!" again, then slumped like all the
fight had gone out of her as she mumbled the
same thing a third time. "She didn't know about
Angus and myself and she was in such mourning. I
thought we could share the pain, so I told her, but
she came at me like a wild thing. I only tried to
push her away, I swear it. I never meant to hurt
her. It's on your head!"

Her fury returned in force and she swung toward Byrne with such strength that the young
guards holding her were pulled in a quarter circle
before they braced themselves. "All of it's your
fault, you manky son of a bitch! You couldn't just
leave Angus and me well enough alone!"

To Megan's astonishment, Sean's face crum-
pled. "You were going to leave me for him and I

can't do without you, Trish. What am I to do now? No one else knows how to run my life."

"You're to rot in hell now," Trish snarled. "I certainly won't be lifting a finger to help you again, now or ever. I've notes on it all," she added to the guards still holding her. "That's what I do, isn't it. I sit in the background and take notes and no one ever notices me because I'm the staff. I told you." She whirled again, or tried to, apparently looking for Megan, because her voice rose again. "Megan Malone, the murder driver, I told you, didn't I!"

The gardaí holding her eyed each other, then rotated her toward Megan, who took a step closer as Trish snarled, "I told you that Sean was desperate for the Flanagans' influence! I've notes on all their meetings, on how Sean promised to make sure the young wan's undrinkable dreck was the winning whiskey. And how they promised to up his own brand that's coming out next year and make him a man among men in the business. Oh, but you don't need me for everything, do you, Sean." She once more tried throwing off the guards' hands, and they cautiously let her, although they stayed pressed so close that all she could do was turn back toward Sean, rather than fling herself at him again. "No, you were able to kill a man without my supervision, weren't you. You knew I'd never let any harm come to Angus, you filthy c—"

Anticipatory silence had filled the theater, but with her last words voices began to rise in shouts of dismay and excitement, until Trish's rage was drowned out. Paul came up on stage as Megan went around the guards to say, "Why put the Harbourmaster recipe on him, though?" to Sean.

The festival manager's expression contorted and he spat, "The plan all along was to trade out Angus's whiskey for Hannah's. But then I realized Trish was going to leave me—"

"You say it like I'm your wife!" Trish howled. "I wouldn't have you if you were the last man in the world, you—"

Megan hastily raised her own voice, trying to keep Sean's attention. "So you killed him and put the recipe on his body, but why?"

"Because Harbourmaster was favored to win!" Sean bellowed. "It's a fine enough whiskey and Rabbie's well-liked! I didn't want to risk him coming out on top, so I thought a bit of a scandal around it would dim his star!"

"All of this." Maggie Keane had come up on stage quietly as Sean and Trish were yelling, and approached Byrne with a shaking voice and teary eyes. "All of this and the death of my own husband, for some stupid promotion on a whiskey that no one's even heard of yet? Three people dead for it? No drink is worth that, Sean Byrne."

He turned a bug-eyed, furious look on her. "It's my *life*."

"It was Danny's life, too," Maggie snarled and slammed the heel of her hand into Byrne's nose.

CHAPTER 25

Paul, at Megan's side, breathed, "Oh shit," and stepped in to flank Trish Dillon as one of the guards, looking rather reluctant, pulled Maggie away from Sean and mumbled something about arresting her for assault. She didn't resist, but from the lift of her jaw and the flash of her eyes, Megan thought she'd be happy to go down for murder right then, if she could get away with it. The supportive murmur that went through the little crowd suggested the several dozen eyewitnesses might all deny they saw anything, too, if she tried.

By that time, Trish had lost her head of steam and sank to her knees, sobbing. Paul glanced toward Megan, shook his head, and took his phone out. The woman on the expert panel pinched the bridge of her nose, then beckoned her fellow judges and walked backstage with them. They reemerged with half a dozen bottles and the woman saying,

"There's no way I'm leaving here without tasting what all this mess has been about." They righted their chairs, eyed the broken table, and collectively shrugged, putting the bottles on the floor around them.

One of the men picked up an unbroken glass from the floor, wiped it with the hem of his shirt, and poured a splash of whiskey from the nearest bottle in. Megan watched with fascination as he sniffed, made a face like his nose hairs had caught on fire, and took a tentative sip before actually wheezing. "Jaysus, that's awful. I've tasted better lighter fluid."

An extremely cultured woman's voice said, "*Feck*," from the audience and Hannah wailed, "*Mummy!*" again before rushing from the little theater in tears.

Hannah's father, in hissing tones that carried across the theater, said, "You might've kept your mouth shut, *darling*," and rose to stalk out after Hannah.

He was met at the door and walked back by a positively seething Detective Reese, who managed to cow him into sitting while glaring furiously at Megan, half the theater away and on the stage. "I leave the theater for *five minutes* . . . !"

"I didn't *mean* to!"

"No one solves a murder case accidentally, Ms. Malone!"

That was difficult to argue with, although Megan genuinely hadn't expected her question to unleash chaos and confessions. At most, she'd anticipated Trish Dillon collapsing weeping into her arms, not a full-fledged assault on the whiskey festival manager. She wanted to say that she was certain Detective Reese would have figured it out, which was true, but she couldn't think of a way *to* say it that didn't sound condescending.

But neither was she going to apologize for triggering the confessions, so in the end, Megan only shrugged helplessly and kept her mouth shut.

"This one's quite nice," the female judge said behind her. Megan glanced back to see all three judges handing bottles of whiskey back and forth, although one of the men was currently eating what looked like a saltine. Megan supposed it and the water bottles they also had were for clearing their palates. The woman had two whiskeys in hand, one lifted so she could read the label over the top of her glasses. "Midnight Sunrise. Whose is Midnight Sunrise?"

Carmen squeaked from the theater floor and came forward nervously. "That is mine, señora."

"It's lovely," the judge informed her. "I don't know if it's award-winning, but it's a very nice whiskey. I'd say there's a market for it, especially if you aren't above a drop of red food coloring to really lean into the name. Oh, shut up," she said as one of the other judges drew breath to protest. "If she was selling it as a bourbon she couldn't use coloring and call it a bourbon, but half the whiskeys on the market have caramel coloring to enhance the golden tones. I don't see why she shouldn't take it another direction. All right, now how about this one, the . . . Keane Edge? Oh, that's yourself," she said to Maggie Keane, who lifted her head sharply.

Paul murmured, "Perhaps you should bring

Dervla up to speed and then excuse yourself," to Megan, who stuck her lip out in an exaggerated pout.

"But I want to hear what the judges have to say!"

"You can listen to Hannah's podcast," Paul said with a slightly ghoulish smile.

Megan sighed dramatically. "All right, fine. Detective Reese looks like she's about to chew nails, so you're probably right." She left the stage with the judges' animated discussion of the quality of Keane Edge whiskey in the background. It was, she gleaned, pretty good. Maybe it would win the competition, if it even was a competition anymore. Megan didn't know if the festival manager being a murderer affected whether somebody got awarded a prize or not. Offhand, she bet nobody else knew, either.

It really only took a moment to explain herself to Detective Reese. "Willow called and said she had seen Trish Dillon at Erin Ryan's last night, so I asked Trish if she'd killed Erin and she flipped out" covered it nicely, and no matter how many questions Reese asked, it came down to that simple explanation. After three reiterations, Reese invited Megan to remove herself from the theater, and moved on.

Megan probably wouldn't have, if Paul, backed by Niamh and Rabbie, hadn't urged her out of the theater and, more importantly in Paul's opinion, out of Reese's immediate line of sight. "I didn't *do* anything," Megan protested as they herded her out.

"No, and yet you snitched a case out from under Dervla's nose and she won't thank you for it," Paul said as they took seats on the steel artwork Viking ship outside the theater. The morning sun had fled and now rain spattered from the sky, with darker clouds threatening more at any moment. Megan thought smart money would be on getting back to city center where they could find somewhere warm and dry, but on the south side of the quays where the theater sat, the one-way system led away from downtown, and apparently none of them was quite prepared to walk until they'd discussed things a little more.

"She doesn't have to mention me at all, I swear it."

"No, but someone will," Niamh predicted.

Rabbie raised his eyebrows. "Aye, and it'll be my own self who does it. I'm never keeping it under the hat that my own niece cleared me of murder charges!"

"I mean, I didn't really," Megan protested, to a surprising chorus of disavowal.

Even Paul shook his head. "I see what you're saying, but you didn't *not*, either, Megan. Rabbie wasn't a serious suspect, but . . . well, he's not wrong. He could also not say anything."

Rabbie, unfazed by Paul's gimlet glare, shook his head. "Sure and people will want to know what happened and I'll never let the truth get in the way of a good story. Especially when there won't be a word of a lie in what I say."

Megan's phone buzzed in her pocket and she took it out to glance at it, then felt her heart lurch as she saw Jelena's name on the screen. She rose and took several steps away, fully aware that her friends were exchanging meaningful glances behind her as she answered. A vone call, video phone, which she hadn't expected. "Hey, ba—uh, Jelena. Are you okay?"

"Yeah, I just . . ." Jelena looked like she hadn't slept well and hesitated before asking, "How's your case going?"

"Ah. I solved it."

There was a heartbeat where Megan could see relief, forgiveness, and hope in Jelena's aquamarine eyes. She felt it, too: maybe it was over. Maybe things could work between them after all. Maybe there was a chance. Megan's heart twisted and she swallowed, making herself add the rest of it: "But someone else died, Yella. It was an accident, but it was part of this whole mess, and . . ."

The light went out of Jelena's eyes and her shoulders slumped as she looked down. "I'm sorry to hear that. I'm glad you figured it out, though. Who, ah . . . ?"

"Sean Byrne, of all people. And his assistant accidentally killed Angus's manager, Erin Ryan, last night. And it turns out poor Danny Keane really did just die of a heart attack. The stress of the event killed him."

Jelena lifted her gaze again, dismay written strongly across her delicate features. "Megan, that's awful. That's . . ."

"That's what you don't want in your life," Megan said very quietly. It was raining harder now, water puddling on the screen. At least she could pretend it disguised the tears in her eyes and voice.

"I'm sorry."

"It's okay. I understand. I wish . . ." Megan's smile felt fragile. "I wish things were different, but

I would have to be different and I don't think I'm going to change that much."

"No." Jelena smiled a little, too. "No, neither do I. And neither am I. I just . . . I called to tell you I was done picking things up from the house. Thanks for giving me the space."

Megan nodded. "Bye, Yella. You . . . you take care, okay?"

"You too, Megan." Jelena hung up and Megan brushed her thumb across the water on her phone screen, over where Jelena's cheek had been. She thought maybe if she just stood there long enough, she would melt away and her heart would stop hurting.

Instead, Niamh came over to put her arms around her, and then so did Paul, and Rabbie, and then to Megan's surprise, Carmen came out of the theater and joined them in the hug, until Megan was at the center of a little bundle of warmth and love. They stayed there for a while, until Carmen, in a prissy voice, said, "Rain is crawling down my spine." With a rumble of laughter, they broke apart and made their way behind the theater to walk up through Temple Bar in search of tea and comfort.

"I'll stay on a bit longer still, if you don't mind, Megan," Rabbie said once they were settled at a café. "There'll be a load of funerals to go to in the next few days."

"I don't mind. I think it'd be good for me to have someone around for a couple days." Everyone, even Carmen, looked slightly relieved at Megan's agreement, and she made a face at all of them.

"I know you were conspiring to make sure I have company."

"Not out loud," Paul assured her. "We just all thought you should."

"I do have the dogs."

"Dogs are not people," Carmen said wisely.

There was a pause before Megan shrugged and smiled. "Can't argue that. What about you, Carmen? Are you in Dublin for a while, or what?'

Carmen cringed delicately. "In all this rain and gray and damp? No, I do not think so. I will go home to España, where I will hire a new head of security, if I must. Ramon is in trouble," she said with a sigh fully directed at Megan. "At least he did not fix the fights himself, but it is illegal to knowingly bet on fixed fights, and I do not know how long the . . ." She snapped her fingers. "Statue of limits?"

"Statute of limitations."

The snapping fingers turned to a point at Megan. "Sí, yes, that. I do not know how long it is for illegal betting. But I am paying my lawyer to help him, and so." She shrugged. "All will probably be well."

"I *am* sorry," Megan said in a low voice. "I like him and I didn't want to get him into this kind of trouble."

"No, but you were willing to get him into trouble for being a murderer, and if he had been, you would have been right to do so, so I cannot say you were wrong to get him into *this* trouble." Carmen clicked her tongue impatiently. "He should not have bet illegally, then there would be no trouble."

"A very practical way to look at it," Rabbie proclaimed as Paul smiled crookedly at his hands. Megan wondered if people often debated the line of where it became ethical to look away from a crime right in front of him. "Do you suppose anyone is going to win this damn competition, or have we all wasted our money and time for nothing?"

"I think money couldn't buy the publicity of being a contender in the Murder Whiskey Festival year," Niamh said wryly. "Even if nobody wins, I think we'll all see our bottles in the off-licenses. Aren't you popular," she added as Megan's phone rang again.

"I don't know why. Everyone I know is right here." Megan got the phone out again, but smiled this time. "It's Raf. Hang on, I'll be back in a minute." She went out into the rain a second time, although at least there was a canopy at the front of the café.

Her best friend's bright grin flashed in the comparative dimness under the canopy. "Hey, Megs. I'm glad I caught you before bed."

Megan checked the time, already shaking her head. "It's six in the morning there, Raf. Why are you calling me now?"

His smile faded into worry. "Because I got your message about you and Jelena breaking up. Are you okay?"

"Um." Megan rubbed her free hand over her face. "Kind of, I guess. Not really. But fine."

"A convincing statement," Raf said wryly. "Look, we were going to keep it a surprise, but I have some news I hope might cheer you up. If it's okay, Sarah and I are going to come to Ireland in January?"

"What? Oh my God! Really?" Megan hadn't thought she was slumping, but she stood up much straighter. "*Really?* Oh my God, Raf, it's been years! Really?"

In the background of his call, she heard a woman's laughter, and then his wife's voice carrying across their house: "I don't know, she sounds disappointed, babe!"

"I told you she would be!" Raf yelled back, then grinned into the phone. "Yeah, really. We thought we'd come see how the other half lives."

"You mean how the murder driver half lives!" Sarah shouted.

"Yes, I mean how the—" Raf stopped calling out to Sarah and ended with, "speaking of which, did you solve it yet?"

"I did, actually, yeah, but that is *way* less cool than you coming to visit!" Megan bounced on her toes, alight with excitement, like she was twelve years old again.

"Only to you. Okay, great, if it's okay then we'll book the tickets and come cheer you up."

"I can't think of anything that would make me happier," Megan promised with absolute sincerity. "Thank you, Raf. You've already improved this week by a thousand percent."

"Yeah, well, what are friends for?"

"They're for going to bed now," she told him sternly. "I bet you just got off shift."

"I did and it was a long one. But I wanted to call before I went to sleep. You sure you're okay?"

"I'm a lot better now, but yeah. I'll be okay. All right. Go. Take care, and I'll see you in a couple of months."

Keep reading for an excerpt of
Death in Irish Accents!

It's been over a year since Megan found herself entangled in a murder—much to everyone's relief, including her girlfriend Jelena and Detective Paul Bourke. So when a body of a young woman quite literally lands in her lap at her favorite Dublin café, Megan tries to do the right thing and leave the crime-solving to the police so she can enjoy the St. Patrick's Day weekend. After all, she has no connection to the victim. Or does she?

Megan's latest client, world-renowned romance novelist Claire Woodward, is fascinated by Megan's own history of catching killers. Claire also just happens to be the murder victim's literary mentor. So maybe Megan can just sort of stay on the periphery of the case while trying to help out? Just a wee bit without causing too much fuss? Even Detective Bourke would approve since he has personal reasons not to trust Claire. The investigation leads Megan to the victim's writing group, who think that Claire has plagiarized the poor young lady's work. And when another member of the group is found dead, Megan will have to step up her sleuthing before the killer decides to write her off for good.

Look for *Death in Irish Accents*, available now!

CHAPTER 1

A body fell out of the closet when the barista opened it.

The barista screamed, throwing herself backward, and landed in a sprawl across Megan Malone's lap. Coffee went everywhere. Megan, too startled to even yell, grabbed the barista to make sure she didn't bounce to the floor the way the—

The way the body had done. Megan said, "Oh god," under her breath. Immediately beside her, her girlfriend made a hideous, high-pitched squeak that was almost worse than the barista's screams. Like Megan, Jelena had grabbed the barista— Anie—but Megan had taken most of the girl's weight. Jelena scrambled backward, right over the arm of their couch, as the body dropped into the couch directly beneath the closet, then bounced off and hit the coffee table with a truly horrible crunch. Then it . . . slithered . . . to the floor, limbs

flopping around with a stomach-turning loose-
ness.

Either it was very fresh, Megan thought with a
sort of clinically investigative detachment, or it
was . . . not fresh at all.

Anie, the barista, was still shrieking. Jelena had
landed hard on the floor and crouched there, hands
clenched against her mouth to stop her own
screams. Everyone else in the café was coming to
see what had happened, people climbing on the
wide arms of the café's couches and pounding up
the stairs from the lower floor. Alarmed faces
started appearing at the top of the stairs, stacked
one above another like a comedy sketch as they
peered around at the nook-like space at the back
of the café where Megan, Jelena, Anie and the
dead girl were. The dead girl had fallen—well,
landed—between two of the deep couches and the
square coffee table at right angles to them.

Jelena, through the fists knotted at her mouth,
whispered, "This is not possible," and part of
Megan had to agree. This was her fourth body in
the past three years. That sort of thing had been
within the bounds of reason when she was in the
military, working as a combat medic and driving
ambulances, but it was not what anybody expected
as a limo driver in Dublin.

The other part of her thought they'd better
clear the room before anybody started taking pictures, although it was almost certainly too late for
that. She got Anie off her lap and stood, raising
her voice. "Max? Can you get everybody out of
here, please?" Her Texan accent sounded particularly noticeable to her right then, but it usually did

when she felt she had to be pushy about something. An American accent worked wonders for being pushy in Ireland.

Another of the baristas, a good-looking young white man, stuttered, "I—yes, okay, yes—" and began to herd patrons out of the café. A third barista went downstairs and Megan could hear him calling, "Sorry, lads, Accents has to close for a while. If you're waiting on your drinks, we'll refund your money at the till."

Somebody downstairs said, "What *happened*," and the barista, Liam, said, "There's been an accident," in a grim tone. After a few seconds, the lingering patrons from downstairs began to exit, craning their necks to see what was going on in the little alcove. One of them said, "Oh, *shit*," and scurried out with their phone already at their ear.

Jelena wrapped her hand around Megan's upper arm. "Megan, we have to *go*."

"I can't." Megan gave Jelena an apologetic glance, seeing the anger and worry in the other woman's brilliant blue eyes. "Honestly, I can't, Yella. Paul's going to have a fit over me even being here, but if I leave the scene before I call him . . ."

"Megan." Jelena's voice filled with strain, and Megan shrugged helplessly.

"I'm sorry. I really am. It's not like I mean for this to keep happening. Let me call Paul." She took her phone out, but Anie, whose crimson-dyed hair made her currently starkly-pale face look desperately unhealthy, clutched Megan's other arm.

"That's right, you've dealt with this kind of thing before. What do we do?" She got to her feet unsteadily, her gaze averted from the body at their feet. Most of the café had cleared out by then, with only the staff and a couple customers getting their money back remaining. "Is this going to ruin the business? Oh, God, I'd better call the owners. What am I going to say to them?"

"I don't know, Anie. I'm sorry." Megan glanced briefly at the body, which didn't seem to be leaking any blood, despite having hit the table hard on its way down. It—she—was young, with thickly curled, naturally red hair, and a host of freckles still visible after death. Megan didn't know if that was normal or not. She looked back across the café, where at least half the patrons were still gathered outside the plate glass front windows, and said, "Does anybody know who she is?" to the handful of people remaining in the café.

"She's a writer," Anie whispered. "Part of a group that's in here all the time. Bláthnaid. She liked a flat white and the peanut butter cake."

"Bláthnaid." Megan mentally spelled the name in her head, because it was one of those that didn't look anything like it sounded, at least to American ears. She heard *Blaw-nid*, but the spelling had a T-H where the W sound was, for heaven's sake. Then, idiotically, she added, "The peanut butter cake is amazing," as if she couldn't quite get her mind to work clearly beyond asinine agreements. "When was—"

"Megan." Jelena's voice sharpened. "Megan, just call Detective Bourke so we can go. You shouldn't get mixed up in this. Not again."

"Right. Yeah, okay, sorry." Megan actually dialed the detective this time, grimacing in anticipation of him picking up. He had once, lightheartedly, said that Megan only rang when she'd discovered a body. The rest of the time, she texted. He was unfortunately pretty much right about that, so she wasn't looking forward to him answering this call.

He did so on the third ring, with a wary, "Megan . . . ?"

"I'm at Accents Café on Stephen Street Lower and a dead body just fell in my lap."

The silence went on so long she checked to see if her phone had disconnected. Then, obviously through his teeth, Paul Bourke said, "Do not *touch* anything and do not *speak* to anyone until I get there," and hung up.

Megan put her phone in her pocket again and said, "He's mad at me," to the remaining people in the café, as a general statement. Then she looked at the set of Jelena's jaw, and thought it wasn't Detective Garda Paul Bourke who was *mad* at her. Although neither of them were exactly mad at her, probably. It wasn't like she planned this. But she did say, "I'm sorry," to Jelena, very softly.

Color rose in the pretty Polish woman's heart-shaped face, staining it pink. "When he comes here, Megan, we have to leave. When he's done talking to you. You can't . . ."

"Solve another mystery?" Megan supplied with a weak smile. "I don't know, my track record is pretty good so far."

Jelena's skin flushed to red. "This isn't your job. It's not the kind of thing you should be getting involved in. It makes me worry for you."

"I know. I know." Megan offered Jelena her hand, and pulled her into a hug when Jelena reluctantly accepted it. "I don't see how this could possibly have anything to do with me, though. It'll be fine, babe. I promise."

"Okay." The word, muffled against Megan's shoulder, sounded resigned. "Next time we're going to a different café after the gym, though."

Megan grinned. "Oh, come on, what are the odds that somebody else is going to get killed here? We're probably safer staying—"

"Killed here?" Anie had come back from calling the owners and stopped, frozen, just before the step leading up to the section Megan and Jelena stood on. "You think she was *killed?* Like, murdered?"

Megan, somewhat insensitively, said, "Well, she didn't put herself into that closet, Anie," and the young woman paled so sharply she had to sit down. A stab of guilt shot through Megan. She generally forgot that she was technically old enough to be most of the staff's mother. Being fortysomething was supposed to feel grown-up, but Megan had come to the reluctant conclusion that most people never actually felt grown-up. They just got older, and spent a lot of their time being vaguely surprised that they no longer shared the same life experiences as a twenty-five-year-old.

And honestly, her own life's experience up to the ages that the staff were was probably significantly different from theirs too, which made unthinkingly callous or cynical statements come a little easier, maybe. She, after all, had been in the Army for five years when she was Anie's age. Megan mumbled, "Sorry," and Anie nodded, although Jelena gave her a somewhat appalled look.

Megan said, "Sorry" again, and meant it.

Anie whispered, "It's okay. Of course you're right, I just didn't think—who would kill Bláthnaid? She was nice."

"I don't know. The guards will be here soon. Detective Bourke is only fifteen minutes away, even on foot." Just as she said that, a tallish, slender man in a camel-colored trench coat strode up to the door, flashing a badge and scattering at least half of the remaining crowd outside. He entered, brushing dampness from sandy red hair with one hand, and glancing around the café in a quick, professional assessment before his gaze landed on Megan and went flat.

Megan's shoulders slumped and she shot Jelena another apologetic look before taking a few steps toward the plainclothes detective. "Paul. Sorry, I mean, Detective Bourke. I'm, uh . . . really sorry."

Bourke shook his head in weary acceptance. "I feel like I should just be grateful it's been over a year since I found you neck-deep in a crime scene. What happened?"

Megan gestured toward Anie. "She asked if we could scoot over so she could get some supplies out of the closet—"

Bourke's gaze went to the closet, which still hung open. Normally hidden behind eight-inch-deep bookshelves, it filled the upper half of the wall above the couches, and was probably a couple feet deep and a good six feet high. Megan said, "I usually sit downstairs. I didn't even know there was a closet there. I thought it was just bookshelves. So we scooted over and she opened it and . . . Bláthnaid fell out."

"Bláthnaid? You know her?" Bourke's notepad

was out now, its orange cover flashing as he flipped it open to start writing. He'd had a different-colored pad for every case Megan had ever seen him work on, and she assumed there was some kind of organizational or file-keeping method to the color schemes.

"No, no, Anie told me her name." Megan gestured toward the barista again. "And then I called you. Honestly, I did," she added defensively, at Bourke's skeptical glance. "You got here fast." It couldn't have been more than four or five minutes since the body had fallen out of the closet.

"I was at the top of Grafton Street," Bourke replied shortly. Megan had a momentary impulse to discuss which end was really the "top" of the street, but given that Bourke had arrived so quickly, he clearly meant he'd been closer to St. Stephen's Green. "What are *you* doing here?"

"Accents is my favorite café. They make better mochas than anywhere else I've ever been. Jelena and I came here after working out this morning."

"And you just happened to be here for the discovery of a body." Bourke sighed and gave Jelena a brief nod of greeting, which she returned before casting an unhappy but accepting glance at Megan.

"I'll be outside."

"Jelena, I'm sorry, I—"

Jelena lifted a hand, cutting off the apology, and went outside. Bourke followed her with his gaze, then raised his eyebrows at Megan. "Trouble in paradise?"

"There wasn't until five minutes ago! She wasn't happy the last couple times this happened, but we hadn't been seeing each other very long then, and nothing like this has happened in over a year now—"

"Exactly fourteen months," Bourke said. "To the day. Cherise Williams's funeral was fourteen months ago today."

Megan looked askance at him. "You just know that off the top of your head?"

"I counted it out on my way over here." He pointed toward Jelena with his chin. "I'm actually going to need to talk to her, you know."

"I don't think that's occurred to her, but I don't think she's planning to leave without me unless I'm here a long time, so . . ."

"You have no reason to be here a long time," Bourke said. "You're not an investigating officer. You're a witness, at most. So tell me what you know and then, for God's sake, go away and don't get involved in this, okay, Megan?"

"This time I don't see how I possibly could. And I've told you what I know," Megan added with a sigh. "Anie opened the cupboard and the body fell out. Everybody screamed—"

"You didn't," Anie put in, and Megan blinked at her, then smiled ruefully.

"Maybe not on the outside. I was trying to keep you from hitting the floor. Anyway," she said to Bourke, "then I called you. That was pretty much it."

Bourke looked down at her for a long moment, nearly-blond eyebrows drawn down over pale blue eyes as he waited for the other shoe to drop.

For once, though, Megan didn't have another shoe. The dead girl wasn't her client, or a friend of her client's, or connected to her in any way. She couldn't blame him for expecting a link, though.

He'd been the investigating officer on her first murder—that sounded all wrong—and they'd gotten to be friends, so she'd called him when she'd found herself neck-deep in a second, and then a third, murder mess.

But she wasn't involved in this one, so she spread her hands in as good an approximation of innocence as she could manage. "Honestly, that's all I know."

"And you're just going to leave instead of hanging around on the edges of my investigation, trying to overhear something and look into it yourself?"

Megan's face heated, although her brief smile was full of admission. "Obviously, I'm not gonna lie and say I'd never do such a thing. I totally would. But Jelena would kill me, and I'd rather have a girlfriend who still speaks to me than another notch on my murder belt." She winced as Paul's eyes popped. "That came out wrong."

"You think? All right." The detective exhaled. "Send Jelena in for a minute to talk to me, but I don't think there's much more she's going to be able to tell me. I'll interview the staff and learn more ab . . ." He trailed off, frowning. "I don't have to tell you what I'm doing for my job."

Megan produced a wide, cheesy grin. "No. But if you wanted to keep me up to date on the details . . ."

"My boss would demote me." Bourke turned away, and Megan, actually feeling a little guilty, scurried out of the café. An Garda Síochána—the Irish police force—was not, as an institution, fond of her, and Paul's boss specifically would be happier if Megan returned to the States and never complicated another Irish murder investigation in her life. Megan thought the ins and outs of the messes she kept getting into were fascinating, but she genuinely didn't want to cause Paul any trouble, and Jelena . . .

Jelena was leaning in the alleyway just beside the café, her arms folded and a worried scowl settling on her delicate features. Megan murmured, "Sorry," again as she found her. "Paul wants to talk to you real quick."

"We go on double *dates* with him and Niamh, Megan, we don't—" Jelena's protest ended in a splutter and a waving of her hands, but she went inside, leaving Megan to cringe guiltily again. Even she had to admit it was kind of weird to be interviewed about suspicious deaths by somebody she hung out with for Friday night pizza, but at least she'd gone through it before. Jelena hadn't.

Of course, if it was weird for them, it had to be a lot harder for Paul, who also probably had to justify to his boss why he spent his spare time hanging out with somebody who kept being connected to murders. Megan said "Ugh," out loud, and thumped her head against the alley wall. Then, also aloud, she said, "But you're *not* connected to this one," and nodded firmly, like all she needed was a good talking-to.

Her phone rang, startling her, and she took it out to see her boss's name coming up with the Leprechaun Limos emblem as the image. Megan answered with as wary an "Orla?" as Paul's "Megan?" had been earlier, and was broadsided by Orla's most an-American-is-listening-to-me Irish accent.

"Megan? Have you plans for the afternoon? I've a new client who's asking for you specifically."

"A *new* client?" Megan echoed, surprised. "Usually only Carmen asks for me by name."

"Oh," Orla said, her voice dropping to a grim mutter, "she's not asking by name, no. She's asking for 'the murder driver.'"